HEART STEALER

HEART STEALER

MELODY WIKLUND

Melody Wiklund

Contents

This book is dedicated to Francis. Thank you for writing with me, and for being my friend.

I

Chapter One

There was a girl watching James from across the ballroom.

It was making him a little uncomfortable. It would have been one thing if it were one of the debutantes getting a little too flirtatious or curious. That had happened before, and it was easy enough to ignore. But this was one of the maids. She should have been busy with her work, keeping the table supplied and the floor clean of spills, and yet time and time again James caught a glimpse of her watching him. Their eyes only met like this once, and she did not flinch away in embarrassment as a servant, or indeed any girl of that age, ought. Instead, she gazed at him coolly until he looked away. When he looked back, she was gone, but only for the moment. And now she was back again, and he couldn't tell if she was watching him or just looking in his direction, gazing out at the crowd of dancers whirling between them. She had not yet met his eyes again. He wasn't sure if he wanted her to or not—it wasn't as if he wanted her to be looking, but if she wasn't, if she really wasn't, then he was paranoid to think she was, paranoid to feel those hard, dark eyes pinning him against the wall—and he probably was being paranoid, he knew that. He was anxious tonight. A lot rode on him behaving right, making a good impression on—

A tap to his arm. "You seem distracted."

"Miss Hunt," he said, "I'm sorry." He hadn't noticed her coming over. The first time they'd spoken this evening since their families said hello to each other at the start of the night, perhaps the second time he'd ever spoken to her with no one there beside him chaperoning—the first time, and he hadn't even noticed her coming over.

She smiled. "You can call me Jenny, you know. Since we're going to be getting married. And you don't have to be so nervous."

"I'm afraid I don't shine at parties."

"No need for you to shine. I only hoped to dance. Or are you going to refuse to dance with me?"

"Of course I won't. I'm on your dance card, aren't I?" Was that too blunt a retort? No, she laughed. Taking it as a bit of teasing, which was how it was meant, or how he meant to mean it, anyway.

She made him nervous, Genevieve Hunt. She was perfect, intimidatingly so. Three years younger than him but far more at ease in social situations, the face and voice of an angel, the fashion sense of a queen. At one gathering he'd attended, she'd played the entirety of Beethoven's *Hammerklavier* on the piano without breaking a sweat. He hadn't been able to sit the whole thing out without leaving to get himself some more punch and a sandwich. When he'd returned to the room, she'd spotted him, and flashed him a short, gracious, little smile before returning her focus to the sonata.

They hadn't been engaged back then. Now they were; not publicly, but her parents and his parents had talked, and he had spoken with her, and the match had been decided. It was an excellent marriage. He had a title, an estate. She had a fortune, relatives looking to make a connection. Only, she was an accomplished young woman with beauty and kindness both in spades, and he was... Well, he had a title and an estate, and a family with an honorable name, a family he loved, but in himself, he couldn't say he was much of a catch. His flaws—his past mistakes—he was well aware of. Some of them were common knowledge to high society, while others he held close to his chest, but did not trust to remain secret forever.

Which ones Genevieve Hunt knew of, he couldn't say.

"You didn't put yourself more than twice on my dance card," Genevieve said. "And not until later in the evening. Don't you want to dance with me before then?"

"More than twice wouldn't have been proper."

"We're announcing our engagement soon enough. A little impropriety is only foreshadowing for the gossips."

He laughed. "The gossips have already guessed, I'm sure. They've been calling us a couple for a year and a half, even when we barely spoke to each other."

The smile tensed on Genevieve's face. "Yes, well. Now that we really are, it wouldn't be bad to give them something real to talk about."

And now he'd hurt her feelings. Clumsy fool. What would his parents say if they knew what a mess he was making of this? *You idiot, James.* He hurried to say, "Well, I'd love to dance with you all night, but I'm sure your dance card is full up."

"The viscount of Emberton has gone home early. He had the next dance with me." She bit her lip. "So, if you wanted to, my next dance is free."

Oh. "All right. I'd love to. Just, um… I'd like a drink first."

"Not intoxicated enough to tolerate me?"

"No, no!" Oh, she was just joking. He grinned. "I'm just thirsty. Hold on a moment—or come with me, I don't know if I can find you again if I leave you. Such a crowd tonight."

"Certainly I'll come with you. Will you give me your arm?"

He offered it to her, and with their arms linked, they wormed their way around the outskirts of the dance floor and over to the refreshments table. They each got themselves a cup of punch—she made a joke about it not being his favorite flavor, and he stuttered for a moment before remembering she preferred lemonade. "So we'll both have to cope."

"Well, at least we have good company."

"Cheers to that."

They drank, each downing their cup in one long gulp. He almost paused at one point, feeling a sting on the back of his neck, wanting to slap at a bug. But it was probably his imagination, and would certainly make him look stupid either way.

The current dance had ended, and dancers were scattering this way and that, finding new partners, the band flipping through their music, readying flutes and violins. James held out his hand. Genevieve took it, and he led her out onto the dance floor.

It was not a romantic dance, nor even a dance for couples. It was a dance for sets of four, so James and Genevieve were not partnered the whole time. They made a set with a woman he didn't recognize and a brother of Genevieve's. The woman was a decent dancer, very efficient. She paid little attention to James, glancing back over at Genevieve's brother whenever they ended up partnered. Genevieve's brother was pretty bad. He had a way of moving that was very stiff and solid, lacking fluidity—it made James remember hearing that he had spent a couple years in the military. But he had a warm smile, and was equally solid in linking arms with James for a moment when the dance required it. His arms were thick and James could feel their muscle even through his jacket. He was careful not to linger touching him, afraid that he, or worse, Genevieve, would think him overly familiar.

As for Genevieve, she was as excellent a dancer as a pianist, steps light and sure, face always smiling, breath steady and even. As for James, he was usually a good dancer, but tonight he was not.

He found himself stumbling time and again, feeling dizzy and over-whelmed. Usually although crowds intimidated him, a dance in a set of four would focus him so that he was quite capable of toning the rest of the world out. But tonight he could not. The colors and the sounds of the ballroom were too bright and loud. When the dance ended, he headed for the edge of the ballroom with great relief.

Genevieve grabbed at his shoulder, and it so startled him that he almost fell on top of her. She started back, embarrassed, and he said, "Sorry—I'm a little dazed."

Too dazed. What had been in the punch? Was it more spiked than usual? But Genevieve had drunk as much as him, and she seemed fine. If it was just nerves getting to him, because of Genevieve and his engagement, how on earth would he get through the party where his engagement was announced?

"Are you feeling all right?"

"I might need some fresh air."

"We could go out on the terrace," Genevieve suggested.

It was a good idea. A romantic idea, and the cold air really might help. But with his head this fuzzy, James couldn't help but think he'd end up saying something to offend her once they were alone. He shook his head. "I'll just step into the hallway. Maybe sit in the library for a bit. Clear my head. I think I should be alone."

"Oh. All right."

"Sorry," he said. "I'll be back. Just, for the moment... I'm sorry. Could you tell my parents where I am if they ask? They worry when I vanish on them."

"Certainly."

"Great. Thank you. I'm sorry." And with this apology, James made his way out of the ballroom and into the hall. There were still people there, and his head was still buzzing. He kept walking until he found an empty corridor, in a corner near a set of stairs.

He breathed in. Breathed out.

His head wasn't clearing in the slightest.

His parents really would be wondering where he was. He was trying to be a more responsible son. When he thought about the kinds of fights they'd been having last month, he really felt like an idiot. Rejecting a marriage with Genevieve Hunt because of some deluded infatuation, when they'd been right all along: She was the perfect woman and he was lucky to have her. He'd acted like a child throwing temper tantrums. Now he was trying to be more reliable, and running off in the middle of a party wasn't reliable behavior, and he needed to get back there, show himself to the crowd, make more conversation with Genevieve, but his head still felt like it was full of cotton, and his chest...

His chest felt tight and empty at the same time. But that wasn't exactly a new thing. He'd been anxious all week.

A sound in the hall behind him. He turned, readying himself to greet an acquaintance, but was brought up short by the sight of the young maid who had been staring at him in the ballroom.

She was looking at him as keenly now, if not more so.

"Do I know you?" he blurted. Which was stupid, because why would he know a maid? And he was sure he didn't recognize her.

She shook her head solemnly. "We've never met before today, sir."

"Oh." His face heated. "Never mind, then. I just thought, perhaps..."

"But I know an old friend of yours."

"...ah?"

She stepped closer, up into his space. "Charlotte Taylor sends her love."

He stiffened. "Charlie? You know Charlie?" As for her love—"Listen, if she sent you, I can't—I've spoken to her about this already. We're through."

"You're not through, James," the maid said. "That's what she sent me to tell you."

She was close enough to whisper in his ear. There was a dizzying scent of lilacs on her, and he had begun to lean away when he felt something like a punch in the ribs. He stumbled back, gasping and clutching at his chest. His hands folded around warm metal, warm from where the maid had been holding it, tucked behind her back. The handle of a knife.

The knife was sticking out of his chest.

He gasped, staring at it. But it didn't hurt. The puncture, the stab itself, had hurt, but the wound did not. And no blood was coming out of it either.

A prop knife?

Then the maid grabbed his shoulder and yanked the knife out of him. It came out clean, not a trace of blood on it. Nor did blood well up from the wound when it left him. No red stained his shirt or jacket. Not a drop fell to dirty the recently-polished cream-tiled floor.

The maid stared at the knife, then at him, somehow even more intensely than before, eyebrows furrowed. "What are you?"

"What are you doing?" James gripped his chest, hands folded over the tear in his shirt. "You stabbed m—"

The maid's hand clamped down on his mouth as he began to yell. She shoved him against the wall, then frowned. "You don't have circulation."

James screamed against her hand. He tried to push her back, but the dizziness was still there, and his arms were weak and useless.

"Sleeper hold's a bust, then," the maid said. "Sorry about this."

She slammed the hilt of her knife against his head, and the world went black.

2

Chapter Two

Natty was not Poor Jane yet, but she would be someday. While she still had her points of weakness, she tried her best every day, every mission, to follow the guidance of the current Poor Jane, her mentor. Angela.

Natty had become Angela's apprentice at the age of seven. It had been a winter night, snow falling soft and fluttery. Her mother called it a lacy miracle when it began—the first snowfall of the winter, come late. Four hours later, her mother was lying on the parlor floor with a slit in her throat, blood staining the carpet, and Natty's father lay beside her.

Angela stood towering over the two of them. Back then Natty hadn't understood what she was, only known her to be a nightmare. She was wearing a thick, dark coat, a straight black skirt, heavy boots, a gray cap, and a scarf that covered the bottom half of her face. Her hair was tied back neatly—"Blood's a bitch coming out of hair," she told Natty later, but she didn't mind getting blood on her coat or her gloves, then as now. She felt Natty's father's pulse.

She'd killed him with a couple strong blows to the head, which was less certain a method than cutting a throat, even though she'd hit him hard enough that his skull was disfigured. Satisfied that he was dead, she turned to Natty.

Natty was lying on the floor too, and she too was bleeding. She'd been hit in the head but not so badly. She'd tried to attack Angela while Angela was struggling with her mother, and Angela had thrown her off, and she'd hit her head on the side of the piano. Now she saw little point in getting up again. Her mother was dead, her father was dead, and Angela stood over her with a still-bloody knife in her hand, and Natty hoped she'd hurry up before she wet her pants and made her own death an embarrassment.

"You're frightened," Angela said, "but you didn't do such a bad job, rushing me. Going for the legs and all that. If your mother had your nerve, you might have finished me together, but she froze up. Pity that, but a lot of nice ladies do. Something to learn from, that. You won't grow up to be a nice lady, will you?"

Natty swallowed hard. *No,* she thought, *I'll never grow up at all.* She didn't bother answering.

Angela crouched down, low enough that Natty could meet her eyes over the scarf. They were pale eyes, a blue that was almost gray in the low light. "You'll never grow up to be a victim. I know that. You've learned your lesson tonight." The sides of her eyes crinkled, the edge of a soothing smile. "Would you like to learn how to defend yourself? How to be the hunter instead of the prey? I've been meaning to take in a student. Now, you have nowhere else to go."

It took Natty a second to realize that Angela expected an answer. "I have an uncle," she said. "He'd take me in."

Angela shook her head. "I'm afraid that's not going to happen."

"They'll take me in. They're good people."

"They won't get the chance." Angela reached out a hand and

gently touched Natty's neck. Worn leather gloves on bare skin. "If you don't agree to go with me tonight, I'll kill you."

Natty felt betrayed. For just a second, Angela had been kind, soothing, like one of those adults that always meant the best for you, one of those women you could ask for directions on the street. "Why?" she asked.

"I've been looking for a student," Angela said. "If you come with me, I can teach you how to be the next Poor Jane. That's what I am, you know. Maybe you've heard the legend. And I wasn't paid to kill you, so I don't really have to."

"You could leave me."

"It's not the way I do things."

"I wouldn't tell anyone about you," Natty said, and maybe it was the truth and maybe it was a lie. In the moment it was the truth. "I'd never tell anyone anything."

"I'm offering you the chance to be like me. To be my daughter," Angela said. "I do have my pride."

"I don't have a choice, then."

"You can choose to die. Maybe you only fought me because you love your parents so much. They're dead now. You can die with them if you want, or you can move on. I'd never take away your right to that decision."

Natty began to cry. Angela's hand moved slightly to cup her cheek instead of her neck. "Shh, now. What do you want, hm? Do you want to come with me?"

"I don't want to die."

"All right then. Get up. We can't stay here long, you know. Neighborhood like this, someone may have heard the screaming and actually sent for the constables—though I doubt it. People don't like interfering, you know. That's one great advantage for a killer: People's lack of curiosity. But I'll teach you all about that later. You won't be in the mood for a lesson tonight."

Despite saying this, she muttered several more guiding comments to Natty on their way out: The best way to exit a window, how to avoid leaving footprints in places or at times they were likely to stay, how to walk quietly, how to avoid notice in the streets. Natty remembered some of it later. Not all of it, but some.

She had a good memory.

***

Natty was not a temperamental seven-year-old anymore. She had progressed far in Poor Jane's teachings, to such an extent that sometimes Angela would even give her assignments all to herself. Most of them were easy targets. Old men who lived alone, women who frequented the bad parts of town. The hardest part of killing them was...

Well, Natty always told Angela that the hardest part of killing them was making sure she followed the clients' instructions. They could be very precise, clients, sometimes even persnickety, and she had little patience for all those details when the point was, or should have been, the death itself. But every client had their own specifications with their own particular reasons. Some clients wanted the death to look like an accident, others like suicide. Some wanted death to be painful, but Angela didn't give Natty those jobs yet, saying she had neither the expertise nor the nerve to carry them out and probably wouldn't until she was Poor Jane herself. Natty felt she ought to object on principle, but never did.

In any case, it was not so easy making a death look natural, not nearly as easy as stabbing someone in the chest and making a run for it. Which perhaps was why Angela had felt confident in handing Natty the current case.

"Miss Taylor wants James Guarin, the son of the Earl of Ilbird, stabbed in the heart. Mark you, it must be the heart, not simply somewhere between the ribs, certainly not in the gut. She doesn't care if he dies instantly, but he must know she was the one who sent you. Charlotte Taylor."

"Charlotte Taylor," Natty repeated. "James Guarin. Knife to the heart. Does she care if the knife stays in or if I take it with me?"

"She did not express a preference. She said his heart was unfaithful and so must pay the price of disloyalty. Presentation matters for the victim but not for the general public. She wouldn't care if it looked like an accident, but I can't imagine that would be easy to arrange, so leave it be. She requested that he be killed, if possible, at a party with Genevieve Hunt, but if this cannot be arranged, she is willing to let it go and have him killed in, I quote, 'some back alley', as long as he ends up dead."

Infiltrating a high society party would be difficult, but Natty had experience blending in with the elite—in the background. She wouldn't have known how to fake the aura, the gentility, of a noble-woman, but being a maid? She could fake that easily enough. Add that to a relatively simple request for method from the client, and the assignment should have been a piece of cake.

Instead, Natty was now supporting James Guarin's body against the wall with one arm while she tried to figure out what the hell to do with him. His live body. Because apparently stabbing this man in the heart didn't actually do anything.

Had Charlotte Taylor known it wouldn't? Was the job a set-up?

Natty gazed at the tear in James Guarin's shirt. With both shirt and coat in the way, she could barely glimpse skin. But she'd felt her dagger pierce flesh, felt the edge of it scrape bone. It had gone in easily but simply had no effect. Not a drop of blood on the linen.

It was enough to make a hardened assassin shiver.

Poor Jane, she thought to herself. Poor Jane would know what to do with this. Angela would know what to do with this. And she'd told Natty before that it was better to get help on an assignment she couldn't handle than blindly try to solve everything on her own.

"You're still an apprentice. And when you kill in my name, my honor's at stake. Your own pride is unimportant in comparison to Poor Jane's legacy. Understood?"

Natty understood. She would go to Angela now, and Angela would fix it. Fix *him*, for good.

She sheathed her blade. Considered taking out a chloroformed rag, but decided against it. If the blow to his head didn't keep James unconscious for long, the drug she'd pricked him with earlier had clearly begun to work its way through his system and would keep him asleep for longer, probably at least two hours—and after that, he'd still be manageable for a while. That would be enough time to take him back to her hideout and dispose of him properly.

He was not a tall man, fortunately. She heaved him over her back, draping his arms over her neck and lifting him up by the legs. There was no real way to be subtle about this. She would just have to be quick instead. There was a side door out of the building right on the other side of the stairwell, and she shambled through it, doing her best to keep James's weight centered so he wouldn't fall off. It was a strange feeling, carrying a live body. She was more accustomed to carrying corpses. But James breathed; his breath against her neck was more distracting than she would have thought. She was unused to being this close to living people, with the exception of Angela. In the maids' quarters the past couple days, she'd been in close contact with a few girls, but that had been different. They saw her as Mathilde, a poor girl, only fifteen, desperate for employment and hideously shy and easily embarrassed. James had for a moment seen the truth of what kind of woman she was, in a way only Angela, clients, and victims were allowed to see her. She did not generally stick around clients or victims for long.

This... she didn't like it.

The manor was surrounded by a wall a little higher than Natty's head, going all around the building. Natty could easily climb over it and back, by herself. Heaving a limp body over it and then following would be more difficult, and extremely unsubtle. Instead, she went around to the back gate of the manor, where the staff went in and out. "He's drunk," she explained to a servant whose path she crossed. "His family wants him sent home."

"The Earl wants to send his son home early, and won't even take him?" The servant tutted. "That family... you do hear those two have their differences."

Natty shrugged and glanced away, all innocent Mathilde.

"I'll help you call a cab, eh? There's a couple hopefuls waiting at the front gate already, but if the Earl would rather be discreet, I'm sure one will be happy to come around the back. You can count on me, Matty."

The "Matty" sounded a lot like "Natty", giving Natty's nerves a jump, but they were settled by the time the servant headed out to the front gate. He returned in a minute, having made the arrangements for her, and a small coach pulled up to the back gate. Natty got in, taking James with her. "They asked me to see him home," she told the servant. "Tell Madam I'll be back in less than an hour."

"Surely you don't need to do that. Just give the man a good tip..."

"I promised."

"Well, you don't work for the Earl of Ilbird, do you?"

Natty shrugged again. "I promised. I'll be less than an hour."

"Well, I'll make your excuses if Madam asks. Hopefully she won't notice. Pretty hectic night, isn't it?"

Natty waved and closed the coach door.

The coachman asked her if she wanted to go to the Ilbird town-house. He knew where it was, had driven the family and some of their guests there before. Natty directed him instead to an alley a few blocks away from Poor Jane's hideout. There she asked him to step out of the cab—"I have some extra payment for you," she said, with a slight blush. When he stepped out, she knocked him out as easily as James.

Angela might have killed him. She liked covering her tracks. But then, there was no contract for killing him, so Natty didn't have to. And Angela had once spared Natty.

She lugged James out of the coach and hoisted him back on her back again. In this neighborhood, no one questioned where she was going with him. In this neighborhood people preferred to be blind to strange comings and goings.

Poor Jane's hideout was a flat on the second story of a nondescript stone building. Natty hauled James up to the door and gave her coded knock. Angela answered and cocked her head, looking askance at James.

Natty said, "Things got complicated. I was hoping you could help."

"Maybe I should have come with you after all. But if there were complications, kidnapping the son of an earl will only cause more of them. Why bring him here? You could approach him again later if circumstances were not in your favor."

Even as she spoke, Angela moved aside from the door to allow Natty in, and then helped Natty to gently lower James's body to the living room carpet. She could have careful hands, Angela.

"The problem wasn't circumstances. It's him. I stabbed him in the heart already, but he didn't die. He didn't even bleed. It was abnormal, so I thought I'd ask your advice."

"Hm." Angela frowned. "Interesting. Let's take a look."

Before doing anything else, she reached into the pockets of the coat she was wearing—long and brown and very warm, the object of great jealousy from Natty, whose own coat was wearing thin—and withdrew her leather gloves. Slipping into work mode, she knelt beside James's body and pulled open his coat, then proceeded to unbutton first his vest and then his shirt. Beneath that there was an undershirt—this she ripped open, starting from the tear where Natty's dagger had pierced it. Beneath all these layers, his chest lay bare. Natty swallowed.

That Natty had stabbed him earlier was clear. There was a gash in the skin, and flesh could be seen beneath as well as bone. But it simply was not bleeding. And there was something else too. Around the wound there was a strange light line, running in a circle. The texture was a bit like stitches, but there were no actual stitches. Angela prodded it and muttered something under her breath, and for a moment the line flared with light, giving off a couple sparks, before dimming again.

"Hm," said Angela.

Natty said, "It's like your sigil."

Angela huffed a laugh. "I suppose I can see the similarities, if you'd never seen anything else like this before."

Every Poor Jane wore the sigil of Poor Jane, inherited from the last Poor Jane (or John) at their death. Natty had seen the sigil on Angela before. It was a mark over her heart, shaped like a skull in a triangle with a circle at each point of it. "The circles are coins," Angela had told Natty before, "and the three sides of the triangle are gain, righteousness, and spite, the three reasons one might desire to kill someone. As for the skull, I imagine it's evident."

It was a grim symbol, the sigil of Poor Jane, but it had a harsh beauty to it. And Natty had seen before that sometimes it would glow or spark when Angela got emotional or when she killed. Natty imagined it did this far more often she'd seen, too. After all, most of the time the sigil was hidden under several layers of clothing, and how would Natty or anyone else know what eldritch things it got up to?

"This isn't a mark of binding, though," Angela continued now. "Or—it is, maybe, but of a different sort. Look at it. It's just a circle. There's nothing it's binding him to. It's more like a place marker than anything else, or... perhaps merely a scar. Something happened here. Something happened to his heart."

She ran a finger along the circle again and frowned. "Give me your knife, Natty. Since it started the job, we may as well try to use it for the finish."

Natty took it out and handed it to her. It wasn't her own knife, anyway. She and Angela shared tools in common; or at least, Natty's tools were partly Angela's. Angela did have a few weapons of her own she wouldn't let Natty touch.

This knife, which Natty had picked out for the job herself, was four inches long and thin enough to stick between ribs with little difficulty. The sheath was dark leather and the hilt unobtrusively black and worn. Not a favorite, but easily explainable if it were found while Natty was in the guise of Mathilde. The kind of knife a woman might carry around for protection if she were young and nervous.

Angela took the knife and unsheathed it. She braced one hand against James's chest, and with the other she calmly and carefully slit the skin open, starting at the gash Natty had left behind and drawing a neat incision first down to the bottom of his ribcage and then up to his collarbone. She cut a little to the side at each end at a right angle, and lifted the flap of skin to the side, just a little, not fully detaching it. Between ribs, she and Natty could get a glimpse of something impossible: the chest was empty. Which was to say, there was still a pair of lungs and some other organs bumping around, but there was no heart to be seen.

Angela touched one of the ribs, and Natty saw that there was a line there too like the line on James's skin. It sparked at Angela's touch. Angela hummed. She pressed the skin gently back into place and turned to Natty.

"Well, it looks like someone's removed his heart," she said. "Makes our task a little difficult, doesn't it?"

"Who could do such a thing?"

"Hard to say. There are more witches and warlocks in this city than people like to admit. Removing someone's heart is a very dark magic, but people don't shun dark magic as much as the general populace would like to think either. Our very existence is the proof of that—and we do good business, Natty, you know that. The kind of motivations that would make a man remove his heart, or make someone else steal it... they're common as dirt." Angela bit her lip. "It would be expensive, though. If he didn't have it done himself, it must have been another noble."

"I don't think he did it to himself. I don't think he even knew it was missing. When he didn't bleed from the stabbing I gave him, he looked as surprised as I was."

Angela snorted. "Knowing you, I doubt you looked surprised."

Natty bowed her head, accepted the compliment. "Well, what now?"

"Now? Well, we can't kill him by stabbing him in a heart he hasn't got, now, can we?"

"No, master." Natty bit her lip. She put her hand on James's chest, over the incision. His chest still rose and fell, even though no heart was beating. "Does this make him immortal?"

"No one's immortal. Some just die harder than others."

"We could try cutting off his head or setting him on fire," Natty suggested. "That works for most things."

"A chop-and-torch solution?" Angela seemed amused. "Charlotte Taylor requested a knife to the heart. It makes us look incompetent if we can't even handle that much."

"She wasn't particular otherwise. I doubt she'd care, given the circumstances, if we couldn't fulfill her orders with complete precision."

"Her lack of specificity in other areas only makes it worse if we can't fulfill the one request she had. Besides, I agreed to her terms. I gave her my word as Poor Jane. That's not something I can take back."

Angela had grown stern now. Natty sighed and looked down, away from her. Of course that left her staring at James Guarin.

His face was still, his skin delicate. Such a delicate man should have been easy to kill.

Angela patted Natty's shoulder. "Don't worry. We'll work it out. First, we'll have to ask Miss Taylor's opinion on the matter. In the meantime, we can't keep a little lordling here in our flat. Find somewhere to dump him—we'll approach him again later."

"I left a coach at Pear Lane. Coachman knocked out. If I put him back in it, they should both come to soon."

"Hm. Should suffice. I'll leave it to you, then, Natty. Let's leave this as your assignment for the time being. After all, it's about time you took on something more challenging."

3

Chapter Three

The day that James Guarin broke things off with Charlotte Taylor, he hadn't been to see her in more than a week.

This was not the first time he'd been absent for a while. Last summer he'd gone home to his family's country estate for a whole month, which had been torturously slow. He hadn't wanted to go. He'd told her he'd refuse to join his family there, and spend the summer in the city with her, just the two of them, even if it drove his parents so mad they disowned him. She told him to be sensible. A month was a month. When he came back, she'd still be waiting.

She had daydreamed a little about going to the country with him, but that was nonsense. She would have had nowhere to stay—no chance of staying at the estate with him, no funds to pay for an inn for a whole month, no reasonable way to explain to her boss why she needed to take a month off work. So she'd stayed in the city, and he'd gone to the country, but they'd been in touch.

Usually, when he couldn't see her, he'd be in touch.

(She had a collection of his letters, hidden under a cupboard in the pantry where she figured her brothers wouldn't look.)

Now it had been a week and four days, and she hadn't seen him and he hadn't been in touch, and he'd said he was going to meet her at the bridge a week ago, at sunset, so they could stand underneath it by the river's edge and watch how the sunset rippled in the water, how it broke when a boat came by. But he hadn't been there, and he'd never so much as sent her a note to explain.

And then, that evening, he showed up at her work. It was a little after six, and often she stayed later to make sure last-minute adjustments got done on time; the tailor she worked for expected that of her, tended to push most of the last-minute load in her direction. (Well, he paid her a little extra for it too, so she didn't mind.) Today she had nothing urgent. She'd been planning on staying another hour to get a head start on a suit due in two days, but when she saw James standing outside the window, looking in at her with a perturbed expression on his face, the clothes went away. Sewing supplies, away. And her, out the door to meet him.

"I didn't know you were coming," she said.

"I'm sorry. Is it inconvenient?"

"No, no, not at all. I haven't seen you all week." She was smiling. Damn it, she'd told herself she'd stay mad at him this time. But here he was, and here she was, and worries flew away. She grabbed his hand. "Where shall we go? Ellie's?" It was a discreet tavern not far from her house, their usual place for lunch or dinner. It had good food, good music, and tables far enough apart to offer a modicum of privacy. For a quiet little affair like theirs, it was ideal.

"Ellie's—yes, I think we'd better," James said, and he smiled at her awkwardly, and away they went.

"Where have you been?" she asked him.

"Home, mostly. I was sick for a while. And then I was... busy."

Ordinarily Charlotte would have been all over him asking how sick he was, what kind of sickness it was, and why he didn't write to her about it—maybe she could have sent him some food, or at least said a quiet prayer for him. She would have been miffed. She would have been concerned. She would have coddled and scolded him until he looked away with an embarrassed grin that said, "my girl is overdoing it", knowing he secretly loved the attention. Today she did not do this. There was something about the way he hesitated before finishing that last sentence. "Busy with what?"

"Certain duties I'd been neglecting. My parents and I had a talk. I had a lot to think about."

"Your parents again? Honestly, James, you aren't half as irresponsible as they think you are."

"I'd rather not talk about that with you," James said. "Let's just go to Ellie's, all right?"

She cast him a glance. He didn't meet her eyes. "All right," she said. "All right, James, if you're feeling down, that's all right. Let's get you sitting down and get a meal into you. You're sure you aren't still sick?"

"I've been better," James said, and she couldn't tell if he meant he was improving or that he still had a long way to go. She didn't hassle him about it. He didn't want to talk.

At Ellie's, they took a corner table. They often did. She ordered lamb and potatoes. He ordered soup, so she guessed he really was feeling under the weather. The waiter brought them each a mug of hard cider to start—he'd stopped asking them what they liked to drink after the first fifteen times—and told them it could be a while. The tavern was full tonight; the kitchen was busy.

"Take your time," Charlotte said. "Don't worry about us. You know we can occupy ourselves."

The waiter grinned. "That I do, love. That I do."

They sat for a while then, sipping their cider. Charlotte was enjoying the chatter of the tavern in the background. She never came here except with James. She was enjoying James too. Even when he was quiet, it was just nice being around him.

"I brought you something," James said abruptly. He took it out of his coat. It was a small parcel. Usually he gave her jars of preserves and jam or boxes of candy, none of them small enough to fit in this box which he could easily hide in the palm of his hand. He handed it to her, and she smiled and said he shouldn't have, and unwrapped it.

Inside was a little box with a brand name on it she recognized. It was an expensive jewelry store. Her breath caught for a moment as she pictured a ring—no, she told herself. *Not likely. He said we'd wait.* She opened the box and inside it was a bracelet.

It was a gorgeous piece. The center of attention was a ring of circles in blue enamel, but around the edges of these blue circles were little diamonds, and as far as Charlotte could tell the band itself was made of gold. She looped it around her wrist, exclaiming over it. In her chest, her heart was flipping and flopping, up to her throat and down to her stomach.

James apologized, sometimes, for his gifts to her not being very expensive. A box of fancy chocolates was about as far as he'd gone, that and once a pair of gloves she'd insisted he return for being too noticeable. That was by her request—left to his own devices, he would have bought her the moon. But she'd told him that she didn't see their relationship as financial. "I can be your lover," she told him. "But I won't be your kept woman. Things can't be like that between us."

"I know," he'd said. "But you know, even if you were my kept woman, it wouldn't change what we are."

"I'd lose your respect."

"How could you? You'd be the same woman."

"I've known enough men, and heard enough of my friends'

stories, to know it would matter more than you think," she'd said, and she'd stood firm on no expensive gifts.

But it had been almost a year since he'd last attempted to give her anything nice. And this was—this was really nice. She felt he was trying to express something he could not say in words, something more than just "I saw this and thought of you", as most of his presents did. Something she could not crush by rejecting the gift. So she accepted, and thanked him, and waited.

He looked her in the eye. "I talked to my parents this week a lot. They're still in conversation with the Hunt family."

"That again?"

"Charlie, I've been thinking about our future. The way we are right now—we can't be like this forever. I need to think about these things more seriously."

Charlotte swallowed.

How many times in the past year had he tried to propose to her, only for her to have to shut him down? He did it most often when he was drunk, but sometimes when the only thing he was drunk off of was moonlight. It always was the same old refrain: "Let's run away together, Charlie. Leave it all behind." She didn't want to "leave it all behind." She had her brothers, and he had a family too for all he fought with them, a family and even a title to inherit. She told him to be patient. They would find a better way.

But the look in his eyes tonight was different from when he made those impulsive proposals. Told her he'd thought things through.

If he'd really thought things through, if he really wanted to run away with her, said it and meant it with all his heart, she wasn't sure she could turn him down anymore.

He looked her in the eyes. "I have to stop seeing you."

"What?"

"I have to consider my position. An earl can't marry a seamstress, and our affair... it's taken over my life. It's holding you back, too, I'm sure. How are you supposed to pursue someone of your own station if you're spending all your time with me?"

"Someone of my own—James!"

"I know it sounds cold. But when you think about it, we really can't go on like this. We aren't adolescents, Charlie. I wasn't even when I first met you and you weren't either. This thing between us has gotten out of hand, and it's more than time we end it."

"You're crazy." Charlotte felt nauseous. "James, are you still sick?"

"I'm fine."

"Then don't joke with me." He gave her a level look. She forced a smile. "You sound like your father, or-or Lord Montroy."

"I'm trying to be sensible for once. The past year and a half, I've been far too childish. We can't just keep on playing games forever."

"Love isn't a game," Charlotte said.

"Love? Do we really love each other, or do we just have a lot of fun? What's love without a future?" James asked. "It's nothing. It's worthless."

Charlotte swallowed. Maybe this was her fault for constantly putting him off. "There can be a future between us. Of some sort. If we just wait..."

"What kind of a future? This relationship only lowers us. The longer we continue it, the more we drag ourselves through the muck."

It was then Charlie felt her first spark of anger. "You mean I'm muck to you, of course."

"I didn't say that. You're a good woman, Charlotte, and we've had a lot of fun together and you taught me a lot of things I never knew. But it's time we move on."

"Taught you things you didn't know? Oh, so fucking me was just so you could learn how to make love to a woman, is that it? Maybe loving me was about that too, learning how to find a woman attractive so you wouldn't act like a cold fish with some elegant proper high society wife."

"Don't be rude."

"I'll be as rude as I want!" Charlotte stood. "You always said I'm not a game to you, James Guarin! How can you talk like this?"

"I don't mean you're a game. I mean this—between us—it's just immature."

"You're immature. You always have been. But the most immature you've been is this. You think what, you can give me a bracelet to buy me off? After what we've been to each other?"

"Charlie. I've said all I can say. I'm ending things. If you don't want the bracelet, you can sell it. It's an apology. I've wasted too much of your time." James got up. "I hope you find someone more suitable for you, who can love you like you deserve. Maybe he'll be a better man than me. But you know we never would have worked. I'm going now."

He stood. Charlotte grabbed his wrist.

She wanted to tell him not to go. She wanted to tell him he'd regret it. She wanted to tell him she'd kill him. She wanted to tell him she'd die. She wanted to tell him she loved him. She wanted to ask if their love had ever been real. These things, these thoughts and feelings and questions, all got horribly tangled in her throat until she could say nothing at all, and he pulled his hand away from her and walked away from their table and out the door and was gone.

She sat. Sometime later the waiter brought her lamb, potatoes and soup. "Gentleman gone for the night? Or is he coming back?" he asked her.

"For the night," she told him leadenly.

"Too bad. Soup tonight is something special."

"Maybe next time," she said.

She still half-believed then that there would be a next time, that

James would change his mind, and a week later they would be sitting in Ellie's together again, and James could try the soup then.

***

Charlotte spent the next week in a daze. At work, she sewed furiously, wishing she could stab her needle into something less yielding than cloth. Leather was more to the point, but even then, it wasn't an animal's skin she wanted to be piercing. Despite her rage, she was careful. Her boss clearly noted her foul mood, but since her sewing was as adept as ever, he made no mention of it, only told her that if she needed some time off, it wasn't a busy season just now. When she refused the kind offer, made sure she had some calming tea to drink each afternoon. He was a good boss.

While she was sewing, she tried to figure out what to do.

For the first couple days, she tried to contact James. Whatever had come over him, how could he really mean to break up with her? They'd been together for three years now. They'd been happy. True, he'd sometimes been frustrated when they talked about the future and failed to reach a conclusion. But they'd always enjoyed a luxuriant present. Evening walks by the river, secret rendezvous at Ellie's and other private bars and cafes. Nights spent at discreet inns, James sneaking out of parties and fancy dinners early to meet her still in his good clothes, smelling of high society wine and flowery women's perfume but largely sober and disinterested in any woman other than her. Little gifts exchanged between the two of them, nothing too grand or expensive, little love tokens that Charlotte cherished more than gold. And she knew that James did the same. She knew that James felt the same

She thought she knew.

Maybe it was her fault. Maybe if she'd agreed to run away with him, or to really become his kept woman, his mistress in some more official sense, this wouldn't be happening. But then again, what if she'd agreed to run off to some other country with him only for him to pull this on her once they were there? No, no, James wasn't like that.

Only it seemed that maybe he was.

When a week had passed by and she couldn't contact him at all, she decided she would be the bigger person. She could be as cold as him. She could need James as little as he cared about her.

"James wasn't meant for me," she said to herself in the mirror. "He was an interesting man and we had fun together, and he taught me a lot of things. Things I never knew before him." She swallowed, thinking of all the things that could mean. They'd learned their bodies together, learned each other's bodies, learned the meaning of pleasure. But also, before James, she'd never known what it was like to have someone look at you like you hung the stars in the skies. She'd never had a person that was always in her mind when she thought about her plans: for the day, the week, the month, the year, the unforeseeable future, always a primary consideration. A person she wanted to be her partner in life. She hadn't known what it was like to have someone you felt that way about.

"But," she said, forcing herself to finish the statement—she could be as heartless as him, damn it! She could, she could! "But we have to move on now. Because all that was immature and impractical. Now we have to be adults. And we can find other people. I can find another man. He can be happy with another woman. That's just the way it has to be."

She stared at her face in the mirror. *Look me in the eyes*, she demanded. *Tell me I can believe that. Tell me I can believe a damn word of it. Convince me you aren't full of bullshit, Charlie. You stupid idiot, Charlie, if you buy some bullshit like that. You stupid bitch, trying to agree with a bastard of a nobleman just because you were in love with him.*

And she didn't believe it, she didn't believe a damn word of it. She stared at her own blank, unbelieving face in the mirror, and felt the urge to scream build up in her throat. But she was at work, so she did not allow the scream to escape. It crumpled back down her throat and into her chest, seeping down through her ribcage into her lungs, her gut, her veins, filtering into every part of her body. She didn't cry at work all day. By the time she got home, she no longer wanted to. The scream had dried itself into bitterness. She no longer wanted to release her sorrow, her despair. She no longer wanted to mourn her love, justify it, recapture it. All she wanted was revenge.

Revenge was a different proposition, with different options to consider. She thought them through. At first, she thought humiliation might be sufficient. With this in mind and acid in her belly, she paid a little visit to Miss Genevieve Hunt and said a few choice words to her about the man she intended to take as her husband. She expected outrage, expected Miss Hunt to go to her parents and demand to beg off, perhaps to even take matters into her own hands and decry James's name to all her connections. Instead, Miss Hunt gave her an icy look and politely told her, "James's past is his own business. As for his future, he has promised it to me. I hope you won't try to interfere with us again."

Charlotte had been stunned by the girl's nonchalance. Miss Hunt had then asked her if perhaps she was looking for money, attempting blackmail. At that, Charlotte had left. Blackmail might have been a nice means of revenge, but she didn't want revenge on Miss Hunt, she wanted it on James. And besides, blackmail was just a slow, steady bleeding of a man. Even if it worked on him, it wouldn't offer Charlotte any real satisfaction. She wanted James to burn. She wanted him to experience the level of pain she herself was feeling. A slow bleeding wouldn't cut it.

If she couldn't humiliate him and destroy his pride, she decided, her last resort was violence. And when she settled on this idea, she realized it was what she had really wanted to begin with. It wasn't enough to ruin James's name, not when he was a nobleman whose name would recover sooner or later. That was only the petty, impotent kind of revenge he would probably expect from her. No, she wanted something irrevocable.

She wanted to kill him.

How to kill him, though? She very briefly considered her brothers. Charlotte Taylor was the only member of her family who had gone into the actual trade of tailoring—her brothers were mostly toughs. Two of them blatantly refused to tell her what kind of work they did, and of the other three, two worked at the docks and the third helped deal with rowdies at a very popular local inn. They knew how to dish out violence. But she discarded the idea of going to them as soon as it came to mind. When she had first started seeing James, they had told her several times they wanted to "have a word" with her new paramour, and she had firmly discouraged them, saying her honor was her own to protect. To go back on that now would hurt her pride. Besides, even the roughest brother, Bartholomew, was more talk and reckless fist-throwing than one for cold-blooded murder, which was what she intended. And she could not bear to get her brothers in trouble with the law if things went wrong. So this would be her endeavor; her family would not get involved.

After that, she considered killing James herself, but even if she could get close enough to give it a go, she wasn't sure she could bring herself to follow through and really stab him. And if she did, how would she avoid getting caught? There was something poetic about the idea of dying with James or hanging for his murder, but it would be better revenge if she really did live on to love another man and enjoy her own life, with him unable to do so. No, no, she couldn't be the one to kill James either. It simply wouldn't do.

Then, a fancy came to her mind. An old legend, the legend of Poor John...

It was nonsense, somewhere between a child's story and the type of story drunks might pass around on a dark and rainy evening. Yet she'd always found the concept interesting: A man who could be summoned to kill anyone for a simple price, a man with supernatural powers who loved more than anything to avenge the helpless. A righteous, ruthless, heartless killer, the type of person she wished more than anything to be at this moment.

If the legend was all nonsense, it wouldn't do any harm to at least give it a try.

***

The summoning ritual varied depending on which version of the story you heard. Charlotte tried the most basic version, feeling that if it worked, it perhaps was proof that it was meant to work. If it didn't work, she promised herself, she would try something else, something more sensible.

First, you had to wait until midnight, then light a candle and open up a window. Charlotte used the window in her bedroom. Then, you had to set out three coins in an equilateral triangle, preferably coins of different denominations. These were easy to come by; Charlotte put two thirds of her earnings into the family's general funds, which they kept locked up in the pantry, but she kept a third for herself, and her savings were considerable. Then, in the center you had to put a piece of bone—not a human bone necessarily, although that was certainly an option, but the quality of the bone was supposed to be related to how likely Poor John was to show up. Charlotte used a nice large beef bone she had gotten from the butcher, the type one might give a dog. Then you had to offer just a little of your own blood. Charlotte pricked a finger for this. Her fingers knew a lot about pinpricks, and barely minded this sort of pain anymore.

Then, the chant:

"On this world I see a blight,

Poor John, Poor John, make it right.

To kill this man I've paid and bled.

Poor John, Poor John, make him dead."

She said it once, twice, three times. The third time, there was a gust of wind. Charlotte rushed to the window and looked out. On the street she thought she saw a shadow shaped like a man. She squinted, unable to resolve the image into a solid form. Then she heard a voice behind her—"You called, child?"

She jumped, but still, she did not scream. Quietly, trembling, she turned around.

A yard behind her stood a tall woman. She wore all black: black coat and straight black skirt, black boots and black gloves, high black scarf and low black hat. Only around her eyes could Charlotte get a glimpse of pale, pale skin. She squinted at this too, trying to make this apparition into a human. After a moment she succeeded in seeing wrinkles. The sight of them made her relax, maybe a bit too much.

"You can't be Poor John," she said bluntly, foolishly.

A dry chuckle. "Really, can't I?"

"Poor John's a man."

"You've never heard of Poor Jane?"

People did talk about a Poor Jane too, especially recently. She'd heard tales that there was a new monster that ran around the city doing Poor John's work, but that was supposed to be a young maiden—the most specific stories said she was a pretty little girl with dark hair and darker eyes, eyes like coals that seemed black at first but burned, up close, with infernal fire.

This woman's eyes were silvery in the candle light. Anyhow, "You're too old to be the woman from those stories."

The woman sat down on Charlotte's bed, comfortable as if she were at home. "Poor Jane has many shapes, as many as Poor John has worn over the years. People don't tell many stories about old women, it's true. And a lot of people take me for a man. And a lot of others haven't lived to speak of me, you know."

Charlotte shivered, and knew, in that instant, that the woman—Poor Jane—spoke the truth.

The woman's eyes glinted. Perhaps, under her scarf, she was smiling. "I see you believe me now. Good. So I'm Poor Jane, and we've settled it. And who are you?"

Charlotte hesitated, remembering old wives' tales about telling faeries your name and being trapped under their thrall for centuries until they got bored of you. But Poor Jane, whatever she was, did not appear to be a faerie, and the stories about her mentioned no stipulation of mentioning a name or not. Testing her ground, she said, "My friends call me Charlie, sometimes."

Poor Jane said, "A woman like me can tell when people lie, you know. Well, not always, but you're pretty obvious. We can cut the crap, can't we? You're asking me to kill someone. You've offered blood and bone and coin. A name won't make much of a difference, now, will it?"

Charlotte wanted to protest that she hadn't been lying, but truthfully she had been. The only one who called her Charlie had been James; even her brothers tended to call her Lottie most of the time, and everyone else called her Charlotte. She swallowed. "My name," she said, "is Charlotte Taylor."

"Good. Charlotte Taylor, what can I do for you?"

"I want you to kill a man for me."

"That much, I got already."

"His name is James Guarin. He's the son of the earl of Ilbird."

"Hm. I've heard of him, I think. Then again," Poor Jane said, crossing her arms, "I hear of a lot of people, in my line of work, and it's hard keeping them all straight. Tell me more about him."

"He's five foot six. He has blond hair—well, I called it blond. He always said it was sandy brown. His face is kind of round, but he's pretty thin overall. Well, he's not fat, I mean. He's not really thin, either, or very muscular. He wears a lot of colorful clothing, but he might stop doing that now. Mostly he wore what I recommended. He might decide he prefers greys and browns now that we are... no longer on good terms."

"A good physical description. Should help me recognize him. But looks aren't everything. Does he have connections? If he's attacked, will he put up a fight? Where does he go throughout the day? What are his habits? Why do you want him dead? Who else might want him dead? These are the kinds of things I'd like to know—if you know them. Tell me what you can, and for the rest, I'll do my own research."

Saying this, Poor Jane leaned back on her hands and tilted her head up, waiting. Even when she lifted her chin, the top of her scarf did not fall a single millimeter down the bridge of her nose.

Charlotte talked.

She answered all Poor Jane's initial questions, and then more and more, elaborating as Poor Jane zeroed in on details and pried her answers open to the light. By the time she was done speaking, Poor Jane knew all about James: his character, his habits, his social position, and most of all, his relationship to Charlotte in all its bittersweet glory. It was surprising how a mythical assassin could be so easy to talk to.

Poor Jane got up at last and brushed her hands together as if she'd gotten dust on her gloves from Charlotte's well-washed sheets. "Thank you, that should be all I need. Of course I'll come to you if I need more. One last thing. How do you want me to kill him? This is clearly an intimate matter for you, after all. Would you like him to die slowly? Or, perhaps you'd like to see his death for yourself..."

"No. No, that won't be... I don't need that," Charlotte said. She bit her lip. She didn't want to torture James, or anyone, for that matter. But then again, it wasn't really revenge if he didn't know what it was for. "If you can: Stab him in the heart. And tell him that it was Charlotte Taylor that sent you."

"Certainly that can be managed."

A jolt of spite hit her, and she added, "If you could do it at a party—maybe one he's at with Genevieve Hunt—that would be a nice touch."

"Hm."

"Well, not necessary. Not absolutely. You can kill him in some back alley if that's more convenient, I don't know how these things work."

"I do my best to fulfill the specifications given by my patron. All of them." Poor Jane touched her hat, not quite tipping it. "Expect the best from me, Miss Taylor. There's a reason I'm a legend."

There was a note of finality to her voice, and Charlotte expected her to make a bow and leave, or perhaps simply to vanish. Instead, she walked past Charlotte and over to the table where Charlotte had set up her triangle. With her back to Charlotte, she picked up the bone from off the table, and pulled down her scarf. Charlotte, looking at her back, got a glimpse of an unnaturally white cheek and jaw. The bone was lifted, and Charlotte heard the sound of chewing, saw the face move. Unbidden, but feeling that she was watching something private or even taboo, she turned away and listened.

"Your blood is full of pain, Miss Taylor," Poor Jane's voice said. "Though you barely spilled a drop of it. I've known patrons much more generous. The stories I could tell you... but we don't tell stories, of course."

"Are you done?" Charlotte asked.

There was no response. She turned around, and saw the room was empty, and the table empty too: no bone, no coins, only a still-flickering candle that had burned down to a stub.

***

Now it had been a couple weeks since her strange, unearthly meeting with that woman, and she began to wonder: Had it been real? Had it been a dream, or a hallucination brought on by days of tense frustration and despair? Had Poor Jane been a vision, a faerie, an illusion—a normal woman playing a trick on Charlotte with no intention of fulfilling her word? When she had thoughts like these, Charlotte reminded herself of every detail of the meeting: The pattern of Poor Jane's words, sometimes quite intellectual and other times crudely blunt, the shadows cast by the candle, the grisly sound of bone crunching between mostly-human teeth. And she tried to remember that before Poor Jane had vanished, she had been filled with a sense of complete confidence that Poor Jane would do as she had promised, the task Charlotte had paid her to do.

And now, on a night two weeks after that meeting, there came a knock at Charlotte's window. When she looked out, she thought for a moment, *it's very dark outside, perhaps the street lamp has gone out,* before realizing the darkness at the window was in fact the dark color of a long black coat.

She opened the window and let Poor Jane in.

"Did you kill him?" she asked, as Poor Jane lowered her booted feet to the floor. Their impact as she straightened was silent, eerily silent.

Poor Jane shook her head. "I made an attempt, but it failed. We've come across an interesting situation, Miss Taylor. A hindrance, a curiosity. Sit down and I'll tell you the details."

4

Chapter Four

James's head ached in a fuzzy way. He felt the way he sometimes did when he hadn't been able to sleep all night and had instead been stuck in a half-waking dream, staring at the ceiling, perfectly conscious of the blanket over his body, and yet partway convinced he was in the middle of being introduced to a dignified elderly gentleman and couldn't figure out how to greet him with the proper level of politeness. Right now he was not dreaming, but as he awoke, he was straining to remember something, something important. Genevieve Hunt and his parents were waiting for him, he thought. But that couldn't be right. He had fallen asleep, so he had to be home from the party already, and it was still dark outside and in, so it was not so late that he had overslept, probably not late enough that he should be up at all...

As he gradually gained consciousness, he realized that what little light he could see was coming not from his usual bedside lamp but from out a window, and the window was not the window beside his bed but the window of a coach. That wasn't right. His chest tightened with panic, and at the same time he became aware that it was already in pain—not the inside of his chest, but the skin felt sore, and when he shifted the wrong way, he felt pain more acute, burning. He squeezed his eyes shut. He wanted to go back to sleep, for all this to have been a dream.

He opened them back up again, and deliberately observed his surroundings. Yes, he was in a coach, and the buildings outside the window revealed no neighborhood he could remember. There was no one in the coach with him, and the coach was at a standstill. This was good, in a sense. He was not headed anywhere he could not control. But he was already somewhere he didn't know, and the stillness of the coach, in the middle of the night, was eerie. He shivered, and realized he was also very cold. His coat from the party was lying over his body like a blanket, but it was thin, and lately the nights had been getting colder and colder. Where had his cloak gone?

He sat up. The movement sent pain screaming through his chest. Certain now he was injured, he unbuttoned his shirt and took a look.

It was worse than he'd imagined. There was a whole flap of skin hanging carelessly off his chest, as if someone had started to skin him and then just stopped midway. Instinctively he squeezed his eyes closed, but he forced himself to open them again and assess the damage. This was no time to be squeamish. He looked, and saw the redness of flesh, skin cleanly cut, brutally white bone, and...

He blinked, squinted, overcoming surface-level nausea and arriving at a deeper horror. There was an empty space between his ribs. Wasn't that...

No, he was no doctor. He was badly hurt, in pain, and still groggy from being knocked out. (He could remember now how his night had ended. That little maid, who had frightened him at first with her eyes and turned out to be deadly in more practical ways.) He could not trust his own perceptions. What mattered more was that he was in a place he didn't know, injured, clearly in danger. He had to get himself together and get to safety. He could worry about possible delusions and empty spaces in his chest after that.

Cringing, he pulled his skin back into alignment with his body as best he could, though he could tell it wasn't going to stick. He buttoned his shirt back up, put his coat on, and got out of the coach. It was a coach high off the ground, and the hop to the ground jolted his chest. He hugged his coat tight around himself and looked at the front of the coach. At the front seat, holding the reins, a coachman sat very still. He was leaning against the back of the seat, his head slumped forward. James took a step forward, then stopped. Anyone who had spirited him away out here was unlikely to be a friend. No need to wake this man up if he were sleeping. Though James wasn't so sure he was sleeping. He seemed too still, as if he slept the sleep of the dead.

In the lamplit dark, then, he walked slowly down the road. He could hear, if he strained, noises coming from down the street that did not sound hostile. If he could find people, he could ask directions. He would just have to keep an eye out for that murderous maid.

When he finally reached the noise, it turned out to be a bar, but by then he had discovered where he was. He was in the west side of town, an impoverished area he rarely had reason to frequent. But he recognized the bar. It was one with a bad reputation. There had been a time, shortly before his first season on the ton, when he'd come to it for exactly that reason. He'd hoped to find a man unconcerned with propriety or morality, willing to give him what he wanted and shouldn't want, and thought he'd be able to know such a man at a glance, or that he'd be approached soon after arriving. Instead, he'd spent an awkward evening sitting at a corner of the bar, being ignored by the regulars. On his way out a man had come up to him—a large, muscular man, a bit older than him, with a dark, well-trimmed beard. His heart had quickened.

"Hey, Mr. Fancy Pants," the man had said in a rolling voice. "You dropped this." And he'd handed James his wallet.

James had looked through the wallet quickly. Mostly everything was in it. There were perhaps a few less bills than he'd remembered, but he couldn't remember how much he'd spent on dinner and a drink and a tip for the bartender. Anyway, he wouldn't make a fuss about it. "Thank you," he said, because the man had lingered, watching him with some amusement.

"No worries. But listen, this isn't the best place for your type. You'd better get back to where you belong, you hear? Take care."

James had thought those words over all night afterward, and come to the conclusion that "your type" probably meant noblemen, that the man hadn't guessed why James had gone there, that no one had guessed. How could they have guessed? All he'd done was sit around, watching and listening, feeling out of place. No, they couldn't have guessed, and that was probably for the best in the end. He had followed the man's advice and hadn't come back. Later, he'd chanced upon a bar that catered more to his interests, but by then he'd met Charlie, and was no longer so free to pursue them.

Now, he would have felt embarrassed to return to this place if he hadn't felt so relieved to see somewhere familiar. He hurried inside.

The bar was much as he remembered it, perhaps a bit smaller. The same dark walls with unidentifiable stains here and there, decorated by peeling paintings of fruit and wine bottles and, directly in the center of one wall, a mounted deer's head. The bar was crowded even at this late hour—not that James was exactly sure what hour it was—mostly with men who smelled of salt. This neighborhood was not very far from the docks. In fact, he'd heard that some of Charlie's brothers worked nearby, which was one reason he didn't come here even when he and Charlie spent lazy afternoons exploring the city; Charlie preferred to avoid them.

James stood at the doorway, looking at the mass of people. His head spun a little. The dizziness from the party hadn't completely cleared, and now he wondered if it had been a natural illness or induced by that maid somehow. Conspiracy loomed high over him, and he was frozen.

The door was open behind him, letting in a draught, and after a moment, people began to notice. A man got up from a nearby table, rolling his eyes, and went to close the door. As he walked by, he brushed against James's chest, hard, and James let out a squeak of pain, doubling over.

Hands steadied him. "Corey, what the devil did you do?" A female voice.

"Nothing! I didn't do nothing! What's wrong with him, I barely touched him."

"You must've done more than that."

"It's fine," James wheezed. "I'm just..." He waved a hand, then returned to clutching at his chest.

"You need a drink." A third voice, on the left side of him.

"Maybe." James straightened up and found a small knot of people bunched around him, expressions ranging from concerned to intrigued. "I-I need a doctor. Or a cab. Maybe a cab."

"Can't get one around here, not this late," a man said. "Alfred Pallison has a wagon with him, I think. Might give you a ride if you paid him, eh, Alfred?"

"No, I won't." A voice from outside the knot of people, old and drunk and irritated. "I'm going straight home, promised the missus."

"Well, you said that an hour ago, Alfred."

"Going straight home, and no stops along the way. Promised."

"Might want to go soon..."

The woman holding James's right arm gave it a squeeze. "Here now, sir, how about you come to the back room for a minute. We'll see what can be done about you, hm?"

"All right," James agreed, and he followed her wearily back, through the kitchen and into a surprisingly well-lit pantry, where she hauled in a stool and sat him down.

"Now, my name's Delia and I'm the co-owner of this tavern. We get a lot of troublemakers around here and we don't like them very much. You don't strike me as one, so if you behave maybe we can help you." She leaned in close to his face and sniffed. "You're not drunk, anyway. What's wrong with you?"

James gave her the brief version: That he'd been at a party and been knocked out and kidnapped by a female assailant, possibly with accomplices. "I think I could walk home from here, or at least to a place where I could stay the night," he said, "if I could get some directions, and maybe a warmer coat. I could pay for it. I have a few coins on me now, anyway, and if necessary I could pay more later. Anyway I don't really need a ride, just some assistance. Also, before I leave, if I could have some bandages..."

"I knew you were hurt. What are your injuries? Maybe we can do something about them."

"My chest was cut up. It's not bleeding much—" Now that James thought about it, it wasn't bleeding at all. "—but it's very tender. If I could bind it..."

"They cut up your chest?"

"A little."

"Beasts." Delia made a face. "We'll have to have a look at it. Here, just a second. I'm not much for binding wounds and all that but there's a man here tonight who is. He's no doctor but he's a decent hand in emergencies. Hold on."

James held on.

The man was fetched. His name was Laurie and he was younger than James had expected, just a bit older than James himself, but he moved and spoke slowly and ponderously, as if he were a much older and wiser man than he appeared. He told Delia to turn her back for the moment, and then requested James bare his chest. James did so.

Laurie frowned. "You should see a real doctor when you get home," he said. "There's something wrong with your innards. I'm no specialist on organs and stuff. But you're right we should get it put together for now. And I don't know as you should walk home like that either."

As he spoke, he opened up the tavern's medical kit. "I'm going to sew you up," he told James, after wiping the edges of the wound off with a wet rag and splashing the open part with some kind of ointment that mildly stung. "The doctor you see at home might pull out the stitches and redo everything, but I'm sorry, you really need more than some bandages slapped over you. I don't know what's keeping you from bleeding but I don't like it and we can't trust it to last. And these are some big, long cuts. Delia, come on over, I'm going to need you after all. You can hold him still for me. Don't worry, sir, Delia's seen plenty of men in deshabille."

"It's fine," James said. "I don't care."

He didn't care about much, after the night he'd been having. And his shoulders were still clothed where Delia touched him. Even his parents and Genevieve probably couldn't object to it as immodesty, not given the circumstances. It didn't matter. Nothing much mattered, until Laurie stuck the needle into his skin for the first stitch and he rediscovered pain.

A whimper escaped his mouth. "Ssh," Laurie said. "Easy. We're going to take care of you, sir, all right? It'll just hurt for a little while and it'll all be much better. Hold still."

James found it very hard to hold still, but he did his best.

The sewing process took a long time. Laurie was careful about it, for one thing, but mostly it was just that the perimeter of the flap of skin was so long, and to sew it up with fine stitches naturally was a lengthy process. By the time Laurie was done, James was covered in sweat. Laurie wiped this off with the wet rag as well, rubbed a little more ointment on the wound, and pronounced the job done.

"That should do you at least until morning. You could come home with me tonight," he told James. "I live very near here, and my bed's large enough for two."

"Ah, I don't think that's a good idea."

"I have a couch, too, if you don't like to share."

"It's not that. I need to go home. My family will be missing me. I just vanished on them. It's inconsiderate."

Laurie and Delia exchanged a look. Delia shrugged. Laurie said, "In that case, I'll walk you home. A man in your condition shouldn't travel alone."

Thanking the two, James began to button his shirt up.

"By the way," Laurie asked, "as your pseudo-physician, I must ask—what's that circle you have? Looks like someone stitched you up before."

"Circle?" James frowned tiredly.

"On your chest, over your heart."

"I don't have anything like that," James snapped. He finished buttoning his shirt, pulled on his jacket, and stood. "I still need a warm coat. Delia, perhaps you can help me find someone who'd be willing to sell theirs."

"Sure thing," Delia said. "For that matter, you might as well buy one from the tavern, if you're in a spending mood. We have a few in the foyer that's been left behind for weeks now. Doubt anyone's coming back for them at this point."

**

They didn't walk all the way. They walked until they got closer to the center of town, where even at this time of night they managed to flag down a cab. Then James told Laurie he could go home if he wanted, and James could take it from here, but Laurie said, "You look like you might collapse at any second. And someone was playing around with your guts. I'll see you to your house, thanks."

"I'll pay you," James said. "For the treatment, that is. And I'll pay the cabbie to take you home. I owe you more than that."

"You don't have to," Laurie said. "Sounds like you've had a pretty awful night. I'm just trying to make it a little better." Then he grinned. "Then again—you don't look like you're so hard up, so if you want to pay the cabbie, sure. But not for the treatment. I'm no physician, and you can get sued for practicing without a license these days if you aren't careful."

James wanted to laugh, because clearly Laurie was trying to joke, but he didn't have the energy for laughing, didn't have the heart for it. Heart. Heart. Now, sitting in the back of a coach again, something came back to him. He cleared his throat. "Actually, would you mind feeling my pulse?"

"Your pulse? I don't know much about pulses," Laurie said dubiously. But he took James's wrist and felt it, and frowned. Put a hand to the curve of James's throat, right beneath the side of his chin. "I can't feel it, actually. It must be faint. You really will have to see a real doctor, though. I'm no professional at this."

"It's all right," James said. "Probably there's nothing to feel."

"I'm sorry?"

"I think I might not have a heart," James said.

Laurie gave him a look, and apparently decided it wasn't worth delving into the subject. Instead he squeezed James's shoulder and said little more for the rest of the ride to the Ilbird townhouse, where he delivered James to Mr. Johnson, the Guarins' blank-faced head butler. Mr. Johnson handed Laurie a handful of coins and bills, roughly the amount James would have given him, for the cabbie and for the trouble. Mr. Johnson always knew what was appropriate, what his employers would want. Knew what James would want, and knew even better—and would always prioritize—what the earl and the countess would want.

In this case, James's wishes coincided with his parents'. He wanted to see his parents immediately, let them know he was home and tell them what had happened, and Mr. Johnson understood this well enough. He headed decisively towards the parlor, and James trudged after him, hoping that he could settle things with his parents quickly and get to bed at a decent hour. Well, not a decent hour, he mentally amended. Outside the sky was already lightening. But soon.

In the parlor, his mother and father were waiting for him. His mother was sprawled across the loveseat, two pillows at her back and a blanket over her lap, a book in front of her that she put down as James and Mr. Johnson entered. His father stood by the fireplace, staring at his watch. He clicked the watch shut and said to James, "Five o'clock in the morning and you finally deign to show up."

James's chest throbbed with a sudden burst of pain. He took a deep breath. "I'm sorry. I know I disappeared at a bad time, and I'm sure both of you were worried. And Genevieve too, probably."

"Explain yourself," his father barked.

"David, dear, calm down," his mother said. She put her book on the table next to the loveseat and sat up briskly, as if she had not been keeping herself awake all night. "Look at him, he's clearly shaken. Sit down, James. You can tell us about it at your own pace."

James sat, and explained.

His mother asked a few leading questions, prompting him whenever he paused. His father was silent. He threw a couple looks of restrained frustration at both James and his wife, but made no more complaints or accusations until James had finished.

"We'll need to get a doctor to take a look at you," he said then. "I'll send for Doctor Candlewick."

"Sure."

"Go up to your room for now. Get some rest. No, before you get some sleep, write a note apologizing to Miss Hunt. It's not good to leave a woman hanging, and she was quite worried."

"I'm sorry," James said uselessly.

"Nonsense. Some damned assassin attacks you and you think that's your fault? Whoever's at the bottom of this will learn not to challenge the Ilbird line. I'll be sending out some feelers to see who it might be—we'll hire a detective if necessary. Now go upstairs. No use standing around talking."

Obediently, James headed up to his room.

He wrote the note, gave it to a maid, and went to bed. An hour later he was woken so that Doctor Candlewick could perform an examination—James, he said, seemed to be about as well as could be expected. He was advised to drink plenty of water after being drugged, and his parents were advised to wake him up every couple hours to check on his condition since he'd suffered a head injury. However, the cuts on his chest, while extensive, were shallow. James was given fresh bandages, expertly applied, and was told not to do anything too exerting until the cuts healed.

"The stitches are well done," Doctor Candlewick said. "Well done indeed. I'd like to meet the young man who did them. You say he's not a doctor?"

"No."

"Hm. Well, I'd like to meet him."

"I'll tell him so," James said, "if I get the chance." He would have to go by that inn to thank Delia properly at some point anyway.

When the doctor had gone, he ran his own hand along the neat stitches lining his chest. Lightly—if he pulled them, it stung. Stitching made him think of sewing made him think of Charlie. It was an unfortunate association. It amazed him, though, that he could think of Charlie now and it didn't hurt, really. He didn't feel anything about it, except vague regret that she hadn't taken their parting well. He remembered, abruptly, that the little maid had said Charlie sent her. But that was unbelievable. Not that Charlie would never do anything dire—in a temper he'd seen her shatter plates, shatter even a vase of flowers—but all this seemed too convoluted for her. Charlie was basically an honest, simple woman. He'd always thought that was one of her better traits, compared to the various debutantes his parents had tried to push him at over the years, all of them silky and well-crafted facades over who-knew-what nastiness. Charlie's meanness, when she was mean, was up front. She didn't go behind your back. She didn't keep secrets.

Well, she'd kept their relationship a secret for three years. But that was different.

She couldn't be at fault for this attack, but if she was in any way connected to it, he supposed he would have to deal with her. At least he didn't love her anymore. He wouldn't feel squeamish about handing her over to the police if he had to.

He'd cut that knot in his life cleanly.

But, he thought, as he drew his hand away from the stitches, still. It wasn't enough. He'd broken things off with Charlie, but he was still flawed, very flawed, far from the husband Genevieve Hunt deserved or the son his parents needed. Even earlier in the evening, half-conscious and in horrible pain, there had been something about Laurie touching him... He'd felt nervous, a little queasy, a little aroused. All feelings he'd promised himself to suppress. He could not be a good husband or a good son if he still had wandering eyes.

Shameful. It was shameful. Guilt surged in him as his mother, who had lingered behind the doctor, fondly smoothed back his hair and helped him into a nightgown.

"You'll be better soon, dear. And these evil people who attacked you—we'll find them and take care of things. Don't worry. Why are you so tense?"

"I've made a poor impression on Miss Hunt."

His mother clicked her tongue. "Miss Hunt's a sympathetic woman. She'll understand. She'll be horrified to hear about all this, really, but she might even find it romantic. Girls like a man beset by troubles. They feel they can comfort him. They like that."

"Maybe." James didn't think he was much the stoically suffering romantic hero, and he doubted Genevieve would see him that way either.

"It will be fine, dear. Don't worry."

She insisted on tucking him into bed and pulling his drapes closed. As she turned to go, he said, "Mama."

"Yes, dear?"

"I—will you feel my pulse for me?"

"Doctor Candlewick did that already."

"He didn't say what he felt," James said.

She stepped over and picked up his wrist. "Nice and strong and steady," she said after a moment. "The same as always. My strong, brave boy."

James sighed. "Thank you. I know it's silly."

"No worries. Get some sleep."

5

Chapter Five

Charlotte Taylor's eyes were distant, but her fists clenched so tightly that her knuckles had gone white. Angela waited. This was part of the job, waiting for clients to think things through. She advised them, sometimes, when she was in one of her kinder moods: Remember, death is permanent. Remember, it's easy to toss a leaf into the river, but impossible to catch it when it's been borne away by the stream. Remember that the choice you make now is irrevocable and for God's sake make it carefully.

She rarely felt that kind. People made their own choices; if they summoned her, they were already resolute. And there had only ever been two clients who listened to her cautioning. The rest had brushed it aside—with hesitance, with arrogance, with active offense, depending on the individual. Warnings in general weren't worth the breath it took to speak them.

But waiting she could do.

At last, Charlotte said, "Do you think he removed it himself? His heart."

"Does my opinion matter, Miss Taylor?"

"I don't know. You have more experience in these things than me, and it's not like I have anyone else to ask about it."

"I think no," Angela opined, "but then, I only know the man by what you've told me." That and Natty's story of his pure shock at surviving the stabbing, but Angela hadn't even mentioned Natty's existence to Charlotte. It wasn't common knowledge that Poor Jane had an apprentice. Common knowledge was that Poor Jane—Poor John—was immortal, and it suited Angela to let that belief persist.

Charlotte's fists clenched tighter. Her eyes flickered down to them, perhaps following Angela's gaze, and she deliberately unclenched them and folded her hands together, restlessly rubbing one thumb against the curve of the other hand as if to improve her circulation, although the room was not cold despite the frigid weather outside. She said, "Do you do other things, besides killing? If required to do so?"

"Poor Jane is a killer, not a man of all trades."

"What if I asked you to kill whoever has stolen James Guarin's heart," Charlotte said, "and to bring his heart back to me?"

"It's a new commission. You would need three more coins, a new bone, some more blood."

"That's easy enough. You'll do it? And bring the heart back, for sure?"

"Nothing is certain in life, but I will always strive to fulfill my patron's requirements, once the commission is accepted."

"We ate fish tonight," Charlotte said. "I can get a bone right now. Stay where you are." And she scurried downstairs, leaving Angela sitting on her bed.

***

As it was now desirable to know more about the subject of missing hearts, removed hearts, stolen hearts and all such manner of things, Angela fetched Natty and together they headed out to the shop of Iris Witherbone.

There were in the city a few notorious witches. There had been more in the past, but in recent years the government had been cracking down on witchcraft, and if it was not always competent at this endeavor—it had sent several innocent men and women on the run, as well as a multitude of bit players who only knew the most rudimentary and ineffective of charms—it still put enough energy into the effort that a couple great witches had been caught and thrown in jail, and more had quietly left the country. However, there were still a few infamous witches at large, protected by powerful connections or spells that made them difficult for an enemy to find. Angela had encountered most of them at one time or another. Iris Witherbone was not one of these.

Iris was not a very old woman. She was, in fact, a bit younger than Angela herself, judging by appearances. Despite this, she had a more than encyclopedic knowledge of just about anything one might ask. Angela had first met her as a client; Iris had requested that Angela kill a rich old man, and given no explanation when Angela requested one. She had offered a magnificent bone in payment, an entire human femur, so Angela had accepted the request. Iris had asked to come with Angela on the mission, and Angela agreed to that too.

It had not been an easy kill. The old man kept several guards around the house, properly paranoid, as well as an alarm system—bells rigged to doors, booby traps in hallways—that would have tripped up a less experienced assassin. Angela killed the guards and disabled the traps, ushering Iris along with her. At last they found the man, and Angela killed him quickly.

Iris ignored the moment of murder entirely. As the old man choked out his last breaths, she was already rummaging through his library. She stuffed a few books into a bag, muttering under her breath, and went through a cabinet, searching until she found a locked box. She murmured a spell over the box to coax it open, revealing a blooming flower of a species Angela had never seen before. Then, eyes gleaming, she lifted the flower to her lips and ate it.

"That is likely a very dangerous and magical plant, you know," Angela observed.

"I know," Iris said peaceably. "It's the reason I needed to kill him. Eight hundred years this plant waited to bloom, and the old bastard snatched it up before I could get a hold of it! Oh well, at least his library proved more fruitful than I expected. Though I don't believe he even knew what he had. Probably thought I came for his Eradicus texts, but it's his Plympeley memoir that's really rare. No idea how he got one of those. I've been looking for it for ages."

At the time, Angela had rolled her eyes and hadn't questioned it further. Most of her clients called on her for aid in crimes of passion or occasionally even self-defense—no one called on a legendary assassin without desperation fueling them. But there were some odd characters like this one, after all, who wanted to kill to advance their own ambitions or wealth. Angela didn't trouble herself about these things.

She hadn't realized then that Iris was going to become a regular customer, but Iris did. She seemed to delight in calling on Angela, and sometimes Angela even got the feeling that not all her kills were entirely necessary to advance Iris's goals, and maybe Iris just liked meeting with her. One time she asked, and Iris grinned and absolutely crooned at her, "Of course I like you, Poor Jane. I absolutely love you. You're charming. You're fascinating. If I knew some other way to invite you..."

"I could come visit," Angela said brusquely, "from time to time. But I don't accept invitations, unless they're standing." You could only summon Poor Jane one way.

"...hm, do feel free to drop by any time!" Iris said. "But I think I will still need your expertise sometimes. And it's more fun to watch you in action, you know. Poor Jane."

Iris knew a bit about what Poor Jane was. A title, a curse, an endowment. She knew a lot about that sort of magic. She knew Poor Jane wasn't Angela's real name, but she never asked what Angela's real name was, or who she had been before she was Poor Jane, what she was outside of it. It was Poor Jane that fascinated and attracted Iris. For this reason, Iris could be considered a friend to Poor Jane, but not to Angela personally. Then again, a friend to Poor Jane was perhaps the only kind of friend Angela could really have. She had acquaintances who didn't know her secret—a certain fishwife at the market place was very fond of her, for example, and a man at the local bar. But they didn't really know the heart of her. Poor Jane really was the heart of her.

Today, Iris greeted Angela with distracted enthusiasm—"My dear, you didn't say you'd be coming!" (Angela never said when she'd be coming.) "How nice, what a surprise. I'm afraid I'm a little occupied at the moment with a wyrm-hunt. Did you come on business or pleasure? If it's urgent, I suppose I can make the time."

"Business," Angela said. "My business is always urgent, as you know."

Iris sighed. (Pleasure, where she was concerned, would have been a more urgent matter.) "Well, of course, anything for an old friend and business partner. Come in, come in, but don't sit down yet. The chairs are covered with papers. No, don't touch them. Centuries old, some of them, and if they flake apart..." She smiled a tight smile. "There'll be hell to pay."

They stood still in the middle of the parlor while Iris tidied up papers, stacking some on a table and brushing others more carelessly into a portfolio. There were nine sheets of paper lying on the floor—irregular in shape—and a few of them seemed to be parts of a portrait of a winding snake-thing, with tendrils that glistened and dripped some fluid that gleamed even when portrayed by dry ink. Iris left all these papers where they were, undisturbed, and at last sat down on a cleared-off loveseat. She patted the cushion next to her. "Sit down, dear."

She was giving Angela her typical enticing gaze; Natty she had barely paid an ounce of attention since their arrival, only a brief glance. Angela gave Natty's still shoulder a push. "Go on."

Natty always read her intent well. Without looking back at Angela or questioning, she sat down next to Iris, close by her on the narrow loveseat.

Iris pouted and moved away, leaning back against the loveseat's arm. "All business, I see. Fine then, Poor Jane. You sit down too. What do you want?"

Angela sat in a vacated arm chair with a single wrinkled and ancient piece of paper still resting on one arm. If she brushed against it and it crumbled, she'd deal with the consequences. Iris needed to get over herself. "Hearts. I want to hear about hearts."

"Hearts? Powerful magic there. Human, animal? I've been thinking about wyrm hearts lately, though not so much as wyrm horns or scales. But the subjects are not unrelated, you know. Are our interests intersecting again?"

"Human hearts. A subject has had his heart removed. I want to know how such a thing could be done, what its effects could be, and how best to locate the heart now that it's been removed."

Iris sighed. "As for the latter, it would be easier to do the opposite. Having the heart, it's not so hard to do a spell to find the rest of the body, living or dead, but the specificity required for one body part among many is not so easy. I suppose your subject would be able to do it himself, it being his own heart, but for someone else it would be much more complicated. If you removed his rib cage and lungs, you might be able to set a sort of compass mechanism within them where the heart would be, but even then, it's not so simple, depending on how the removal process went, and whether the heart was still intact, whether it still maintained its original form or had been transformed, and in my experience it's far more likely it's been transformed than not. People don't like carrying around a vulnerable hunk of human meat with them most of the time. Most people consider it grotesque, I suppose, more's the shame, but besides that, if you remove a heart you probably want to use it to either control or protect the former owner, and if the heart's damaged by accident, well, it obviously puts a damper on those plans. In my experience, it's most expedient to transform the heart into something hard and crystalline—a jewel works well, or a stone. Only a heart wants to beat, you know, and a beating stone can be conspicuous. On the other hand, it makes your task easier, doesn't it? If you find a culprit with a pulsing stone, I think it's pretty likely you've found your heart."

"The subject's heart," Angela corrected her.

"What—Oh, of course dear. My apologies for suggesting you have a heart. I'm aware of your objections to the subject." Iris tittered.

"Very well. A pulsing stone."

"Or something of the sort."

"But you've taken my questions out of order. What do you think would be the purpose of such a removal?" Identify a motive, and finding a culprit would be much easier. Or it could be made clearer whether James Guarin would wish to do such a thing to himself.

"Well, if he undertook it himself, he might be doing it to achieve immortality. People have done that in the past. I don't know why they'd prefer to live without a heart, especially for so much longer," Iris pondered. "I mean, I've never heard of anyone doing the same with their brain, though it's equally feasible to live with no thoughts. If someone else did it—well, to control him, of course. If you have someone's heart, it's a relatively simple matter to sway their emotions. Your very possession of it, with no further effort on your part, will cause them to feel a strong, strong, and stronger affection for you, and an impulse to be loyal and obedient to you. Quite a lovely thing, really, but removing a person's heart is not easy, or else I suppose it would be done quite often. They'll have called in some expert, in either case. Do you want me to do some reconnaissance for you?" This last part doubtfully, hesitantly, reluctantly.

"I wouldn't say no," Angela said. It wasn't in Poor Jane's nature to ask favors, either. Even asking information was stretching it.

Iris hummed. "Wellll... if I have time, or if I chance on the information, I'll let you know. This wyrm business does have me very busy, though. Can't say when I'll get around to it."

"Well, whenever you do. I'm also a busy woman, you know, but I've always made time for your requests."

"Yes, well, I do pay you though, dear. And pay you well. Besides, it's in your nature. Speaking of," Iris added, "have you given my offer from last time any further thought?"

It had been some time since Angela had last seen Iris, and she'd forgotten the terms they'd parted on. Deliberately forgotten, for that matter. If Iris had an ounce of tact—"I believe you offered to pay for a real dinner next time. I wouldn't be averse."

"Not that one," Iris said impatiently. "Your sigil, Poor Jane. Your... burden. I offered to take it from you. You needed time to think."

Angela's hands clenched. The leather of the gloves she was wearing stretched tight on her knuckles. "Did I say I needed time to think?"

"You left. I assumed."

Angela stood. She walked across the room to stand in front of the smirking Iris, and slapped her hard across the face.

Iris sucked in a breath.

Angela had never hit her before. She didn't hit clients, as long as they let her fulfill the commission without interference. She never hit friends. She'd hit Natty, now and then, being her mentor and having once been something like her jailer (before she fully got used to her apprenticeship, she had an understandable tendency to run) but in general, she wasn't very violent outside of work. Still, there were some things that required it. Some lines that shouldn't be crossed.

"I left so I wouldn't have to do that," Angela said. "You know, I thought you were smart. I thought you knew me better. I thought you understood what Poor Jane is."

"Just an offer," Iris said, a bit hoarsely. "If you'd wanted it, it could have been mutually bene—Damn, I think you broke a tooth." There was blood dribbling out the corner of her mouth.

"I doubt it. And you deserve worse." Angela shook her head. "Natty."

Natty got to her feet immediately. She gave Iris a little respectful nod, and headed for the door, preceding Angela out.

***

"I could take it," Iris had said, all those months ago.

"Hm?" Angela had been distracted. She was sitting next to Iris's window, sharpening her knife on a whetting stone that Iris had just given her as a "little case bonus" this time around. But Iris was in bed, half-dressed, half-asleep. Angela liked to sit here, near her, sometimes focusing on her knife and other times looking over, never quite watching Iris but always aware. And Iris, in the same way, was clearly pondering some arcane matter in her bed, but she liked being able to glance over and see Angela sitting there, silent supporter and almost confidant even though Iris had yet to say what problem she was mulling over tonight. Until now.

"I can see them, now," Iris said. "Ever since that last potion, I can see the curses, the gifts, the potential of everyone around me. I can see your sigil too."

"Well, you'd already seen it on my flesh. I trust it is impressive as an aura too?" Angela had the impression that was more or less how Iris's new "gift of seeing" worked.

"Gorgeous," Iris said. "If you could see it, honey..."

"Trust me. I carry it. I know."

"Glowing, full and bright and dark and hungry. It devours you and weighs you down, thrums in your veins and carries you forward. It energizes you and controls you at once." Iris sat up, eyes summoning Angela closer. When Angela put her knife and whetting stone aside and stepped over, she pulled Angela into a kiss. "I can taste it on you," she whispered. "The blood."

"That's no vision. You still haven't allowed me to go home and wash it all off. Does it get you hot, seeing just what a butcher I am? Don't bother answering. I know you well enough by now."

"It consumes you," Iris said. "It's so strong." She shivered. Her eyes glistened. "When I was young, the sight of it would have terrified me. One of those old gifts that thinks it will perpetuate itself forever. Now I'm its equal. I could take it. I could consume it, make its power my own. I wonder if I would inherit its hunger, or if I would satisfy it and it satisfy me..."

She leaned in, trying to kiss Angela again, but Angela pushed her away. "You're ritual-high."

"Poor Jane, Poor Jane, I could do it and you know it. Let me try. The kind of bleeding I could offer is probably the only kind that could make you well."

Angela looked at her, gorge rising, heart quickening. But Iris's gaze was hazy. An hour ago she'd been sprawled out on her cellar floor in the center of a spell circle, repowering the wards of her house and absorbing all stray magic and ambient energy inside. Blaming her for something she said in this state would be unfair.

"I'll talk to you sometime when you're more yourself," she said.

"Oh, please. Won't you at least stay for dinner? Or we could go out, and I'll buy you something for once. Or would you hate to be seen with me in public?"

Iris was a five-foot tall, shapely, golden-haired, barely-wrinkled beauty. Her outfits varied by function, but Angela knew she was well capable of dressing at the height of fashion. Angela was a tall woman, stiff and muscular, who tonight was again wearing all black including her gloves, and who underneath those gloves bore the calluses of a fighter. There was no question which was more suited for the public eye. Angela couldn't help but smile wryly as she shook her head and opened up the window, looking down to see where to first place her foot.

At the time she was forgiving. But even high on magic, Iris should have known better. Should have known, should have seen, how integral Poor Jane was to Angela—how Poor Jane was Angela, was all she had ever fought for, ever truly longed to be—

She'd told Iris the story of how she became Poor Jane, once. Had it wormed out of her—she hadn't intended to tell, but Iris could be persuasive. Other than Iris, she'd only ever shared with Natty, figuring the girl should know the history of her line. She had told Natty the story of how the previous Poor John, Matthias Baker, had become Poor John as well. History, history, history. But the story of her own ascension, she had told Natty over and over again, until Natty probably knew it better than the fairy tales her late mother had told her as a child.

Angela had been a street rat before she met Matthias, a street rat among street rats. There had been nothing special about her, except perhaps that even as a young girl she'd been unusually tall for her age. In fact, Matthias had recruited her and her friend Thomas at the same time, brought them both back to his house, which had been a decent and well-furnished house for a poor sort of neighborhood. He'd given them bread and soup and told them all kinds of impressive things about who he was, about the legend of Poor John. He'd told them that Poor John was a righteous man who was unafraid to kill the rich and powerful, who could be crueler than the cruel and kinder than the kind. The cruel could not stand against his knife, and who else would be so kind as to take blood onto their hands in order to help the oppressed? And they could be his special assistants who would help him with all his important work. Someday, they might even become Poor John themselves.

"Really?" Thomas had asked him, wide-eyed. And Angela had elbowed Thomas, making him shut up, because clearly Matthias was a decisive man, and if they wanted to impress him, they should come across as certain too. Naivete or incredulity would make them look like dumb kids who wouldn't be very useful at all.

They weren't the only children Matthias had recruited. He had seven others living with him at the time. The oldest had been four-teen already, voice getting husky, not really a child anymore. The youngest had been five.

"One of you will be Poor John someday, when I pass away," Matthias had told them. "The best one of you, the one who is most suited, the one who is the most helpful to me, will be the one I choose. Don't worry. I'm always watching. When you do a good job for me, when you show those important qualities that make you Poor John material, I certainly won't forget."

He had never told them what truly made a person Poor John, how the power and the obligations of Poor John were truly passed down. But Angela had been young, and she didn't think to ask. Magic was magic. Thomas had felt the same.

The older children, now. Some of them were more curious. The fourteen-year-old, for example (Angela couldn't remember his name anymore) had sometimes asked Matthias when he would be good enough, if he was good enough, if he could share in Matthias's power at least to some extent, if Matthias could explain some things to him that he didn't yet understand. Matthias told him time and time again that good things came to those who waited. "Don't push yourself. You're not ready, son. Not yet."

That fourteen-year-old. He died a few weeks before his fifteenth birthday in a botched job—the target had still died, but Matthias, who had gone along to help his protégé that time, saying he would show him some new pointers, needed to take over halfway through, when said protégé took a knife to the gut. "He pushed himself," Matthias told the rest of his children sorrowfully. "Too reckless, too hasty... I hope you'll all remember. It's important to know your limits."

He didn't tell them what mistake, exactly, it was that the dead kid had made. And Angela didn't understand then that the mistake hadn't been made on the mission, but in the weeks before. His curiosity and ambition had been his mistake, and Matthias had dealt out the consequences.

Perhaps Matthias should have explained it to them then, and Angela would have known better, years later, than to make the same mistake.

Or perhaps some things were inevitable.

***

Some of Matthias's street rats took to the profession of assassin's assistant better than others. Those who were failures tended to die fast—or run away, in which case Matthias killed them anyway. There was only one girl who Angela was inclined to think (in retrospect) actually got away, since there was never any evidence of her death provided. But in general, they died in accidents or in fights with their targets or under Matthias's knife, or they learned the rules of the trade, both practical and philosophical. Philosophically, the rules were simple: Obey Matthias, kill without remorse or hesitation, respect the name of Poor John. Practical matters were harder, and, apart from outliers like the fourteen-year-old, were where most of Matthias's "apprentices" fell down on the job.

Of all apprentices, Angela was most excellent in practical matters, while of those that survived, Thomas was worst.

Angela's excellence was easy enough to explain. She was not squeamish, and she was a fast learner, and she had a good body type for fighting (if a little tall for stealth). Thomas's survival was perhaps more of a mystery, for he was both squeamish and clumsy, but in fact it found the same explanation as the former—since Matthias had recruited Angela and Thomas at the same time, they took many jobs together, and while Angela didn't care much who she killed in the course of her job, she had grown up alongside Thomas like a brother, and always made a point of protecting him.

There was one night, for example, when Thomas was assigned to kill a certain old general. Old, and not in the best of health anymore, but still an experienced fighter with many guards stationed around his house. Not an easy task by any definition.

Angela wasn't really supposed to be there.

"Thomas has handled several assignments on his own," Matthias said. "He is fully capable without your assistance, Angie dear. And this is no job for a girl."

Matthias knew just how good Angela was, or he should have. Yet he rarely acknowledged it, and in fact rarely talked to Angela at all when he could help it. The older she grew, the fewer tasks he assigned her, until she was mostly given information gathering and little actual Poor John work.

Angela knew Matthias didn't consider her a worthy successor, knew it was because she was a girl, and rapidly approaching womanhood, her femininity becoming more physically evident every day. Matthias kept fewer girl assistants than boys, and didn't teach them well or watch them closely. Most of his girl assistants died fast, and Angela could tell Matthias was getting a little uncomfortable with how many years she had survived in his service.

Angela also knew she was a worthy successor. Worthier than anyone else.

She didn't need Matthias to tell her that—only she needed him to choose her, eventually, so that she really could become Poor John. So she needed to prove herself. Another reason she needed to go on this job, aside from the fact that however much Matthias liked Thomas, if Thomas went by himself this job would be a miserable failure. Angela respected the tenets of Poor John's calling. Commissions ought to be fulfilled promptly, thoroughly, and neatly, not bungled.

And there was protecting Thomas too, though Matthias didn't much like that either.

"I won't interfere with Thomas's task," she told Matthias. Lying, but nothing in Poor John's code prevented lying, except to a patron in the moment of a deal. "But I could still be useful. I can watch for interlopers, and distract anyone that comes near the general's room while Thomas is working. Even a girl can do that much."

(If the last sentence was a bit sarcastic—well, Matthias's brow furrowed for a moment, but he didn't mention it.)

Matthias sighed. "If I tell you no, will you sneak out later and do it anyway?"

"Of course not."

"Angie dearest, someday someone is going to bash your head in, and I won't weep over your grave."

Angela bristled. Matthias didn't weep over anyone's death; was she supposed to be offended that she wouldn't be an exception? It would be more embarrassing if it were the other way around.

"Do what you want," Matthias concluded, "but if you distract Thomas, and he messes up, I'll give you a caning."

Five hours later saw Angela standing in the general's garden, right outside his window, dressed in dark brown and gray rags and periodically glancing in every direction, keen eye watching for light and motion, ears listening for any sound apart from the wind in the trees.

The first noise to break her concentration, however, came not from the garden but from inside the house. And it was a loud crash.

Typical Thomas.

The window was a high one, the general's room being on the second floor, but Angela was a good climber. She was in the room in a blink, and saw Thomas pinned under the aging general's body. The general had a rope wrapped around his neck—the patron had requested a strangling—but it hung loose, while the general's hand around Thomas's skinny neck was wrapped tighter.

"Who sent you?" the general asked hoarsely. "Damn brat. Answer me!"

Angela moved.

The first thing she did was kick the general in the head. She wore heavy boots but walked lightly; he hadn't heard her coming, but certainly felt the kick. The second, now that the general was off Thomas, was to lunge for the door and jam a fallen chair under the doorknob. She could already hear footsteps hurrying closer.

The third was to grab the rope, now fallen, loop it around the general's neck again, and pull it tight, bracing a foot against the general's back. "Thomas," she said, "out the window. Now. There's no one to cover for us, and we'll have bodies here in less than a minute."

"But Angela, I haven't killed him yet."

Angela pulled a little tighter, shoved a little harder with her foot, and the sound of the general's neck cracking was audible. Not exactly what the patron had requested, which was a shame, but strangling had been involved, and they were short on time. "He's dead," she said. "Now let's go."

Mostly the servants and guards had swarmed to the hall, and they had not yet broken in when Angela and Thomas jumped out the window (Thomas falling in a stumble, Angela landing a smooth crouch). However, where the garden had been previously empty, one guard had emerged. Thomas pulled a pistol from his belt and shot him twice in the chest, and he and Angela sprinted for the garden gate, and, after vaulting it, down the street, turning one corner after another until they considered themselves a safe distance from the general's manor.

"What the hell were you thinking?" Angela asked Thomas, as they stood in a corner panting.

"He was bigger than I thought—I didn't use the proper leverage..."

"I'm not talking about the general," Angela snapped. "Strangling a military man was a tricky proposition to begin with. It's why I thought you could use some backup. I'm talking about the gun! Why the hell did you have a gun with you? You know the client asked for strangling."

"Well, I did strangle the general. You saw I did—it's why I had trouble to begin with, it's a stupid method."

"The client picks the method. We're supposed to rise to the challenge."

"Well, I did! Obviously! You saw me!"

"Then why the gun?"

"In case of others," Thomas said indignantly. "As you saw—as you also saw! The number of people he keeps around his house is ridiculous."

"Guns are loud. They call attention. Now everyone in that house knows we escaped through the garden and will be out chasing us. If we'd just killed that guard more quietly, this would be much easier."

"We had to get out quickly."

"Thomas, if a gun is the only way you know how to kill quickly, I seriously wonder how you think you're going to make it as Poor John. They're a crutch. You know how to break bones, how to stab and slice and strangle and even just bash someone over the head. What do you need a gun for? Even long distance, a throwing knife is just as practical as that little toy pistol you had—not an ounce of range on that thing. It's because you're squeamish," Angela said, "and you just don't want to have to draw blood."

"Shooting people draws plenty of blood, Angela. And Poor John doesn't have any issues with me using a gun. He gave me that one, remember? You're just jealous he never gave anything like that to you."

Angela bit her lip. Any retort she made would sound stupid. He wasn't entirely wrong, but he also was wrong, very wrong. She disliked guns due to their lack of finesse, the lack of skill required. Not everything was about Matthias.

(Later in life she would come to appreciate guns more for their range and practicality.

They would still never be her weapon of choice. A difference, perhaps, between Poor Jane and Poor John.)

Later that night, after they had made their circuitous way back to Poor John's hideout, she stood silently outside the door of Matthias's study and listened to Matthias lecture Thomas on all the mistakes he had made over the course of the night. The difference between the way Matthias treated Thomas and the way he treated Angela was that he actually told Thomas what he should have done differently, how his mistakes could have been fixed. Angela, he never gave anything so helpful.

The conclusion of Matthias's speech:

"You can't be Angela's little pet forever, you know," Matthias said.

"I'm not her pet."

"You rely on her too much. Trust that she'll always be there for you. Women are all the same, Tommy boy. Sooner or later she'll either betray you or weaken and die. You should not give her all your heart or invest yourself in her wellbeing."

Angela, having heard enough, departed.

It didn't annoy her that Matthias had told Thomas not to rely on her. That Thomas needed to be more independent, more able to protect himself and attack without any backup, she had known for some time. But that Matthias had called her a woman like other women, that he had said Thomas's failing was putting Angela in his *heart*, as if they had a love affair rather than a friendship or a working partnership—that infuriated her more than perhaps any demeaning comment Matthias had ever made to her face.

"I'm not a wilting flower," she muttered as she headed back to her quarters. "I'm not a lady. I'm no fucking Juliet!"

What she was—what she would be, or be damned—was Poor Jane. The time had come, she decided, to stop wasting her time waiting for Matthias to see her, and claim her inheritance by force.

***

She still did not know, then, how the line of Poor John passed down. She still believed the lie that Matthias would choose the next of his line, but she figured there had to be a method to his choosing. Maybe there was a mark he would put on his successor—maybe he placed on his successor the sigil that Angela had once (only once) caught a glimpse of on his own chest. Maybe there was some sort of ritual, or maybe there was a secret lesson that he would teach only the chosen one. If the answer was any of these things, Angela figured she could claim it as her right. She could carve the sigil into her own chest, perform the ritual by herself, or force Matthias to teach her his secret lessons at knifepoint. (Gunpoint, if she had to, even if it was too crude for her taste.) She just had to know what the answer was.

To that end, Angela decided to enlist the aid of another legend, the spirit of Cruel Therese. Despite her name, Cruel Therese was known as a more benevolent spirit than Poor John. She was said to be the ghost of a maiden who had been murdered by her husband when she had discovered her husband's affair. She had then returned as a shade and forced her husband to relive every sin he had ever committed, and in turn to witness every sin ever committed against him, every spoken aspersion, every betrayal, every piece of petty malice. Her husband had died within hours of the ordeal. Ever since, Cruel Therese had hovered between life and death. She would appear sometimes to those who summoned her with a gift of wine and the petals of a white lily. To these lucky few, she would offer a gift of knowledge, but only knowledge with a certain weight and price. Many regretted ever learning the secrets she had told them, but once asked, she would reveal the whole truth, and there was no way of stopping her halfway, no matter how harsh or unwanted that truth might be. For this reason she was called cruel. But Angela was unafraid of the truth; she had seen more cruelty in her brief time than most. So she found a quiet corner in the city park, poured a bottle of wine on the ground, tore up a dozen lily petals, and waited.

The lilies and wine looked like bloody snow. Their odor was intoxicating. Angela stood over them for a long time before a mist began to rise up from the ground, and slowly gathered into the shape of a woman dressed in white.

"Poor Jane, Angela Parker," the woman intoned. "I see you've called on me to ask for some advice."

"I'm Angela," Angela said. "Poor Jane—not yet. And I don't have a last name."

"Parker is the name of the man who fathered you, though he never met you and knows not of your existence. Gentili would have been your name if your mother kept you, and if she had kept her own last name. But those possibilities are but will-o-the-wisps built on a past that will have little effect on your future. For the woman you will become, you will become of your own volition. Eve made by Eve."

"Right," Angela said, "so I'll become Poor John. I wanted to ask you how. Matthias doesn't seem likely to pick me from among his apprentices." She didn't bother explaining who Matthias was, for it had become clear to her that this woman, Cruel Therese, knew more about her life than Angela herself.

Unfortunately Cruel Therese did not appear to be very focused. "Poor Jane is what you will call yourself. And you're not the first woman to go by the name, no, not the first Poor Jane in your curse's line by a long shot. The very third Poor John was a Poor Jane, and in total there have been eleven Poor Janes in the Poor John line, though four of them were very short-lived. Then again, many a Poor John does not long live under the title. A total of fifteen Poor Johns have died within a week of gaining the title of Poor John, and three were not aware they had gained the title in the first place."

"So you can become a Poor John without even knowing?"

"The process of becoming Poor John is very simple in its beginning, though taking on the title is not the same as adjusting to the new abilities, instincts, and needs that accompany the curse. But to take the title, all one needs to do is kill the current Poor John," Cruel Therese said. "The curse passes from victim to killer. Thus it is designed so that only a killer may carry the title, and a weak assassin will not carry the title for long. Although the current Poor John is something of a misnomer. He has carried his title for years with little challenge or even effort to fulfill his commissions, depending on the strength of pawns and killing only through treachery. He has been responsible for the deaths of many people stronger than himself, but then, strength is not the only desirable quality for a killer. Manipulation and cleverness are qualities that can be very useful as well. Although I see you do not esteem him highly, Angela Gentili Parker."

Angela didn't answer. Most of what Cruel Therese had said had gone in one ear and out the other—the only thing that had really struck her was "kill the current Poor John", a phrase which was now repeating in her head over and over again.

Cruel Therese frowned, academic displeasure coming over her

face. "Perhaps a more visual demonstration would be helpful, as I see you are having difficulty following." She reached out and placed a cool, long-fingered hand over Angela's eyes. For a moment the world went dark, and then the visions began.

Angela saw, then, how the line of Poor John had been passed on from the very beginning.

She saw the first Poor John, a bandit who had made a witch queen angry. A curse meant to enslave him to the witch queen's will went astray, and left him rather a slave to anyone with hate in their heart, a man who lived only on murder, who could eat nothing but human bones and never felt satisfied except in the aftermath of a kill. She saw the man who killed that first Poor John, watched the rejoicing at the death of a monster—saw that second man slowly corrupted until he was almost a revenant, saw the revenant killed by the man's former wife. Who became Poor Jane, starting the cycle over again. And she killed by her son. The first three Poor Johns were all killed by people who had loved them, who hoped against hope to save their souls from further corruption and save their people from the death that followed in their wake. The fourth, now, was killed by a prospective victim in self-defense, and the cycle began to tilt in new directions.

The curse loosened a little as time went by. Poor John, or Poor Jane, didn't always lose their mind, depending on how rampant their killing was, how much they indulged their itch. They didn't have to eat only human bones. Other bones would do most of the time, and they could be supplemented by more ordinary food. But the need to seek out those with hate in their hearts, make bargains, and kill, remained strong, unabated through the centuries.

And Poor John, or Poor Jane, always died by violence.

Angela saw the deaths from every angle. She was a bystander in the shadows, a voyeur; she was the killer, righteously destroying the monstrous Poor John, unaware of the consequences; she was

Poor John, dying over and over again a hundred different ways. She strangled and was strangled, burned and was burned, stabbed and was stabbed, shot and was shot. She fell off cliffs and pushed others off cliffs, drowned and killed others by drowning. The vision passed faster and faster. Through it all, she felt a cold pressure on her forehead, until at last this pressure overtook all other sensations, and the vision again went black.

She thought for a moment, *I am dead now. The cycle is complete.*

But then she opened her eyes, and saw Cruel Therese still before her, wavering and translucent over the dried wine on the ground and the pile of shredded lilies.

"You have seen it all?" Cruel Therese asked.

She nodded.

"You understand, then, how the line of Poor John is passed down?"

She nodded again.

"And did you have any other questions?"

She shook her head.

Cruel Therese smiled. "Then may you use the knowledge well, and may life be kinder to you than it was to me."

With those words, she faded into thin air, leaving Angela stunned and blinking. She had no chance to respond. Had she responded, she might have said that she did not expect life to be kind, nor did she wish it to be. She only wanted to be Poor Jane, and now she saw that it would be a far easier task to achieve than she had imagined.

***

She walked home at a slow, thoughtful pace, considering Cruel Therese's words and the vision she had seen. She was not unaffected by the experience. While she saw Matthias on a regular basis, he was the only person she knew with supernatural abilities, and he rarely flaunted them. She'd never met a ghost before, or experienced magic practiced on herself personally. And while killing affected her less now than it had in the past—and the prospect of suffering a violent death had to her been certain for years—to see and experience so much death in such a brief span of time was still enough to leave her in something of a stunned haze.

But a haze was not enough to dull Angela's senses and leave her off-guard. If anything, it did the opposite. Unfocused, she let the sounds, sights, and smells of the city waft by her, into her, through her, absorbing little of it but observing all. The smell of sewage as she passed a certain alley seemed stronger than usual, and the call of an owl louder. When she walked through the door of Matthias's house, she could not muster a response to the young girl who greeted her from the parlor, chirping out that she hoped Angela had had a good walk and that she had been practicing knots all evening if Angela cared to have a look—no, she couldn't even remember the girl's name. But the nuances of the voice she absorbed in their totality: friendliness, a little hopefulness, a little fear. (Most of Matthias's apprentices were scared of Angela, at least a little. They knew the things she'd done. Some were jealous, some admiring; all intimidated.) She gave a nod. Absorbed, too, the smell of strong tea from the kitchen. Someone was planning on staying up all night. She walked towards her bedroom, automatically avoiding the boards in the floor that creaked and that one nail that stuck up on the staircase.

And when she came to her room, the sound of someone breathing behind the closed door and a body quietly shifting—of course she heard that too.

It wasn't one of the younger apprentices pulling a rare light-hearted prank. The sound of the breath was too high up for that. The person breathing was tall, and breathing deeply, trying to calm themselves and not quite managing. Matthias, she thought (although Matthias's breath was generally more shallow, even when he was out of breath after a coughing fit—he smoked a lot), and it flashed through her mind that Poor John had somehow learned where she was going tonight and why, that he knew what she now knew and knew she intended to kill him, and had come to her room tonight to kill her first. And the time for her to kill him therefore would have to be now. Now, now, now, before he could kill her and end her before she could fulfill her destiny. She flung open the door, dodged a knife strike and grabbed hold of a wrist, flipping a body to the floor and pulling a knife of her own from her belt.

The knife was at Thomas's throat before she even realized who had been attacking her. She froze.

"Thomas," she said, "why are you here?"

"I won't be soft anymore," Thomas panted. His eyes were bright with terrible fear and resentment and determination. "I have to cut you loose, Angela. I have to kill you. If I want to be Poor John, I have to kill you."

He was pinned under her on the floor, wrist at a tricky angle, but he still twisted.

"You idiot. You think you'd be good enough to be Poor John if not for me? Stop. Don't make me kill you."

Thomas let out a soft keening cry and continued to twist.

Angela broke his wrist.

In another house, maybe, with another team, the screaming that ensued would have brought the other apprentices running, or at least summoned Matthias, the house's master. Here it went ignored. Angela could probably kill Thomas and dispose of his body and never even face disapproval; Thomas losing to her was a sign he didn't deserve to live. But, "I don't want to kill you," Angela said. "We've been friends since we were kids. You're never going to be Poor John. It's not my fault you're incompetent. Even without me..."

"Matthias said I was his first choice. He said my attachment to you was the only thing making me weak. He said he'd make me Poor John."

"Did he."

Angela stood. She wondered if Matthias had really hoped Thomas would be able to kill her, or if he'd hoped Angela would kill Thomas. She didn't see why Matthias would hope that. Maybe he'd take it as an excuse to get rid of her after all, but since when had he needed excuses? So either he'd really wanted to use Angela to get rid of Thomas or he'd believed Thomas far more capable than he was, and Angela far stupider.

Either way, it was insulting.

"Get out of this house," Angela said. "I'll spare you, but I think it's clear you can't beat me. You're not Poor John material. I am. And I won't forgive you a second time."

She took the knife he'd brought with him. It had fallen on the floor, out of his nerveless hand, when first she grabbed him. She put it in her belt, along with the other knife she carried. Then she left the room. He was still lying on the floor—maybe rethinking his actions, probably just trying to catch his breath and bemoaning his broken wrist—and did not follow her.

She went to Matthias's study, unsure if he would be there or not. He was there, sitting in a chair facing the fireplace, facing away from the door. She would have thrown a knife at him had he been standing, but this way, the back of the chair blocked her way. She had to circle around to look him in the eye.

"Angie," he said, "you're in late. What have you been doing this evening? Getting into brawls?"

She drew a knife and stabbed straight at him. He blocked, but didn't quite manage to catch her wrist, and she slid down his arm, flipping the knife's position on her hand as she went, and stabbed him in the shoulder, right under his neck. The spot wasn't lethal, just a couple inches off.

He rose, grabbing at his belt for a gun. (This was where Thomas was picking up bad habits, she thought distantly.) She poked at his eyes, was blocked again, kneed at his groin and missed, hitting the inner thigh. He had the gun drawn now. She hit at his hand, sending a shot intended for her heart into the floorboards instead. Kneed him again, this time hitting where she aimed. Grabbed her second knife and thrust it into his jugular.

It was done, then. He lived a minute longer, clutching at his throat. Well, maybe not a full minute. But when he had breathed his last...

Ah, then the feeling took her.

It was a burning, seizing in her chest. She pulled her blouse open and saw her skin writhing, darkening into the shape of Poor John's sigil. *I did it*, she thought. It had been easy. Well, she could have died, had she been any slower, had Matthias not been sleepy. But it had been the work of a moment. She was Poor John now—or Poor Jane, rather, as Cruel Therese had predicted.

All changed in a night.

She learned Poor Jane's instincts and abilities and needs later, testing herself little by little until she figured out what parts of herself were still human and which were changed, cursed or strengthened. That night, she gathered all the apprentices together and told them the truth: That she had killed Matthias, that she was Poor Jane now. And then told them that she was releasing them all. She did not intend to have any helpers. She would be a Poor Jane who worked alone, and if they wanted to inherit her position, they would have to get it honestly, by slaying her. But she did not intend to make that easy.

She moved out of Matthias's lair, found her own hideout in a neighborhood where nobody knew her. In the months that followed, two apprentices tracked her down and tried to kill her. She killed both of them. One tracked her down and tried to persuade her to take him on as an apprentice after all. She fought him and sent him away when she won.

Thomas never showed up. Maybe he looked for her, maybe he didn't. She didn't look for him. She forced herself not to.

If she ever had an apprentice, she swore, there would be only one, and it would be one she chose, one suited for the position and carefully trained. Not just a tool, but a true disciple. What she had hoped she could be to Matthias, what Matthias had never given any of his apprentices a chance to be.

But at that time she was young, and such a future was still far away.

***

Angela had fought for the position of Poor Jane. Had claimed it. Killed for it. Lost her only friend for it. Sacrificed the majority of her life to it.

Iris damn well knew that too, the greedy incorrigible bitch.

She had deserved the slap and a good deal worse.

Still, Angela would have to make up with her at some point. Fortunately, Iris didn't hold grudges against people she liked—Angela probably wouldn't have to kill her or stop using her. She would go see Iris in a few days and see if she'd actually gotten around to any of that reconnaissance.

In the meantime: "Someone who would want to control James Guarin's heart," Angela said. "Natty, you can tell me the obvious suspect, can't you?"

"Genevieve Hunt," Natty said.

Angela smiled. "Good girl. Now, how about I get some tea together and you can draw up a plan for how you're going to get a heart out of her?"

"Yes, master."

Natty's ideas had gotten better and better lately. Angela still insisted on hearing most of them before she put any of them into action, but she was a good planner, and a skilled hunter when on the job. She was everything Angela had hoped her someday-apprentice would be.

6

Chapter Six

James Guarin disappearing in the middle of the Kenbers' party was about on par for Jenny's luck. If anything, it was above par for the general course of their relationship: he'd at least danced with her first, and even said a few words. Then he'd vanished, telling neither Jenny nor his parents nor the hosts nor any of his friends that he was leaving. Only a couple people commented on it to Jenny's face, asking if she knew where he went and remarking that it was rather thoughtless of him to go running off like that. But she heard the real rumors circulating from her friends: James Guarin had a lover—some rumors even said it was a male lover—and so of course could barely stand to spend time at a party with the woman he was only marrying for her family's money. And who could blame him, the upper elite tittered, when Genevieve Hunt was a coarse, untitled, jumped-up middleclass wannabe, desperate to pretend she could be on the level of a future earl? Truly pathetic on both sides, the Ilbird family allowing a commoner into their ranks and the Hunt family begging for scraps of aristocracy, teaching their daughter to sing and dance and play piano like some trained and pampered cockatoo. But such arrangements were increasingly common these days—still, it was clear James had a distaste for it all, and really no one could blame him, the poor dear.

Jenny's friends were entirely on her side, of course. They all told her so, especially Tiffany Botts, who was eager to ingratiate herself with the season's richest debutante after their latest tiff.

Tiffany, the little snake, knew more than most about James Guarin's alleged lover. That was what had caused their latest fight in the first place. It had happened a couple of weeks ago, only five days after the Ilbird family and Jenny's mama had finally come to an agreement about their engagement. Finally, after two whole years of negotiating and wrangling and drawing things out, they'd settled on an amount of money for Jenny's dowry, an equitable arrangement for the Hunt shipping company to set up a port on a river on Ilbird land, some cooperation on logging in the Ilbird forests, and a generous monthly allowance for Jenny after her marriage as well as several other concessions to do with whom the Guarins would introduce the Hunts to in high society and what Jenny's manner of living would be within the Guarin household. All that was minor, actually, given that the Ilbird family and the Hunt family had long wanted to form an alliance, the current Earl of Ilbird and Jenny's papa being good friends and seeing the benefits of a more formal bond between them. What had taken all that time was talking James into accepting Jenny as his future wife.

(But of course neither family would talk about that in public. Mama and Papa would barely discuss the situation with Jenny, unwilling to admit that with all they had trained her and all the Hunt family had to offer, they couldn't provide her with the husband they wanted. It was embarrassing.)

Five days since the betrothal was made official. Mama and Papa were over the moon. Jenny at first had felt stunned by the sudden change. She had been planning how to convince her parents to consider other suitors in the coming season, and now their plans had come to fruition when she had begun to think them hopeless. And James, who had always been polite but distant with her, polite and distant and sometimes a little fidgety, had looked her in the eyes when he proposed and told her he was sorry for having pushed her away in the past and hoped now with all his heart to be worthy of her and make her happy. Her own heart's pace had quickened when he said that, and when he took his hands in hers and pressed into her palm the Ilbird family ring. A subtle piece, a diamond in the center and garnets framing its edge. And he kissed her knuckles, gently, and she realized his hand was trembling. It had all been so tender as to seem unreal. The only further thing one could have asked for, to make it a scene from some romantic play, would be for him to tell her he loved her, maybe that he had loved her all this time and would love her forevermore. He did not say that, though, which was for the better, since indeed they barely knew each other and Jenny would have been a fool to believe it. But she had looked into his eyes and felt that perhaps, in time, such a declaration might hold true. He was a good man, an honest man, and such a gentleman. She had always thought so. If it was James Guarin, in time she was sure she could love him back, too.

Five days, and she went from stunned to quietly, ambitiously hopeful. Began to picture her life as Countess of Ilbird. As James Guarin's wife.

On the fifth day, she had gone to visit Tiffany Botts. Tiffany had recently promised to introduce her to a trendy dressmaker. Jenny's clothes were always fashionable among Papa's circle of friends, but in high society the fashion was a bit different, and she was glad to meet someone who could help her stay on top of the newest looks. If she was going to be James Guarin's fiancée this season, she didn't want to embarrass him.

The seamstress had come to Tiffany's house. Her name was Charlotte Taylor.

Miss Taylor had been, for the sum of half an hour, the picture of professional courtesy. She had taken Jenny's measurements in that businesslike way that seamstresses always did, that way they had of reducing a woman to figures and shapes that left Jenny barely present in her own body. After a fitting, Mama would often make some comments about how Jenny should lose some weight—was bound to lose some weight before the next party, actually, so could the seamstress please take that into account and take off an inch here and there?—and it always left Jenny mortified. But in the moment, she never felt that the seamstress really saw her, only some inhuman human form to be bound up in measuring tape. And Mama wasn't here today and couldn't say anything to the seamstress afterward, another reason she'd jumped at the opportunity to come over and get things done at Tiffany's.

But when she was done measuring, Miss Taylor straightened and gave Jenny a hard stare. Jenny found herself noticing, as she had when they were first introduced, that Miss Taylor's eyes were a little red, with bruise-like circles beginning to form under them. And her jaw was clenched so hard it looked like it had to hurt.

"Are you done now?" Jenny asked her.

Miss Taylor nodded.

"Thank you, I appreciate it. Now if we could look over some designs, I need something formal but celebratory, and not too stiff but still traditional. My engagement is going to be announced soon, and for the occasion I need something that will stand up to close scrutiny. The family I'm marrying into runs in quite a high social circle."

"James Guarin," Miss Taylor said.

The words came out strangely, as if they had been blocking Miss Taylor's throat, and she had managed to wrench them free but not quite to free any other words yet. It struck Jenny that most people not in high society themselves didn't know James's name or reputation very well—he was known only as the son of the earl, but didn't do much to draw attention to himself. It struck Jenny as strange, also, that anyone should have heard of her engagement when the two families had been doing their best to be discreet until the official announcement. Although certainly there had been rumors spread about them before. She smiled. "Yes. James Guarin, son of the Earl of Ilbird."

"My lady, is he the best man for you to marry?"

Jenny blinked.

"James Guarin won't be faithful to you," Miss Taylor said. "He's not a trustworthy man. He had a lover, you know. He has not been waiting patiently for the woman he marries. A lothario isn't a worthy match for a woman like my lady."

No one had ever said this so bluntly to Jenny before. Jenny felt her cheeks heating. "James is a quiet man. People talk about him, but he never had a lover, not before me. Not really. It's just talk."

"He did. I should know." Miss Taylor paused. "His lover was me."

Jenny stared at her blankly.

"I was his lover," Miss Taylor said. "And if you'd seen the way he made love to me, the promises he broke, you'd know there's not a faithful bone in his body."

Jenny swallowed. "You—you say you *were* his lover. Were, but not now?"

Miss Taylor's jaw clenched again.

Jealous, Jenny thought. No, not now.

She lifted her chin. "James's past is his own business. As for his future, he's promised it to me. I hope you won't try to interfere with us again."

"You're just going to ignore it? And marry him anyway, despite knowing—you can't just ignore it. If people knew, you'd be a laughingstock."

Jenny knew what it was to face derision already. It stung, but it was hardly enough to break her. Still, this would hurt her parents more than her. They were from a different time, a different class, and might not understand the way it was with aristocratic men. (Jenny, on the other hand, had heard many worse stories about many men of high position.) She reached for her purse, which she had put down on a nearby table while Miss Taylor took measurements. "What do you want?"

"I want you to know what kind of man he is."

"What do you want to keep quiet?" Jenny said. "I can understand the... favor you'd be doing me."

Miss Taylor drew herself up. "I'm not a blackmailer!"

"Indeed? Then what else can I do for you?"

"I—" Miss Taylor's teeth ground again. "Nothing, it seems. Have you no pride?"

Jenny smiled thinly. "I think it's best if I have another seamstress make my dresses for this season after all. I won't keep you here any longer."

She hadn't mastered the art of dismissal as perfectly as Mama, but her tone was still sufficient. Miss Taylor's shoulders stiffened, and she strode out.

Jenny turned to Tiffany Botts, who had been watching the whole fiasco with her mouth hanging open. She stormed over and grabbed Tiffany by the hair, fingers sinking into a delicately twisted up-do and pulling it back, tilting Tiffany's chin and making her squeal.

"Miss Hunt!"

"Did you know she knew James? Did you know that was why she wanted to see me?"

"Jenny, I didn't, I didn't, I promise! I didn't even know she particularly wanted to see you—she just said she'd heard I was friends with you and asked if you needed any dresses. Let go!"

"So you just thought it was fine to introduce me to some slut off the streets?"

There were tears in Tiffany's eyes. "I didn't mean to, Jenny! Miss Taylor's a respectable dressmaker, she comes from an established shop, she does a great job usually, I didn't know! It's not unusual to—well, you have a good reputation, and your family's rich! Why wouldn't she want an introduction?"

Jenny gave Tiffany's hair a last contemptuous yank and let go. "You've embarrassed me. If it's not on purpose, you must be an idiot. I'm not sure I can associate with someone with such poor judgment."

"Jenny, I'm sorry, really, I'm sorry. I didn't know it would go like that." Tiffany rubbed her head. Then, apparently not having exhausted her poor judgment, she asked, "Are you going to really stick with James Guarin now, after hearing that? Yow."

Jenny shoved her and departed at almost as brisk a pace as Miss Taylor. They were similarly disgraced, after all, by a shameful association. But no, she told herself as she walked home, she was not going to think that way. Miss Taylor had sought her out because James had broken with her. That meant James was not unfaithful, did not have a mistress he intended to keep now that they were engaged. Unless there was someone else. But there was no proof of anyone else. And frankly, she could barely believe the politely nervous James Guarin had managed to have one mistress in the first place. A second one would be incredible.

The fight with Tiffany bothered her too. She couldn't be sure Tiffany really hadn't known anything. But perhaps what bothered her more was that Tiffany had seen her humiliated by a common seamstress. Tiffany, whose family was not terribly rich but at least aristocratic, who flitted around Jenny like a moth attracted to the light of the season, but whose roots in the world of the elite were in fact far deeper than Jenny's own. Jenny had wanted to be real friends with her, but there were times when she felt a clear distance between them. And if there had ever been a chance, she'd wrecked it today. Or Miss Taylor had wrecked it. Or all three of them had wrecked it together.

There was a strand of long blonde hair left on her hand when she took off her gloves after getting home. She remembered how soft Tiffany's hair had felt. She'd always admired the way Tiffany arranged her hair, had hoped Tiffany might give her some tips. Maybe she still would, if they made amends. But she had turned something beautiful into something crude.

Just Tiffany Botts, she reminded herself. She had many more discreet and tasteful acquaintances, even if she'd been fond of Tiffany's enthusiastic cheer.

The issue with James Guarin was more significant. But she was not sure what could be done about it. She'd learned a hard truth about him. She knew it couldn't be shared, not with her other friends nor with her parents. Nor brought up with James himself either—oh God, she would die of shame if she had to look him in the eye and ask him if he'd had a lover before her. Make herself a jealous wife before they were even known to society as fiancés. No. No, she certainly couldn't do that.

He had broken things off with his mistress. He had promised himself to her. That had to be what mattered, now. As for his past, well, it was the custom of aristocrats to push such unpleasantness under the rug, right? Jenny had been trained her entire life to be a proper aristocratic wife. She could learn this principle as well.

And now James had disappeared in the middle of a party. The first time she'd seen him since meeting Miss Taylor. He'd danced one dance with her, a set of four, and disappeared. He'd seemed out of it that night too, flushed and nervous and a little clumsy in the dancing.

She was sure he had his reasons for vanishing. She was his fiancée. She was supposed to trust him.

When she got a note the next morning from him, she still felt relieved. Only to be expected, Mama said. Even if the dance had gone well, it was customary to send a note to one's fiancée or the woman one was courting the night after a party. There should have been flowers, too. Roses or lilies. But ah well, times were not what they once were, Mama said, and maybe that wasn't the custom anymore, she really didn't know.

Mama would have liked to hover over Jenny's shoulder as she read the note too, but Jenny excused herself and went to her bedroom, where she carefully cut the envelope open at the top so she would not have to damage the Ilbird seal on the flap. The note she pulled out was written on heavy cream-colored stationery. Its simplicity, and the rough handwriting on its lines, had a masculine appeal that brought a smile to Jenny's face.

She quite liked James, when it came down to it, even with all his bumps and rough edges and his hidden thorny past.

The contents of the note, however, were dubious.

Dear Miss Hunt,

My deepest apologies for abandoning you at the dance. I would not have done so by choice. After stepping away from the dance floor this evening, I was assaulted and rendered unconscious by a servant, who appears to have been a disguised assassin. This assassin removed me from the premises and brought me to another area of the city; however, I have now escaped and am safely with my family. I realize this sounds incredible and do not seek to excuse myself from your displeasure at vanishing. I hope to make things up to you at the soonest opportunity.

Sincerely yours,

James Guarin.

Quite outlandish. Could someone possibly have attacked James at the party—could kidnapping really have been the reason for his disappearance? If that was the case, to say Jenny would forgive him was beside the point; there would be nothing to forgive. Only it was a little—no, it was very hard to believe such a thing could have happened mere yards away from such a crowd of people. And what reason would anyone have to attack poor James? He was no earl even if his father was, and he was in general such an inoffensive man.

Then again, she did know at least one person who was furious enough at James to attempt to ruin his marital prospects. But a common seamstress, hire someone to kidnap her former lover? That idea was also outlandish.

Jenny frowned and folded the note back up. The writing started almost halfway down the page, so that when it was folded in half, the only line visible on top was "Dear Miss Hunt". She sighed. How many times had she told James to call her Jenny? Then again, few people did. Her own parents insisted on calling her Genevieve these days. And she and James, despite being fiancés, were not intimate.

She needed to spend more time with him. She needed to get to know him better.

When she received another letter from the Ilbird household that evening—this one from the countess, formally inviting her to spend the week with the Guarin family at their estate in the countryside—she accepted instantly.

***

The Ilbird estate was less than a day's travel from the city. She arrived there the next day in the late afternoon, and was met in the parlor by the Countess Ilbird, who offered her a warm welcome.

"James will be down to greet you in just a minute," she promised brightly. "He's been sleeping most of the afternoon." A bit graver, she asked, "He told you about the attack?"

"He said someone kidnapped him from the party the other night."

"Yes, quite. I'm glad you'd heard some about it. Well, the ruffians injured him. It wasn't bad, so no need to worry, but he's been needing some rest. To be honest, that's why we're here. City life is too boisterous and he needs some peace and quiet. That and—I can trust your discretion?"

"Of course."

"We aren't sure yet who attacked him, or what motivated them. There was an assassin disguised as a maid involved, but it seems like she didn't act alone. Until we find out who's at the bottom of this, the city may be a dangerous place for him." She offered Jenny an apologetic smile. "I hope you won't think I've brought you into danger by inviting you down here. It's not common knowledge we left the city, and I don't think any assassins will follow us. But I felt it best to warn you."

"I doubt I would be targeted in any case," Jenny said. "I'm glad you invited me down. James is my future husband. Any trouble he encounters, I must support him."

She still felt the situation quite extraordinary.

The countess said, "You're such a dutiful young woman. When I was your age, I'm sure I was far more caught up in fashion and other nonsense than in worrying about my husband. I'm so pleased my James will be marrying someone so virtuous and brave." She took Jenny's hands in hers and gave them a light squeeze. "I'm hoping you and James will still be able to spend some time together this way, even if there won't be any dances or other occasions. I'm glad you understand."

"Well, one does not live for dancing," Jenny said. She'd had to send regretful notes to a couple of friends whose parties she'd be missing, but what of it? Probably they'd have more fun gossiping about her absence than they would have had chatting with her about less exciting topics. Time spent with James would be more valuable.

James emerged from his bedroom upstairs some minutes later. That he'd just roused himself from bed was clear—his eyes were still sleepy and his hair was slightly wet from having splashed water on his face to wake himself. And his clothes were ruffled—he must not have taken much time dressing. He was moving stiffly, and after giving her a polite bow in greeting, he winced and clutched briefly at his chest.

His story of getting attacked at the party finally solidified in her mind at the sight. "Please sit down," she told him. "You're still recovering. I didn't come down here to put a strain on you."

"It's no strain," James said, but he sat down as soon as she did. "I really am sorry about the party. I missed those two dances on your card."

So he remembered that. "Don't mention it," Jenny said. "A kidnapping is a good enough excuse for me. I'm more concerned about your health."

This launched James's mother into an in-depth analysis of the state of James's health which lasted for several minutes. By the time she was done, the initial awkwardness between Jenny and James had passed, and James was awake enough to ask Jenny what she'd been doing the past couple days, and Jenny responded, trying her best not to make it sound either like she had spent them obsessing over what James had meant by vanishing on her or like she had been heartlessly enjoying life while James had been suffering from his injury. Whether she struck that balance or not, James didn't appear offended. He listened with a small smile on his face, occasionally glancing over at his mother when Jenny made a joke or a remark he found notable.

She was out of harmless remarks within an hour, however—James's exhausted silence didn't make for great conversation—and was relieved when James's parents dominated talk over dinner. She could do the heavy lifting of "getting to know James" tomorrow, she decided.

As it turned out, James was not quite so sickly as either his mother or that evening's impression made him appear. The next day, he was feeling better. "I mean, it still hurts," he said. "I was stabbed. But I'm improving. So, if you would be interested—you enjoy the outdoors, don't you? I mean..."

Jenny's feelings on the "outdoors" were fairly neutral. She enjoyed hunting, especially hunting parties, but that was clearly not what James had in mind. It was a cold day, with the morning painting frost on the windows. But she was open to suggestions, particularly suggestions from her fiancé, who perhaps might like the outdoors a lot. (She didn't know him well enough to say, but she could confidently say that he didn't like parties, and those were inside, so perhaps he preferred the reverse.) "Are you suggesting we go for a ride?"

"Perhaps not a ride. Too bumpy for me." James grimaced. "No, I was thinking a stroll. Not very far, but there are some nice woods around the east side of the estate, and there's a nice spot I'd like to show you. Mr. Johnson would come with us to chaperone."

Jenny had met Mr. Jonhson, and considered him equal to whatever situation might come up. "I would love to go for a stroll," she said. "Just give me a few minutes to change into something suitable."

"Well, we might wait until after lunch, though. It will be warmer then, and I think Mother has some special dessert prepared. Although she won't tell."

"All right. After lunch."

The dessert that the countess had prepared turned out to be raspberry and strawberry jam tarts. She informed Jenny conspiratorially that they were James's favorite. If so, his mood might have been worse than Jenny had thought, for he ate them with no enjoyment, although he did warmly thank his mother for them. "They're excellent," he assured her, chewing them slowly and blandly. They were, actually, excellent. Jenny wondered if being injured had ruined James's appetite.

James's mother proudly told them there would be more at tea, but James informed her that he and Jenny might be late to tea or miss it altogether, depending on how their walk went. Oh, so they were going on a walk? How delightful. But they would—oh, good, Mr. Johnson was going along? Very good James, you think of everything.

Jenny changed into something warm, woolen and walkable, and met James and Mr. Johnson at the back door of the manor. From there it was a short walk into the woods. There was a thin, well-trodden path in the woods, easy to walk on with only the occasional root interrupting it. The trees were thick, but not so thick as to keep out the sun. Half-light filtered down through their branches. James's face in natural lighting, a little bit shadowed, looked soft and mysterious, and Jenny hoped the lighting flattered her too.

"You play a lot of songs about nature," James said.

"Oh, do I?"

"The seasons. There was a long one about spring, I remember. Maybe you'd rather be going on a walk in spring." He smiled self-deprecatingly.

Jenny thought more about the abstract emotions evoked by the music she played than she did about their titles, or the imagery they were supposed to concretely represent. For that matter, when she played for an audience, she paid more attention to getting the notes and the tempo right than anything else. Spring was nice, though. "I love the flowers," she said. "Especially when the first snow melts. But summer is my favorite season."

"Ah. Not summery at all today."

"No."

A moment of silence.

"In the summer," Jenny suggested, "We could come back here and see how the plants are different. There would be different birds about too."

"Birds, yes." James sighed. "I do like the birds around here. When we're staying at our townhouse, I only ever see an assortment of pigeons or crows. Though I suppose there are some gulls by the river, or the docks."

"When we get back to the city, perhaps we could walk by the river."

"...perhaps."

"I love the river," Jenny said. "Even in the city, I love it. There's such power in the way it rushes by there. It's so loud, drowns out everyone talking, so none of my friends really like going by there. But sometimes I like being drowned out. I don't know, maybe it's silly of me." She laughed lightly, and James forced a chuckle in response.

Maybe thinking of the river had summoned it, but as she spoke, a mist began to rise around them. Funny, since it hadn't been a very damp day, and mists like these were more common in the morning. "Do you get a lot of fog here?" she asked.

"Ah, some. Not much. Peculiar weather, this. Look." James frowned up at the sky. Between the branches, Jenny saw clouds. "Looks like it might rain."

"Surely not. It was so clear earlier."

"Perhaps we should go back."

"But we just came out. We could stay out a little bit longer."

"If I get you caught in the rain, my parents will kill me," James said, "and yours too, for that matter."

If they got caught in the rain, Jenny imagined, James might give her his overcoat. She only had a shawl with her: warm and woolen but not made for bad weather. Or they might run back to the house, panting—maybe he would give her his hand to pull her along faster. She and her sister used to book it back home every time it rained, and end up sprawled on the porch sobbing with laughter. She wasn't sure she'd ever seen James really laugh.

She kept walking, and James kept walking to keep up with her. "I imagine you can survive them."

James snorted.

"I want to see the spot you told me about. You haven't given me any details. I'm curious."

"Well, it's nice. It'd be less nice wet."

"I don't think it will really rain, though," Jenny said. "Come on. You won't abandon me again, will you?"

Properly chastened, James hurried alongside her. Until suddenly he paused. "Miss Hunt..."

Jenny. How many times did she have to tell him? "What is it?"

"I think we've lost Mr. Johnson."

"Oh?" She hadn't looked behind them for some time now. Mr. Johnson had been walking a few yards back, far enough to offer some privacy for conversation without allowing for any impropriety. Now, glancing back, the butler was nowhere to be seen.

"We must have walked too fast," Jenny said ruefully. "He's an older man, after all."

"Hm. Mr. Johnson is usually a frighteningly fast walker. In the halls, I struggle to keep up with him."

"You don't suppose... he fell behind on purpose? So we could..."

James laughed. "You're assigning Mr. Johnson a much more tender heart than resides in that iron chest. No, he would never allow an unmarried couple to go wandering off alone. He's much too punctilious. But..." He sobered. "It's not like him to fall behind by accident either."

"Well, it must be one or the other," Jenny said, trying her best not to sound impatient.

"I don't know." James gazed down the path. "I don't like this mist."

"There's only one path, James. No turns or even any clearings. To get lost on this route, he'd have to put in some effort." Jenny couldn't help but wonder if James was underestimating his butler. She'd known many a stern-faced servant to have a secretly mischievous or romantic side in the past.

James shook his head. "Well, we shouldn't be alone without a chaperone."

"It's only been a few minutes. Nothing to worry about."

"I know. I'm not worried." James was clearly worried. "I think I'll just go back a little way and see if I can find him. Suppose he tripped on a root and can't get up."

"You said he was in excellent shape."

"Nevertheless, we shouldn't leave him behind."

"Fine." Jenny sighed. "Go on. I'll wait for you."

She leaned against the smoothest tree in the area, close to the path and without any low branches. James turned and headed away, and within minutes the mist had swallowed him up.

The mist was getting thicker.

Aristocrats and their massive estates. She'd visited many of them since her coming out, but her mind returned to the first time she saw one, the first time her father took her to visit a friend of his who was a lord. She was seven then. The lady of the house took her to sit in the parlor and chat with the women who were visiting that weekend (there was a bit of a house party going on) and she'd been so terribly bored that she'd thrown a temper tantrum. She'd yelled at the lady of the house and yelled at the other guests and absolutely screamed at the servant who was eventually tasked with taking her away until she could control herself.

Her father had come to find her soon after that.

"Thought I heard your voice, dearest."

"I want to go outside," she said. "I want to go riding. You said we could go riding. You said there were horses."

"Yes, Lord Genvere offered me the use of his horses for the weekend. You want to go riding? I'll take you riding."

It was on horseback that Jenny got an idea of the size of an aristocrat's estate, even a small one. ("And Genvere can barely afford its upkeep," her father noted—not a new comment from him, as he had a tactless tendency to discuss the financial state of all his friends.) Her father took her from one side of it to the other, finally stopping at the top of a hill where they could survey the estate in its entirety.

"You like the view, Jenny?"

"It's very pretty."

"Someday you'll have your own estate, just like this."

"I'll be a lady then, Papa?"

"You'll be queen of the world," her father said solemnly. "But Jenny, you have to promise me something. The queen of the world has to be patient and kind, understand? I hope my little girl can try her best to be more patient and more kind."

She felt guilty then. "Yes, Papa."

The view of that estate, grassy lawns and orchards and manor, lay before her eyes as clear as day. Yet at the same time, she could see the mist, and beyond it, squinting, see the trees. She could feel rain on her skin, beginning to soak her fine dress and shawl, and couldn't place whether it was raining on the hillside, droplets gathering on her horse's hair and saddle, or raining here in the forest as James had dreaded. James, that was a distant thought. Where had he gone? Had he really been here to begin with?

A hand touched her shoulder, and for a second she thought it was her father's. But it was too small for that. It tugged her hand until she began walking at a stumble, dreams still before her eyes. A voice said, "My lady, come. We have to get you out of the mist and rain. It isn't good for you."

"Ah," Jenny replied, figuring it would be clear to her companion what that meant even though it was not quite clear to herself. She followed, half blind, rain making her shiver. And as they walked together, the mist thinned and slowly cleared, and Jenny found that she was only staring at trees now, the mirage of a long-past hillside gone from her eyes. And while it was still raining, the rain was not as heavy.

There was still a hand in hers.

She looked over at what she had thought for a moment was her father and discovered, instead, a young woman a bit shorter than she was, with dark brown hair and tanned skin. She was wearing an orange gingham dress and a brown woolen coat, and looked to Jenny's eyes like a maid on an off day or perhaps a shop girl. Though more likely she was some farmer's daughter, out here in the country.

"Who are you?" she said. Her voice came out croaky.

"You're going to catch a cold in this weather," the girl said. "Come with me. I have a room at an inn nearby. We need to get you out of those clothes."

"I—Thank you, but I shouldn't. I'm staying with a family near here." Somehow she didn't say it was the earl's family. That would impress this girl a lot, no doubt, if she was the daughter of a local farmer. Somehow she didn't want to impress her, not that way. The girl's hand was warm. "I should get back..."

"The inn is close. You shouldn't be wandering through these woods right now, my lady. The mist is dangerous."

"The mist?" Jenny shivered.

"It's a bad mist," the girl said. "It steals your mind and will. Makes you remember the past. There's a bad magic in it."

"Oh," Jenny said. That seemed about right, actually, or at least very similar to what she'd just experienced. "Does that happen often around here?"

"No, not often."

"How do you know about it? And why—you seemed fine."

"My mother taught me about these things," the girl said. She didn't expand, instead tugging on Jenny's hand and repeating, "Come."

Jenny obeyed.

"Who are you?" she asked again. Not a local, perhaps, if she was staying at an inn.

"My name's Rachel."

She did not elaborate on where she was from, why she was staying at an inn, why she was in the area, why she had been in the forest. But her name was still enough to transform her from stranger to friend. Jenny smiled at her. "You rescued me."

"The mist is dangerous."

"Thank you."

Rachel shrugged. "You're welcome."

It was indeed a short walk to the inn, though it might have only seemed that way to Jenny because she was still a bit dazed. At the front, Rachel said a few words to the innkeeper, and then she led Jenny up to her room.

"They're going to draw a warm bath for you," she told Jenny. "It should be ready in a few minutes."

"Oh, that seems like a lot of trouble to go to. And I should really get out of your hair soon."

Rachel squeezed her shoulder. "Sit," she said, and she nodded toward the sole chair in the room, a handsome wooden thing pulled up against a flimsy, aged writing desk. Jenny sat, wet skirts squelching against the chair seat.

Rachel sighed. She pulled a suitcase out from under the bed—brown and bulging. Rummaging about for a minute, she took out a fluffy pink towel. "Actually, stand."

Jenny stood and stepped sheepishly away from the seat, assuming Rachel was giving her something to sit on. Instead, Rachel came over and untied her moist shawl. She then tossed the shawl to the corner in a careless manner that left Jenny sure that, whatever Rachel's profession, she was surely no maid on holiday.

"Arms out," Rachel ordered. Jenny, perplexed, held her arms out, and Rachel took the fluffy pink towel and began to pat her shoulders with it.

"Ah—that's not necessary, you know. I could do that myself..." She began to reach for the towel, and Rachel slapped her hand.

"Arms out, I said."

"...right, sorry."

Rachel, apparently suspecting further rebellion, restarted her efforts with Jenny's arms. She slowly patted the towel along first Rachel's upper arms and then her forearms. As this was a dress with fitted sleeves and only the slightest puff of fabric at the top, there was not all that much to work on here, but Rachel was thorough. She worked with just one layer of towel, although it was fast dampening, and squeezed the arm as she worked her way down, finally giving a peremptory pat to Jenny's already-dry hands. Then the other arm, and then, the back and chest.

She patted off Jenny's bare neck and collarbone, which were mostly dry, having been covered by the shawl, but had a few beads of moisture and were very cold. The feeling of the now-damp fluffy towel against her skin was gentle but made her shiver.

"I hope you're not cold," Rachel said.

"I'm fine."

"The water will be brought up soon. The bath will warn you up."

Jenny was silent, because Rachel had already moved on to patting down Jenny's upper chest, and then, finally, to applying that same gentle, meticulous pressure to her breasts.

She didn't linger, but Jenny fought the urge to push her off. Her arms were still up, as Rachel hadn't directed her to bring them down, and her hands clenched into fists midair, the muscles in her arm starting to complain about maintaining the position. She shifted uneasily, bringing her legs together.

Rachel moved on, patted down Jenny's waist and stomach and sides. "You can put your arms down," she told Jenny. "They won't be in the way anymore. Just keep them to the front."

Then she began patting down Jenny's skirt, which fortunately was a simple make without too many layers of fabric to have gotten soaked. It still had to be a wearying task trying to cover it all, while Jenny stood there silent, trying not to react whenever Rachel's hands pushed towel, and fabric, up close against her legs.

It was a lot of effort to go to when Jenny would be changing in a minute anyway. For a good Samaritan, were such lengths really reasonable?

Mama would have scolded a maid for wasting such time or for touching Jenny's body so much. The former was irresponsible, showed a lack of efficiency, but the second was indecent. Any properly trained maid would know that.

And now she was kneeling at Jenny's feet and had begun squeezing out the hem of her skirt in the towel. There was a knock on the door. It was a couple of the inn workers, here to ready the bath. They had brought a small tub and hot water. And, they said, if there was any other way they could help, they would be only too happy.

Jenny folded her arms around her chest. More strangers to witness her embarrassment. Just what she needed.

"No need," Rachel said coldly. "Thank you for the assistance."

The workers exited; the door closed.

Rachel and Jenny were alone again, and Jenny cleared her throat. "These buttons will be difficult with wet fabric. Hard to reach anyway. If you wouldn't mind...?"

"Of course," Rachel said.

And Jenny held still as Rachel undid the buttons down her back. It would have taken ages for her to undo them herself, fumbling and reaching. Mama encouraged her to choose the most impossible dresses these days. Showed class. And usually she had her maid to help her, so it didn't really matter.

Rachel was nothing like a maid, or like a seamstress. There was nothing impersonal about the concentration which she applied to carefully undoing the buttons and peeling wet cloth off damp skin. When she helped Jenny step out of the dress, Jenny noticed her eyeing the cavernous shell left behind by the empty skirt, and then eyeing Jenny's legs.

She helped with Jenny's corset, too, which was also difficult, but also in a more compromising position than the buttons down Jenny's back. Jenny watched her, watched her fingers and her eyes. If she could pinpoint whether those eyes and fingers strayed too much, then perhaps she'd know. She could say, for certain, "This is a very kind stranger, just a bit awkward," or "This is a woman with indecent intentions."

And then what?

She was stranded in an inn with her either way. She was still going to bathe and change and perhaps wait out the storm before leaving.

Still. She wanted to know.

But how did one judge when a touch lingered too long, or whether a neutral—guarded?—look was simply wearily empty or concerned or hiding appreciation? Jenny struggled, wavering this way and that, and finally gave up.

A final test, she pulled off her shift quickly and carelessly, and checked to see if Rachel was shocked. She did not appear to be, but she did not hurriedly look away as would have been proper. Instead, she gave Jenny's body a once-over, and said, "I'll help you take down your hair."

Oh, that was right. Her hair was still up.

And now she stood still again, shivering, as Rachel's warm body stood close behind her bare back, and Rachel's clever fingers worked at her hair, removing pins and releasing strand after strand. "It should be brushed," Rachel said when she was done, "but that can wait. Will you need help in the bath?"

It was on Jenny's tongue to say yes, but shocked at herself, she bit it back. What on earth would she need help with? There was nothing. Now she was the one going too far. Rachel would guess—what?

Guess Jenny's suspicion. Jenny's keen curiosity. Perhaps too keen, perhaps even hungry for Rachel to do something that would seal it.

Rachel, who was probably a perfectly normal, kind, innocent good Samaritan, with nothing on her mind but a desire to help.

But what on earth would she help with in the bath? Why was she offering?

"No," Jenny said, realizing she'd paused for too long in answering. "Thank you for your help, but from here I can manage."

The bathwater was warm, though it had cooled from when it was first brought in. Jenny sank into it and groaned, hoping that as it eased the tension in her body, it would free her mind of tangled thoughts as well.

***

When she got out of the bath, it was still raining, but unexpectedly, Rachel declared Jenny should go home anyhow, as soon as she'd put on a change of clothes (she was a bit bigger than Rachel, but ought still to be able to squeeze into one of her looser dresses) and dried her hair off. Jenny blinked. "Are you too tired?" Rachel asked.

Jenny, not about to admit she'd been imagining a quiet evening of conversation, perhaps dinner brought in by the innkeeper, said, "I'm quite fine. Very well, I suppose we should go."

"I didn't have an umbrella before," Rachel said, "but I've got one now. You said it's a quick walk? Who are you staying with?"

At last Jenny was obliged to admit that she was staying at the manor.

"I see. You're right, that's really not so bad. Well, let's go then," Rachel said, and in that brisk way of hers, she had herded Jenny out the door in minutes.

At the manor, they were met by an underbutler who appeared flabbergasted to see Jenny back. "Dear lady, how excellent that you have returned! But where is the young master?"

"James?" Jenny asked.

"Mr. Johnson returned to us an hour ago, saying he was separated from the two of you. He was feeling sick and unable to search for you, so we sent out some people to look for you. But now you're back and the young master is not."

It had been hours since Jenny had last seen James. At least two since she'd gotten to the inn. She'd taken a bath and changed out of wet clothes. She'd obsessed over a stranger's kindness. She'd barely spare a moment's thought to her future husband.

But James had been caught in the same mist as her. He should have been her first concern.

"I—We were separated too. I assumed he'd already gone home. I was lost—this woman here found me..."

Rachel said, "I'll go find him."

"Ah?"

"This mist isn't something just anyone can handle, or even find, for that matter. I'll find this young master of yours and bring him back." She gave Jenny a smile, closed mouth, eyes glinting. "Don't worry."

7

Chapter Seven

James couldn't say how long he'd been sitting underneath this tree.

He knew he'd been looking for Mr. Johnson, peering through the mist and trying to see if he could spot him. And before that he'd been walking beside his fiancée, a woman so perfect she barely seemed real to him. But all that seemed far away now.

In the present, he was curled against a tree trunk, back pressed hard against wet, sappy bark. In the present, he was wet and cold and his chest ached like hell. But even the cold and the wet and the pain were still distant.

And in his head, he was years away. He was once again a boy just become a man, and he was standing in the manor's stables pretending he wanted to go for a ride. He didn't want to go for a ride, not really. He had never loved horses as much as his father seemed to, although he was fond of Gray, the stallion his father had gifted him two years ago, and tried to take him out riding often. In the past, though, when he'd forgotten for a few days or even a week or two to see to Gray, he'd never worried too much about it, knowing the stable hands would exercise all the horses regularly, and Gray would remain well exercised and fed and groomed no matter how much James neglected him. But over the past few months he'd been going riding almost every day, and the reason was so he would have an excuse to go down to the stables, slowly and painstakingly put all the tack on his horse, and afterwards spend upwards of an hour over-grooming him. And the reason he wanted to do that was because of the new stable hand, a man two years older than him, a man who had discarded thoroughly the boyhood James was still casting off.

The man's name was Eric. (Even now, the name held a strange significance to James, even now that it had been years, even now that James had spent his feelings just as strongly on another foolish venture, even now that James had cast aside such foolish sentiment altogether... the name's significance lingered strange and strong in him.)

Eric was almost a foot taller than James. He was red-headed and freckly in the summer, and as it was now the end of summer, his freckles were still at peak. He wore the same livery as all the Earl of Ilbird's servants, but since the stablemaster wasn't particularly strict on uniform, his coat was usually cast aside, his vest left in his room all day, and his shirt half unbuttoned. He had only one civilized pretension, and that was that he always used the same strong after-shave, which to James was the most smoothly masculine scent he'd ever smelled, when it mixed with his sweat in the early morning and the smell of horses. (He'd never liked the smell of horses until now, but now he was becoming fond of it.) James thought sometimes that when he "grew up", he wanted to be just like Eric. It would drive his parents mad, of course. Eric was a servant, and not even a particularly dignified one. He squeaked by on formality in front of James's parents and the stablemaster, but when he was alone with James and James got him talking—flattered by attention and curiosity from the Earl's quiet, standoffish son—he could be very rude, even very crude. He was the only person who'd ever told James about sex in graphic detail, though James's high society friends would be keen on the subject in a year or two. He was not the only person James had ever met who would comfortably cuff him on the back of the head or slap him on the back and teasingly call him an idiot when he made a carefully stupid joke, but he was the only one James cared about.

James's feelings for him had been fresh, sharp, humiliating, and overwhelming. He'd had little crushes in the past, but nothing like this. Maybe they hadn't been crushes at all. There had been girls he'd liked, daughters of his parents' friends, and his mother had laughingly asked him if he liked them when he'd tell her he hoped they'd come visit again. The word "love" had seemed to fit well enough then for the boy he was. Ten years old, thirteen years old, he'd thought they were pretty and he'd thought they were smart and nice, and he'd wanted them to like him. Was "love" anything different from that?

He still wasn't sure, but falling for Eric was different, at least. And he did call it love, in his head, over and over again. He didn't talk to anyone else about it, of course. And he hadn't used the word "love" with Eric. Not yet.

Eric might laugh. Might scoff, or be disgusted.

But Eric wasn't mean. And he wasn't concerned with what other people thought about things, wasn't concerned about propriety. And he was fond of James. It was clear in the way he acted around him, frank and unguarded. And there had been a couple times he'd laughingly said, "You know, kid, you're all right."

And when he said things like that, James really didn't know how much longer he could keep quiet.

At the same time, he didn't know how he could dare to say anything to Eric's face.

It was the most daring and stupidest thing he'd ever done in his life, maybe, when he locked the door to his bedroom and took out a piece of paper and tried to write a poem about how Eric made him feel. Over the course of a month, he wrote it once and twice, three times and four, ten times and twenty. Some of the poems were very similar, only small differences in iterations of the same imagery and metaphors. Some of them were very different. Mostly they were very bad. James thought so at the time. Later, he showed a couple of them to Charlie, and she said she thought they were beautiful, but James wasn't sure she ever really got it. Now he couldn't remember quite how he'd felt writing them, and certainly he couldn't understand what had made him go insane. It all seemed idiotic. But at the time, it was the longest concentrated artistic endeavor of his life.

Then one day, he quoted a line of poetry at Eric, a line from Shakespeare—"Cowards die many times before their deaths"—and Eric scoffed.

"What's that from, the Bible?"

And James found himself muttering excuses, and Eric laughed and said it was okay, he knew James liked books and was an educated kid, would be an earl someday. As for him, he wasn't much for poetry! But then, he was just some dumb stable hand, huh? Stop blushing, kid. What's that about cowards? So stop overthinking things.

Well, after that, James knew he couldn't give Eric one of his poems. What would he think of it? Still. He didn't dare to say any of it to Eric's face, yet couldn't bear to hold his feelings inside. He could from day to day, but the thought of carrying them quietly around forever was unbearable.

He wrote it, then. A letter—prose, not poetry. It wasn't even very poetic. But it said everything clearly enough. He brought it down to the stables with him on a late summer day. Kept it in his pocket while he went for a ride, and then slipped it to Eric when he got back in.

"Eh? What's this?"

"Nothing. Just read it."

"What's so important you can't tell me?"

"Just read it," James said. "That's why I wrote it. I can't say. I'm going."

But Eric grabbed him by the back collar of his shirt and hauled him back. "Hold on. Let me read it."

"Eric, let me go."

Eric fumbled at the envelope of the letter one-handed, not letting go of James's shirt. "I can barely write, kid. I'm not going to write back to you when I could just read and tell you. Hold on."

"Eric." James bit his lip, hard. But when Eric let go of his shirt, he didn't leave. He just stared determinedly at a corner of the stables that hadn't been cleaned yet today and was full of dirty hay. Once he glanced back at Eric to see a concentrated frown on his face. He quickly looked away again.

Finally, Eric touched his shoulder. He flinched, hard.

Why had he thought this was a good idea? He didn't feel like he was breathing. And yet he felt wildly free at the same time. There was no going back now. If Eric said he was stupid and disgusting, and Eric could never feel the same way, he'd just go ahead and die.

"Shh, there. Calm down, bud." It crossed James's mind that Eric's voice at this moment was a lot like the voice he used when he was talking to a nervous horse. "This is a... pretty serious letter."

"I'm sorry." James, who had embarked on this resolving to feel no regret or shame in facing Eric with his feelings, found these words escaping his mouth regardless. "I didn't mean to... well, it's nothing that serious, I guess. I just..." He shrugged. "I wanted you to know that I felt that way about you. But you can forget it now that you've read it, I promise. I'll never bring it up again."

"Hey. It's nothing that dire." Eric laughed awkwardly. "Listen, I don't think I'm really the guy you think I am, and I'm definitely not the person you should spend such elegant words on. But, I mean, I'm not offended or anything. Calm down."

"Oh," James said dimly. Then, "I'm calm. It's fine."

"You're clearly pretty worked up. Here, sit down." Eric squatted on the floor, and James did too, heart still beating out of his chest.

"I didn't mean to make a big deal out of anything," said James, who had been feeling like his world was about to either end or explode into light ever since he first met Eric, who had perhaps never felt like anything was such a "big deal" as handing Eric this letter, who felt grateful that Eric could tell that and was treating it seriously, and who was at the same time mortified that anything could really be such a "big deal" as this to him.

Eric had told him about sex before, about having sex with pretty girls whose identities he didn't mention. Even that never seemed like a "big deal" to him, but here James was going crazy over a guy occasionally patting his back.

Eric said, "I think you're probably confused about some things."

"I know," James said. "I know we're not supposed to—I know you're a guy, but I've never felt anything this strong for a girl. I don't know..."

"Ah, well." Eric cleared his throat. "Maybe you fancy men. Some guys do, and—no offense intended—you do seem like the type. And you know, that's fine. Plenty of gentlemen have a guy on the side, doesn't usually bother their wives any. Well, they can be unsatisfied —I've known some women... But maybe more on that later," he said, apparently sensing James's lack of interest in tales of unsatisfied wives at his moment of crisis. "I just—I mean, I'm just a stable hand, you know me. What you see is what you get. I'm not—" he gestured with the letter in his hand. "All this."

"All that is about you," James said, "and no one else in this world."

Eric gave him a long look. Then he stared up at the ceiling and let out a sputtering laugh. "All right, all right. You win. Well, thanks for the letter, kid. I guess it's pretty flattering."

That was it, for then. James didn't ask him if he felt the same way. But it still felt like a weight off his back that Eric knew, and so he did not regret having made his confession.

The brief time after that was the most thrilling part of James's life so far. It was the closest he'd ever come to requited love, and this was the extent of it: He saw Eric every day, and Eric knew he loved him and did not object to it, and still slapped him on the back and ruffled his hair and laughed at his horrible jokes, and didn't object when James sometimes daringly found excuses to touch him back.

He was happy. He thought they both were, in a way.

And he thought about doing what Eric had said and finding a wife who wasn't too invested in love and keeping a lover (an Eric) on the side, and sometimes it didn't seem so bad. Though when he thought about it deeply, it sounded like torture. It was only the "Eric" part of it he liked, and he wasn't sure he could ever convince Eric to be in on it in the first place, to really be his lover. But that was all right. All he wanted, he told himself, was Eric around. The rest might happen or might not. It didn't matter. He didn't allow it to matter.

Then one day Eric told James he was leaving.

"What? Why?"

"My brother's got a position with the Duke of Roppon," Eric said. "He thinks he can get me one too."

"You've got a good position here already," James said. "And everyone says the Duke of Roppon's kind of a mess even if he's a duke. His household is much less..." Organized, by the gossip James overheard from the servants. And it had bad retention too. But then, Eric had never been one to care much about organization. And if he left now, he would only have worked for the Earl of Ilbird's household for a spring and a summer. Maybe he didn't like to stay in one place too long.

Eric shrugged. "It pays well."

"What, we don't?" James bit his lip. "I could talk to Father if you think you're being paid unfairly."

"Oh, god. No, for crying out loud don't mention me to your father."

"Why shouldn't I? He's always saying I need to be more involved with how the household runs."

"James, if you aren't more fucking careful, you're going to get me sacked without references, all right? Don't you get that?"

James blinked.

"Do you think people don't notice the way you act around me? Servants aren't blind, you know. People talk. Mr. Johnson spoke to me the other day. I'm lucky he didn't go to your father first and is giving me a chance to quit."

"Eric, you didn't do anything."

"I'm apparently a bad influence on you. That's enough. You're an earl's son. You really don't get it."

"You're the farthest thing from a bad influence on me. You—"

"Don't," Eric said, "start that again."

A moment of silence.

"I'm sorry," James said. "I can be more discreet. I can tell Mr. Johnson it's a mistake. You don't have to leave."

But Eric did leave.

James heard, later, that he did get that position under the Duke of Roppon. He sent him a letter, full of apologies and other things. He didn't expect a letter back, but he got one, short and to the point.

"Dear James,

"I didn't expect you'd write to me again. It's a nice letter. You don't have to be sorry. It's really not your fault. The world is just like this, but it's not your fault and I know you never meant any harm.

"Your letter was nice, but please don't send any more. People might get a hold of them before I do and you know the kind of things you write wouldn't be good for other people to get a hold of. I can keep your two letters pretty safe as-is but I don't know what I'd do with a bunch of them. Thanks for the letters and thanks for the good times. I hope you're doing well.

"Yours truly,

"Eric."

James read this letter over and over again. He thought Eric's letter was probably nicer than either of his had been. His hadn't been as longed-for, nor even wanted. But Eric still kept them, and that was nice too.

But while in the past he had been able to live off scraps, he found this letter of Eric's, so kind and written in such careful handwriting, did not make him happy at all.

***

That fall was his first coming out in society. For a man, perhaps a first year as "debutante" was not as important as for a woman. After all, men waited much longer before getting married, and so they might spend their first year simply socializing and playing around rather than ardently seeking a mate. Still, James couldn't help but feel a bit overwhelmed by it all. He knew a number of nobles his age—had met them over the years when they came visiting at the manor—but this was society on a different order of magnitude than before. A couple of years ago he used to think this day couldn't come soon enough. Now, however, it was hard to care as much. Coming out in a society that did not include Eric (except somewhere in the background, waiting on a dissolute duke's horses) didn't seem like much fun. A world without Eric was an empty one.

In the city at the beginning of the fall, he tried to find excitement in other ways. He visited a bar with a poor reputation once, and went walking by the docks, hoping to find something to take his mind off Eric. And then, just as the season was about to begin, he met Charlie.

Looking back now, he could just barely remember that Charlie had been there on the first visit with his parents to the tailor's, to get a new fall wardrobe. She hadn't been Charlie to him then, though, hadn't even been Charlotte Taylor, had been nothing more than a part of the furniture, one of the assistants that the master tailor had running here and there and back and forth and to and fro. She was not the one to take his measurements. She simply fetched various samples of fabric for the family to look at. Most of them were brighter than James would have chosen on his own, but the tailor assured him that these were the colors currently in fashion, and James supposed that even if he had no great expectations for the season, he still didn't want to make a fool of himself.

He got a note a week later, saying that two suits were done already whenever he wanted to come down and pick them up. Having nothing better to do, and a great restlessness in his heart, he headed down to the tailor's within the hour.

The streets were bustling. The tailor shop was in a fashionable quarter of the city, and all over town were young ladies and gentlemen recently arrived for the beginning of the season. Apart from that, there were the city folk who actually lived in the city, including many who profited from the influx of rich young people—merchants and beggars and performers—who were currently out in the street in force. James spent a solid ten minutes standing in a square listening to one such performer play a fiddle and sing a song about being in love for the first time. The song ended with two young lovers promising faithfulness, and James walked away with an aching chest. He could have been faithful to Eric. He was sure of this with the certainty one can only have of a hopeless proposition. If Eric had loved him, he would never have loved anyone else.

At the tailor's, James was asked to wait for a minute. The tailor wanted to see to him personally but he was in the middle of another fitting; he hadn't expected James would really come today. What kind of gentleman came running so promptly when summoned? James blushed and sat in a corner, willing the tailor's assistants to ignore him as they bustled back and forth. Why indeed had he come so soon? It wasn't as if he was eager to get his clothes, unexcited as he was about their design and coloring. He had simply lacked anything else to do, and his parents had always encouraged him to avoid procrastinating. But now he looked like a fool.

(Eric must have thought he looked an overeager fool as well, a nasty little voice in his head whispered.

It was impossible, these days, for him to go ten minutes without thinking about Eric.)

At last the tailor was free. James was dragged off to a back room and undressed and redressed, remeasured, scrutinized at every angle. The tailor decided one pair of pants and a coat were adequate. Everything else needed minor adjustments. As for the satisfactory pair of pants and coat, James could take them home today.

James reached for them, but the tailor snatched them away so fast that his hands only just brushed the fabric. "Sir, I'll have these boxed for you. Or maybe a bag?"

"Whichever is fine," James said, not wanting to cause any trouble.

"A box and a bag then," said the tailor, apparently deciding that going to the most trouble possible was the safest option. "Charlotte! Take care of these, will you? Young Mr. Guarin has been here for some time now. He'll be wanting to get to the docks soon to watch the beginning of the boat race, no doubt."

He bustled off.

"Boat race?" James repeated blankly. Where had the tailor gotten the impression that he was headed towards a boat race? He didn't think he'd made any comment to that effect.

The question was meant to be rhetorical, but he got an answer from the girl who had taken his clothes and was currently folding them. "Aren't you going to the Autumn Boat Race this evening? It seems like everyone has been talking about it today."

James tried to remember if his parents had mentioned anything like this and came up blank. Maybe they didn't know about it; maybe they didn't consider it a suitable activity for a future earl. If it started at the docks, there would probably be a lot of common-folk around—"riffraff", as his father would call them, not the type of people a young noble should associate himself with.

This didn't seem like something to say to a girl who was probably common enough herself, so instead he laughed and said, "Isn't it a bit early for 'autumn' anything?"

"Maybe so. But do you have a better name for it?"

James shrugged. "Uh... the End-of-Summer-But-Not-Quite-Autumn-Yet Boat Race?"

The girl laughed. "Call it the Summer Boat Race and have done with it, then."

"No, no, it's not really summer either. But not really fall. Forget seasons—what else is there about it? Anything in particular? They could name it after whoever runs it..."

"Old tradition. And the current host, as far as I know, is named Haggisthorpe, which doesn't feel very festive to me personally."

"No, not really. Ah, nothing against him, I've never met him, just..."

"Well, me neither, but what a name. It's barely fit for a person, never mind a boat race."

"Call it the Capital Boat Race?"

"Boring. Worse than Haggisthorpe."

James shriveled for a moment, but the girl's eyes were dancing, as if to say she believed he could do better than that, as if to say she believed that whatever he was—and how could she know, having only just met him—he could certainly do better than bore her.

He bit his lip. "Ah... The Apple Boat Race."

"Apples?"

"The apple season is just beginning now," he said. Or was that basically the same as saying it was autumn? Apple season was long. And apples had nothing to do with boat racing. He felt an imbecile.

But she smiled. "That's true. Ah, here in the city you rarely see an apple tree. I used to live in the country, and I paid closer attention to these things."

"On a farm?"

"Yes, we used to have a farm. A small one, but in the fall we'd help larger farms with their harvest. We knew the season for every crop. Now I think I'm already forgetting some of them."

"Well, at least you can tell by what they have in the market," James offered.

"Fair. I try to buy the fresh fruit whenever it's in season and make preserves. But these days I don't always have time anymore. It's a pity." She sighed. "We do well enough all winter, it's nothing to worry about. But I love preserves."

"That's too bad."

She shrugged. "We make do."

She glanced down and seemed to realize she hadn't finished folding the clothes. Flip, flip, flip. It was done in an instant. And then she was placing them neatly in a box, just the perfect size, and wrapping them up in brown paper. And then a bag. And then...

She started to hold them out to James, then pulled them back. "Are you going to go to the boat race, then, or are you headed home?"

"I don't know. I don't really have plans lately."

"Well, would it interest you?"

"Maybe. I don't know—the docks will probably be so crowded."

"The boats will pass under the bridge," she said. "It's a nice place to watch."

"The bridge? Maybe."

"There's a nice place to sit under the bridge. I often go there," she added. "If you want, I can show you a good vantage point. I see the race every year."

"Oh. All right."

On the way out, he asked her her name, and she said it was Charlotte. He told her his was James, and she said she knew already. James Guarin, Future Earl Ilbird. "Just call me James," he told her.

The spot under the bridge was not very beautiful. It had a view of the river, but it was shadowed by the bridge over it, and it was moist and mossy with nowhere dry to sit. But it was cozy to sit there with a companion, feeling conspiratorial. He put his bag beside him, and Charlotte opened up a bag that she herself had brought along to reveal a bottle of whiskey.

"I was going to share it with my brothers tonight. They'll be down at the docks, probably, mixed up in all that hullabaloo. But they'll beg a drink off someone else. Much better to share this with the future earl."

"Please just call me James."

A laugh. "You drink, right, James? You can hold your liquor?"

"Well enough." Actually not very well at all, but she said he could so confidently that he found he couldn't contradict her.

"All right. I don't have any cups. I hope you don't mind sipping where I've sipped. Or you could just drink first..."

"I don't mind. Why would I?"

A smile, and this time, a look that was almost demure, and at the same time almost impudent. "Oh, I don't know. Earls and all."

"Really. Earl this and earl that with you. Cut it out." He already felt then, having known her for less than an hour, that he would never stand on rank with her. That he wanted to be her friend.

She opened up the bottle and took a brief swig, then handed it to him. Her warm fingertips brushed his on the cool glass, and he started a little. She didn't seem to notice.

They passed the bottle back and forth and back and forth, mostly just sipping. It was half gone when the boats came by, boatmen stirring calm black water into a white, frothing frenzy, and James was relaxed enough to join Charlotte when she stood up and began yelling encouragement to this one and that one. She knew some of them by name, and in between yells told him some details of who deserved to win, who she hoped would win, and who might actually win. He didn't absorb most of it except that the person she thought would win had not yet reached the front of the pack and was still in the middle of the pack of boats. That was common enough in a foot-race, but he wondered if in a boat race it would be more difficult to pull ahead later on.

Then the boats had moved on, and James half expected Charlotte would want to run after them, or find another place to intersect their route—perhaps the finish line? But she sat down, pulling James down with her by the wrist. They finished the bottle, slowly, and sat and talked.

Somewhere in those hours, he began calling her Charlie. Somewhere in those hours, she began leaning against his side, head resting on his shoulder. James couldn't remember that anymore, but he could remember, after a moment of silence, Charlie asking him, "So, James, why are you so melancholy anyway?"

"Mm?"

"This afternoon, and when you first came to the fitting. You looked so distant and sad. Made a girl want to cheer you up. So tell me why you were so sad. Maybe there's something I can do about it."

He wasn't quite drunk, but he was tipsy. And Charlie was warm against his side. He told her, "I was in love with someone and they left."

"Oh." A moment of silence. He thought she'd ask him who or

how or why, and then he'd probably lie to her. But instead she said, "Well, that's something I can fix."

And then she kissed him.

**

James could remember all these things, and yet, at the same time, he couldn't.

He could remember, objectively, that he had fallen apart under Charlie. He could remember that he had thought his heart would beat so fast it would rip itself apart. A shifting heat. And then more visits to the tailor shop, asking Charlie when she got off work, walking with her down to the marketplace, dinner at an inn. The first time they booked a room—for the afternoon. It was a while before he was bold enough to stay out all night.

His season went very differently from how his parents had planned.

He could remember all these things, but they came to him distantly. As if he could look up at the stars and see the sparks coming off of them, smell their gas, see the rocky surface of the planets, and yet know they were still very far away, worlds away from him, too far to even offer heat or call to him with their gravity.

And he was here in the woods, and he was cold, and he didn't understand why he had acted so foolish.

Eric had been a stableman. Nice enough, but common and frankly smelly and a touch condescending. And Charlie had just been a shop girl, an assistant seamstress who happened to have a bottle of whiskey and thought it would be funny to play games with a gentleman. How could he have been stupid enough to fall for them both? To take those cold and distant stars and treat them as his sun, his moon, his very earth.

The rain was cold and wet, and his mind was about to travel down another winding road, another intimate night, when he felt a hand on his shoulder. He looked up and it was her, the girl from the ball, the girl who had stabbed him in the chest. Yet he was as incapable of feeling fear now as he was of feeling warmth. Was she even really here? He thought probably not.

This mist was doing something to him. Maybe it would kill him. Maybe this girl, this assassin, was part of the mist, or had brought it here to destroy him, and he would be consumed by it.

"You're far gone," the girl said. "My mistake." She patted his cheek. Her hands were as cold as his skin, and as wet. He stared at her without comprehension as she fumbled around in an inner pocket of her coat before pulling out a little bag, the size and shape of a sachet, and out of that a round, black pill. "Open," she said, and holding the pill with one hand, squeezed his chin with the other, forcing open his mouth. She popped the pill inside and told him to swallow.

He swallowed, then asked her what it was. He had a feeling he should care more than he did.

"Something to dispel magic," she said. "The mist has almost cleared, but it has a strong hold on you. The pill will help you shake it."

And it did.

After a moment, his head was clearer. Thoughts of the past were gone, and the present was clear. The mist was real, but it was subsiding. And this girl was very real, dark hair and dark eyes that pinned him against the tree trunk as surely as they'd pinned him in that dance hall.

He stood shakily. Took a deep breath, prepared himself to make some kind of declaration. He wanted to steady his breathing, steady his heartbeat...

Wait.

He couldn't feel his heart beating.

He couldn't feel his heart beating.

That had to be wrong. He was imagining it again—the doctor,

Mother, they'd both told him his pulse was fine—but Laurie hadn't, had he? Laurie hadn't, and he'd said...

Fingers trembling, he unbuttoned his coat and then his shirt, pulled it open to see his chest. The stitches Laurie had made were still there. The half-healed wound was still red and scabby. But now he could see something else, also, a pale circle right over where his heart should have been. A scar. He didn't have any scars, he was sure of it. But it was too old to have been from the other night. It looked as if it had been there for years.

The girl was still watching. Abruptly he didn't care if she killed him. He had to know. He grabbed her hand and put it on his wrist. "Can you feel my pulse?" he asked. He had to sound crazy.

She looked him in the eyes. "How could I?" she said. "You don't have a heart."

8

Chapter Eight

Natty's original plan for getting James Guarin's heart away from Genevieve Hunt involved a housebreak, a couple of knockouts and possibly some threats delivered to the young mistress if Natty couldn't find the heart in Hunt Manor alone. This, however, was before she and Angela learned that Genevieve Hunt, along with the Guarin family, was paying a visit to the Ilbird Estate in the countryside.

On hearing this, Angela spread a fresh sheet of paper on their parlor table and twirled a pen between gloved fingers. "New plan," she said. "Your old one would have worked well enough, but as things are, I think this case calls for a little 'divide and conquer'. What do you think, Natty?"

"One of us tackles Hunt Manor and the other trails Genevieve Hunt?"

"We don't know yet whether there is a single hiding place for the heart or if it is necessary for the thief to keep the heart on them. If we search Hunt Manor while Genevieve has the heart on her person, it's a waste of time. On the other hand, there will be no better opportunity to search her room than in her absence—and no better opportunity to accost her than while she's away from her family. From what I've heard, the Hunts are a protective bunch."

"So," Natty repeated, "one of us tackles Hunt Manor and the other trails Genevieve Hunt."

Angela nodded. "I think... You, Genevieve, and me, the manor. You need more experience in locations outside the city. Not all targets will politely stay within city bounds, you know."

Natty was aware of that much already. And despite the fact that often their missions did stay within the city, Angela had hoarded up maps of most towns in the country just in case, as well as maps of every other country where she'd ever had to travel for the sake of a patron. The map of the area surrounding the Ilbird Estate consisted mostly of one small village and a lot of forest.

Angela pursed her lips. "The village may seem promising—lots of alleyways and quiet corners—but remember, villagers talk. They remember every stranger passing through and what they looked like and what they did. If you can get Genevieve in the forest, that would be far preferable."

"Indeed," Natty said. "But Genevieve Hunt doesn't seem the type to go wandering by herself. She's a proper lady."

"Hm," Angela said. "Well, you'll have to think carefully about your approach."

Natty had a stroke of luck, then. Iris Witherbone, apparently in a contrite mood despite Angela having been the one to smack her in the face and possibly break a tooth, sent them a bouquet of apologetic flowers via messenger raven, along with a note saying that if Angela wanted to come and visit, perhaps Iris could help her with her latest mission after all.

Angela hmphed at the note and hmphed at the flowers, but she went to see Iris anyway. The mission took priority; if Iris could help,

Angela could swallow her pride. (Besides, Iris was one of the few people in the world Angela cared about, almost as much, maybe, as she cared about Natty. Not that she would ever admit it.) She didn't take Natty with her, saying she expected Iris wouldn't really be of much use. But she came back with two little jars, both of which she casually tossed to Natty, calling out, "Careful!"

Natty caught them.

One of them, Angela said, contained a highly concentrated batch of nostalgic mist, a mist which would quickly spread fog and rain over an area and cause disorientation, trapping anyone who inhaled it in a maze of wistful memories of happier times. The other contained pills that would negate the effects of any spell or magical presence. (Angela and Natty already owned some of the latter, but it was always good to have more.) Much better apology material than flowers, at least, and Angela was quite on good terms with Iris again. And, she said, she hoped that Natty would find one or both of them useful on her quest.

"We'll see," Natty said.

She watched Ilbird Estate from a distance—well, she watched the road from Ilbird Estate into the woods, figuring it her best option as Angela had agreed. And on the first opportunity, the first time she saw Genevieve heading into the woods, she took one of the anti-magic pills to immunize herself and then opened the jar of nostalgic mist and let it do its work. Within minutes, Genevieve was separated from her companions, and soon she was confused enough to be easy prey.

Genevieve Hunt. She was and was not what Natty had been expecting. On the one hand, the proper lady was as courteous as people described her, and she was as pretty up close as she had appeared at the party from a distance. On the other hand, she had a strange, nervous humility about her that reminded Natty of her observations of James Guarin. A pretty pair, she thought, and found the thought tinged with acid. Perhaps she was becoming too invested in her client's jealousy. At any rate, she was not as disdainful as many a young lady Natty had met before. She also was a bit clueless. Not naïve, precisely—she could clearly tell there was something off about Natty's commanding manner, and there was a good deal of suspicion in her eyes when Natty, under the guise of drying her off with a towel, thoroughly frisked her. But she didn't stop Natty all the same, or protect her clothes when she got into the bath, leaving them for Natty to paw through them just in case there was something small there she had missed.

Natty wondered if someone so clueless could really have stolen James Guarin's heart.

James Guarin, now. That man was still pretty much exactly the same as when Natty had seen him last. She found him huddled against a tree with his brain miles away, eyes full of anxious confusion.

But when she'd given him the pill (she wasn't going to carry him all the way back to the manor—better if he could just recover himself and they could part ways), his attitude changed almost instantly.

He even reached out to her, grabbing her wrist so hard it was almost violent. She thought he was attacking her for a moment, and prepared to chop at his throat with her other hand. But he put her hand on his wrist, fingers on an artery, and said, "Can you feel my pulse?" and she knew his urgency had another source.

Absurd, though. "How could I?" she said. "You don't have a heart."

A sharp intake of breath. (Though his heart was not beating, he still breathed somehow. She still wondered if he would die if that breath was restricted.) "You," he said, "you stole it from me. How—why would you take it?"

"I don't have it. Don't be stupid. You were there when I stabbed you. That was the first time we met, and your heart was already gone then. How could I have it?"

James's eyes closed. "You said Charlie sent you. Does she have it? Or did she send you to kill me?"

The urge to reply, to answer all his questions, was unexpectedly strong. Natty pushed it aside. "I said what I was told to tell you that day. Today there is no need for us to converse. You should return to your manor."

Today would not be the day she killed him—unless she had some unexpected stroke of luck. She still had to search Genevieve Hunt's room at Ilbird Manor, but from her observations of the woman, she now thought it unlikely the heart would be there. The thief, she thought, was probably someone else, though hell if she knew who. She would still search, but most likely, James Guarin would live another day. So there was no need for him to look so desperate, no need for him to grab her wrist again as she turned away, and cry out, "You can't just leave!"

"You'll be fine," Natty said. "I gave you a pill to ward off the mist's effects. They should wear off quickly. No permanent damage."

"I don't care about the mist. Where's my heart?"

"I don't know," Natty said. Except that by the way he was acting now, she could be pretty certain it wasn't with him, in his possession.

"You obviously know something. You kidnapped me that day, and here you are again. This is part of some larger scheme. I don't think Charlie was the one who sent you, either. That was a lie to throw me off. What do you want? What game are you playing?"

"I don't play games," Natty said. "This is work. I don't waste time on pointless conversation either."

"You know what I mean," James said frustratedly, and then, again, "Where's my heart?"

"Stolen," Natty said.

"Stolen—if not by you, by who?" he demanded. "How? Why?" She tried to pull away again, perhaps half-heartedly, and his grip on her wrist tightened, stronger than she had thought him capable of in his mist-addled state. "You can't leave. Not until you explain."

She could still have escaped him easily enough. As a last resort, she could have broken his wrist.

But as she looked at him, his desperately confused eyes and half-parted, panting lips, it occurred to her that a man so desperate and so naïve might be useful.

"Take me back to the manor," she said. "Tell no one who I am. I'll explain what I can. I'll help you," she added, and James's eyes narrowed, half-suspicious, half-hopeful.

He nodded. "Yes. Come back with me. We can talk in private there."

***

There was a silly amount of confusion at the manor when Natty returned with James in tow.

Natty understood that large households were always this way. She could vaguely remember her own mother fussing when she got lost in a crowd and was spotted a few minutes later, and James had been missing for hours. But these days, her household solely consisted of Angela, and while Angela used to keep a hawklike eye on Natty when she was young, these days she trusted in Natty's common sense and rarely fussed over her. Recently, for example, Angela had sent her out on a mission to assassinate a young soldier who was on leave and visiting a bar. She hadn't gotten back to base until the early morning hours, and had been much more damaged than James was right now: knees and knuckles scraped and bruised, forehead and lip bleeding, pants and coat ripped. The night hadn't gone well.

Angela had given her a once-over, and sent her to the bathroom to wash off her injuries. Fetched her some bandages and antiseptic to make use of. And, when she was done, had asked her for her report: had she killed the man or would Angela need to go in herself?

Natty had killed her man. Angela had been satisfied.

Here, James's return was treated with no such efficiency. His mother was exclaiming over how she'd been so worried, what with his recent injury and the assassin still on the loose, and how could he just go off on his own and disappear like that? Really, how could he?

"I'm fine, Mother," James said. "I'm sure the assassin is still back in the city, anyway. There's nothing to worry about." He offered Natty a queasy smile. "I just got lost in the mist. Did Miss Hunt make it back? I lost track of her, and I'd hate to think she's still stranded out there."

"Ah, she didn't tell you yet? Rachel brought her back safely, too. No need to worry about it."

"Rachel?" James's brow furrowed. He glanced at Natty. Natty looked back at him. "Oh. Well, good."

Big, overprotective families. It was ages before James was able to squirm his way free of his parents, and by that time, Genevieve had shown up. She beamed at Natty, and walked over and gave James's arm a squeeze. "Hey."

"I'm glad you made it back, Miss Hunt. Sorry I just left you like that. I got lost."

"It was the cursed mist. Nothing to be done about it," Genevieve said. "And I told you to call me Jenny."

James smiled shakily. "Right. Jenny. Forgive me."

"What is there to forgive? Oh, so you've met Rachel now?" she added, gesturing at Natty. "She saved me. She's very smart."

"We spoke," James said.

And now Genevieve was looking at Natty again, with a keen interest Natty could not allow. She wouldn't be able to search Genevieve's room if Genevieve was present, nor have a private conversation with James. She cleared her throat. "The mist has affected James worse than you. He was stuck in it for longer."

"Oh dear," Genevieve said, face dropping. "Oh no. What can we do about it?"

"There's a treatment I know," Natty said. "But I'm afraid it's a bit... I'd need to be alone with him. I know he's your fiancé. I hope you won't object."

Genevieve's face did something interesting. She gave Natty a long, suspicious look, then looked over at James, who still looked quite bedraggled and miserable. "Perhaps if you told his mother what must be done..."

"It's delicate. I doubt she could handle it."

"It's fine, Miss Hunt," James said. "We won't do anything improper, I promise. I hope you can trust me."

"Of course, James. It's not that I don't. It's only..." Genevieve wavered.

James glanced over at his parents, who had retreated a distance so Genevieve could speak with him more privately. "It will be fine," he said. "Rachel seems to be quite knowledgeable. We might as well take advantage of that."

So it was that Natty ended up in James Guarin's room, at his own invitation, rather than having to break into the manor. It was convenient—although this would not be a good chance to search his room, she was sure by now he didn't have his heart hidden somewhere within. More important was being given access to the manor, and even more than that, if not to James Guarin's heart, to his mind. For all that he didn't trust her yet—had no reason to trust her—he had brought her here to speak with him, wanted to listen. Wanted her to explain the strange events unfolding around him. Might accept any explanation, no matter how false.

The feeling of power she had with his eyes fastened on her,

looking up to her, was enjoyable. She ended up telling him mostly the truth regardless. Mostly.

"So you don't have my heart."

"No."

"Charlie really did hire you." A twist of James's mouth; distaste.

"Yes."

"And now you're seeking it instead of trying to kill me, but you don't actually know more than I do."

This was the simplest thing for James to think, so Natty nodded. "However, it's a good bet that it was stolen by Miss Hunt or Miss Hunt's family. Who else would benefit from being able to control you or make you fall in love?"

James sighed. "I don't agree."

"Setting your feelings aside," Natty said, "am I not logical?"

"No," James said. "You aren't." A hand raised. "Don't look at me like that. I won't fight with you. I know physically you can win, and you're probably cleverer than me too, what with your profession. But there are three points you have not considered."

"Three points." Natty raised her eyebrows. "Go ahead."

"First," James said, "if the point of stealing my heart is to have me fall in love with her, why am I not in love with her?"

Natty snorted. "You're not?"

"I'm not."

"Sure. You're not."

"I would know," James insisted. "I don't... Genevieve Hunt is beautiful and talented, and I admire her greatly, but to call my feelings for her love... I really don't know."

"You start by saying you know and end by saying you don't know," Natty said. "You broke off a relationship that had been going for three years so you could marry Genevieve Hunt. How is that not love? It's not nothing, anyway."

"To an outsider, I can understand my actions seem irrational, affected. But it wasn't like that," James said. "It's not that I became suddenly infatuated with Genevieve to the point of abandoning Charlie, though I can see why she might think so, and be bitter as a result. I left Charlie because I didn't love her anymore. How could I stay with her? I wasted so much time on her already. Ignored anyone who worried about me. Damaged our family's reputation, rejected a pure and honest girl like Genevieve..."

"You barely know Miss Hunt but call her pure and honest. You say you're not infatuated? You're not objective either."

"There's no point in discussing this if you aren't going to listen to me."

"Fine. I'll suspend my disbelief. Go on. Your second point?"

"As to the second point, Genevieve wouldn't have needed to bewitch me in order to make me marry her," James said. "That's ridiculous. Our parents already agreed on the match, and she's... well, there are plenty of men who are interested, many better prospects than me. In terms of money and power, her family is hard to match; in terms of beauty and talent, it's hard to match their young mistress. Witchery? Superfluous."

"And yet you rejected her for more than a year, and now you're praising her beauty and talent."

James ignored her this time. "Finally: It's just not something Genevieve would do."

Natty waited for him to add to this proclamation, but apparently that was it. She tilted her head, gesturing for him to go on.

James shrugged helplessly. "She's a very patient and kind person. I thought that even when I was in love with Charlie. I really can't imagine her ripping someone's heart out."

"So your reasons for believing Miss Hunt didn't enchant you," Natty said drily, "are: she's too pretty, she's too nice, and you aren't in love with her. You don't see a contradiction."

James made a frustrated noise in his throat.

"I can tell you three reasons it is her," Natty said. "One: her family is rich and powerful and could afford to hire a witch. They're more expensive than Poor Jane, you know. Two: Again, she is the only one to have benefited. Three: Every single thing you just said."

"If that's the only lead you've got, this was a waste of time," James said. "I should have just left you in the forest."

Natty would have been the one leaving him, but apparently he'd forgotten his desperate clinginess already. Feeling a prick of annoyance, she gave James a harsh twist of the ear, making him yelp.

"You're really going to take it on trust?" she asked. "Even knowing you're biased? You're an idiot."

"He's not an idiot."

This voice was coming from the other side of the bedroom door. Someone had been eavesdropping on a very incriminating conversation. Natty's reaction was instant—she whirled James around in front of herself, snatching a small knife out of her sleeve and holding it close against his neck while her other arm snaked around his chest to hold him in place. James let out a little whine of complaint but held still, back against her chest.

"Who's there?" Natty called.

The door opened, revealing Genevieve Hunt, a miffed expression on her face that froze when she saw James's position.

"Come in and shut the door," Natty said. "Quickly."

Genevieve obeyed.

"You were listening in on us."

"Of course," Genevieve said. "I wouldn't leave my fiancé alone with a suspicious stranger."

"Here I thought you liked me."

Genevieve flushed. "Let James go. He's not—we're no threat to you, obviously. And from what you said, stabbing him wouldn't have any effect anyway."

This was true, but it seemed to make Genevieve and James

nervous enough all the same, which was for the best when they had Natty outnumbered. Not that she couldn't take them both out in ten seconds, even with James's freakish immortality in the mix. She released James, and he stumbled away from her, breathing heavily.

Genevieve gripped his arm steadying him. "Are you all right?" As she spoke, she moved one hand down to his wrist, checking his pulse for herself. Her lips pursed at its lack.

"Fine," James said. "Genevieve, you shouldn't get involved in this."

"Clearly I already am, as your top suspect," Genevieve said drily.

"I don't suspect you," James said. "As for whether Rachel does, it's irrelevant. She's hardly a close confidant."

A smile flickered on Genevieve's face. "Well, apart from that, I am your fiancée. I don't particularly want to marry a man without a heart."

James bowed his head. "My apologies. There is time before the wedding—I really do hope to retrieve it before then."

"That's not what I meant. What I mean is I have a vested interest in its return. I'm involved. Let me help you," Genevieve said. "After all, a wife is meant to be part of her husband's life. Isn't she?"

"It could be dangerous."

Genevieve smiled more firmly now, and said, in a voice wistful and chiding, "Sickness and health."

James swallowed. "...well."

"Well, if Miss Hunt wants to help," Natty said, "she could start by submitting to a search. She should be your top suspect, even if she isn't."

Genevieve folded her arms. "You already searched me."

"Not your room."

"Fine. Search my room. I don't disagree that I'm the most suspicious person here, but as I did not steal any hearts—I don't know any black magic to begin with—continuing to suspect me is a waste of time. Better to settle it here and now. Shall I lead the way?"

Natty held out her arm. "Please go ahead."

James was still muttering protests, but as Genevieve strode decisively out the door and Natty followed, he trailed along behind them, unable to let the search for his own heart go without his attendance. Just as well. Natty wanted to keep an eye on him until she was well out of here; Genevieve too, preferably. Just in case either one of them decided that a more sensible way to deal with an assassin was to report her to the authorities.

At Genevieve's room, she turned to James, who stopped walking abruptly as soon as she looked at him. "You. Watch Miss Hunt while I search."

"Rachel, I don't..."

"If you don't suspect your fiancée, then there's no problem with me checking her things," Natty said, "is there?"

"Well," James said, "a woman has her privacy."

Natty rolled her eyes. "Watch Miss Hunt and only Miss Hunt. Then you won't violate her privacy, will you?"

She began searching.

Genevieve Hunt had not been staying in this room long. She would have had little time to find or manufacture an especially clever hiding place for a small object: a loose floor tile or some secret compartment in the wall would be beyond her. Nevertheless Natty was meticulous about her search, emptying every drawer of wardrobe and dressing table, emptying Genevieve's bags and even her smallest purse, containing only some money and feminine products. She found nothing terribly surprising, though a few items that might have given James pause: Genevieve's taste in literature, for one thing, and her taste in undergarments for another. But nothing all that shocking to the seasoned eye. The most suspicious objects were a locket (but too small, she decided, to be the enchanted heart, even if there was a precious stone in the center) and a pair of earrings (also too small) and a makeup compact (which appeared to be quite old and worn, while the heart would have had to be new). Nothing she found had a pulse, anyway, so even the most suspicious objects could be eliminated.

She finished. "James, you've been watching Miss Hunt this whole time?"

"Yes."

"She hasn't picked anything up?"

"No."

"I'll frisk her, then," Natty said, "and we'll be done." Although it was possible Genevieve had hidden the heart somewhere else on the manor, Natty didn't have the time for that extensive of a search, and the servants—or the Earl or Countess themselves—were too likely to intervene. She could have waited until late at night and carried out a search anyhow, similar to what Angela was doing in the city, but the likelihood of Genevieve secreting it away somewhere in this manor was low. Too easy for someone to stumble upon it, besides which, she barely suspected Genevieve at this point. Genevieve's parents, now... perhaps. If they could have found a way to tie the spell to Genevieve despite Genevieve not possessing the heart.

Genevieve said, "You frisked me earlier."

"Hours ago. You've changed clothes too. I should be thorough if you want to eliminate any suspicion."

Genevieve glanced nervously at James, who bit his lip. Natty rolled her eyes and began patting down Genevieve's arms. Genevieve silently complied.

James, relieved of his duty, looked away.

***

"You should have told me about this earlier, James," Genevieve said.

They were now all sitting out in the garden, Genevieve having declared that she didn't want James trapped with Natty in a closed space where no one would see if something happened. The first sensible thought she'd had today, but a nuisance. Now Natty had to spend a lot more energy watching for prying eyes and ears.

James muttered, "I wasn't sure... I didn't know if I was just imagining things."

"You don't have a pulse. You saw your own ribcage. How would you imagine that?"

"Well, you know I can be very nervous sometimes, and at that party I was nervous. I'd been stabbed, choked, hit on the head—my perception was not very reliable. And there's a circle on my chest I actually couldn't see until now. A man had even mentioned it to me, someone who helped me after I got kidnapped—" Side glance at Natty. "—but until now I couldn't see it. I don't know why."

"Part of the enchantment," Natty opined. "The pill I gave you counteracted magic worked on the mind, so the illusion broke, and you could see what had been done to you."

James shuddered.

Genevieve nodded. "Very well. But now you know, and we both know. What next? Rachel, did you have any other leads?"

"James's cooperation opens up some avenues," Natty said. "If he's willing to answer some questions, it could help. James?"

James nodded.

"We can assume you had your heart when you last felt love for Charlotte Taylor," Natty said. "When was that?"

James frowned. "That's a hard thing to pinpoint. Feelings are feelings, after all. Since I left her, I've wondered if ever loving her was a delusion I had, whether I was fooling myself about really caring for her at all."

"They weren't and you weren't," Natty said. "You're wasting time. When do you last remember loving Charlotte Taylor?"

Frowning harder, now. "I suppose," James said, "About a week before we settled my engagement with Miss Hunt." He glanced at

Genevieve apologetically. "I'm not sure whether my feelings for her were ever really..."

"Finish," Natty said.

"We had dinner together then, and... spent time together as we usually did," James said. "I remember being very happy to be with her. We laughed a lot. I suppose I thought I loved her at the time."

"And after that? When did you start feeling love for Miss Hunt?"

"I've always esteemed Genevieve highly."

"Fine. When did you decide to marry her?"

"The day before we settled it and I proposed," James said, "I finally came to the decision. But I don't know if..."

"And between these two dates? What did you do? Where did you go? Who did you see?"

"I think I went to the opera the night after I saw Charlie last," James said. "I would have liked to take her but she doesn't like the opera much, and I was going with friends. I stayed out pretty late, and we stopped at a bar. The day after that I had a fever, and I was sick for maybe four days. Afterwards, as I was recovering, I came to the decision to marry Genevieve. It was being so sick that did it, I think. I really felt like I might die, and so much in my life suddenly seemed childish. I wanted to do something worthwhile."

Natty waved a hand. "That's irrelevant. But we can build a time-line. Most likely you were attacked the night you went to the opera and the bar. A ritual was performed on you to remove your heart. Afterwards you were sick for four days—that had to be the after-effects of the enchantment setting in. Do you disagree?"

"Reasonable enough," Genevieve said.

James looked uneasy. "Genevieve, you do know that whatever spell this is, I still—I liked you before, is what I mean. I always admired you. I was just very caught up in Charlie and my own foolishness. It's not—this doesn't mean I don't care for you."

"These matters are better discussed when we've retrieved your heart," Genevieve said. "Your feelings may change."

"Maybe," James said. "I doubt it."

On Natty's impatient questioning, he told her what friends he'd been out with that night at the opera and what bar they'd frequented afterwards. She made a mental note of the answers; she would not forget a single name. But that could be better investigated back in the city than here. And for that matter...

"If you're willing to cooperate a bit further," she told James, "there is a way we could pinpoint the location of your heart, if not ascertain the culprit."

"Oh? What is it?"

"There are spells for finding things," Natty said. "For a body part, it's much easier for the owner to perform one than an outsider. If you cooperate with us, we could find it much faster than searching each of these people one by one."

"What is it? The spell."

"I don't know it," Natty said, "but an associate of mine back in the capital does. Return with me, and we'll see what can be done."

James and Genevieve exchanged a look.

"Do you have any better ideas?" Natty asked. "Or do you think you can handle this on your own? Or that the authorities will be helpful? Chances are they won't even believe you, or if they do, will wash their hands of it. Cops hate dealing with magic."

"It's your choice, James," Genevieve said. "I'll help you either way. My father has resources for finding things out. But if you want to go with Rachel, I won't stop you. Just let me come with you. You shouldn't do this alone."

James slowly nodded. He looked at Natty. "We'll head out tomorrow, then, or the day after at the latest. I'll need a little time to make excuses to my parents. If it can be helped, they shouldn't be involved in this."

9

Chapter Nine

Iris Witherbone had finally found the entrance.

She'd spent months researching dragons lately, the past two months focusing on wyrms, and several weeks on one wyrm in particular. It would not be entirely accurate to say that legend had it that there was a wyrm sleeping under the capital city. "Legend" indicated a general knowledge, and people didn't really talk about wyrms anymore. But Iris had found mention of this particular wyrm and the catacombs it lay in within several authoritative bestiaries. She had decided it was worth looking into further, given how hard it was to find any dragons these days, and given the magical value of dragons' body parts, especially wyrms.

Now, after tens of stolen, excavated and overpriced books, several spells of location and analysis, and three shots of rum mixed with lime juice, she had finally found the entrance to the catacombs. It was hidden in a remote alley, covered with a grate that made it look like it led to the sewers. Well, there was enough rubbish and waste at the bottom of the entrance to give that impression. But this tunnel did not connect to the sewer system at large, and after a few turns, the waste petered off, and instead one found oneself in tunnels more full of dust and dirt that to the practiced nose smelled of corpses, magic, ancient knowledge, and even more ancient beast.

So, although some of the books had offered maps to the cata-combs—conflicting maps, but they agreed on some basic points—she did not try to force her memory down those routes, but instead followed drunken, highly experienced and magic-guided instinct, and wended her way in the direction her gut dictated.

As she walked, the tunnel changed from plain gray stone blocks to a more ornate structure. Crumbling gargoyles and saints smiled at her from the sides of support pillars, with benevolent beams and grotesque grins. Flowery sculpted vines played along the sides of the passageway. She saw a couple actual tombs, fewer than she would have expected. They had tantalizing inscriptions in a forgotten alphabet, one she could have deciphered with enough time. But that was not her purpose here today.

She followed the smell, and as the tunnel grew more ornate and more tombs showed up, the smell grew stronger as well, until at last she came to a doorway and saw through it a tunnel blocked, en-tirely filled by a huge, tube-shaped, sinuous body covered in scales that, in the light of the lantern she was carrying, appeared a dirty olive green.

"Wyrm," she whispered in delight. She'd found him.

She laid a hand on the serpent's side. There was a thick layer of dust, but underneath it, the scaley skin was cool to the touch. She wondered how long it had been since this beast had lain in the sun. Perhaps it had been centuries. Perhaps millennia.

If woken, the havoc this creature could wreak...

She played with the thought for the moment. It had amused her for weeks. She had been considering, too, the potential bene-fits of killing this wyrm in its sleep and cutting its heart out. The powers one could grasp from eating a wyrm's heart were immense. Unfortunately they had the side effect of half-transforming the consumer into a wyrm as well, and while Iris was not averse to prolonging her life or gaining strength and magical ability, she had lived long enough in her own body to know she preferred her skin without scales, her skull without horns, and her body temperature more bio-regulated than a serpentine form would allow. More than that, her research indicated that the presence of this wyrm in these catacombs was a large part of what fueled the ambient magic of the whole city, even the whole country. Killing it would disrupt a delicate balance. She didn't mind disrupting balances, but she thought it might be better to do some further calculations first so she could better predict what the results might be—what would be lost by the wyrm's death, and also what magical forces or beings might rush in to fill the void it would leave behind.

For now, she would content herself with harvesting a few of the wyrm's scales. These were an essential ingredient in many potions she had never been able to try in the past, and an optional strengthener in several potions she made regularly. She could sell them at a high price to many potion-makers, too, she was well aware—but whether she would, ah, that was the question. She liked money, but power was far more addictive. When she gained the ability to make recipes other witches could only dream of (she pictured them gnashing their teeth and groaning in crude jealousy), what greater satisfaction could she get out of life?

***

That night, Poor Jane visited Iris.

She was in the process of refining one of the huge scales she had carefully peeled off the wyrm's hide. She had chopped it up and grated it, and now was boiling it in water to make a sort of jelly. But the jellifying of the scale powder would take a long time, and she was glad of a distraction. And a chance to boast. "Poor Jane! I didn't expect I'd see you again for ages. Come in, sweet, sit down. I'm making an extract here that's very potent and delicate so I'll have to stay at the stove for the moment. But do sit down and tell me how you've been and what you've been up to. You always have such delightful stories."

Poor Jane sat down. "I've been searching a house."

"And killing its owner?"

"No deaths tonight," Poor Jane said, face sour with disappointment. "Only a search, and that fruitless."

"Oh?"

"I'm still looking for that poor sap's heart."

"Oh, that." Iris shook her head. "How dull. I was considering whether to take a wyrm's heart tonight or not, but eventually settled on not. If I can hold back from even taking the heart of a wyrm, how much more should whatever villain stole this poor boy's heart have held back from the same? I can't imagine it's doing them very much good. A wyrm's heart can grant you immortality, you know. Among other things."

"So you've said," Poor Jane said.

"Is that sarcasm? My dear, it doesn't suit you."

"Then why do you look so endeared? Practically purring."

"Got me," Iris said ruefully. "Ah, Poor Jane, Poor Jane. It will be another hour, maybe, I have to keep a close watch on this jelly. Then it will have to sit for a good long while by itself. Do you plan on staying long?"

"I have no firm plans for the night."

"Would you let me firm you up?"

"Anatomically inaccurate," Poor Jane said. "Really, Iris. Have you been flirting with men lately?"

"Would you like to know? Jealousy *does* suit you."

Poor Jane pursed her lips. She was an aloof woman, only truly attached to her mission and her young apprentice. She always refused to be jealous, and even when she was, would never admit it. Ah, sometimes Iris just wanted to bite her. If she ever did allow herself to become half-wyrm, she imagined the impulse would become irresistible.

As for Iris, she was made for jealousy. She was possessive of things that were hers, things that weren't hers and never would be, and things that should be hers and yet lingered just out of reach. Poor Jane was probably one of those. She wasn't sure which.

Poor Jane had told Iris once—in a maudlin mood, a mood for indulging Iris's fancies—that one of her closest experiences with a magic outside her own curse had been summoning the ghost Cruel Therese and asking her a question about Poor Jane's inheritance and death. Iris had listened, smiled, and sighed.

"Cruel Therese, ah yes. I suppose you know that no one talks much about her anymore? No new rumors of people summoning her and learning forbidden knowledge?"

"These are not the old days, when magic was gossiped about on every street corner," Poor Jane had said. "Those who actually use old magics tend to be more discreet about it. And who wants others to know the forbidden secrets they learned? I've told very few about summoning Cruel Therese myself. Only my apprentice, and now you."

"Hm. I suppose that's true," Iris had conceded. "But that's not the reason people no longer even whisper about seeing Cruel Therese— except in old anecdotes. It's my fault, actually. I scared her off."

"Scared off a ghost centuries old?" Poor Jane's eyebrows raised. "Cruel Therese?" She even sounded a little defensive. Whatever her experience with Cruel Therese had been like, it must have been precious to her.

"To be fair," Iris said. "I didn't do it on purpose."

Summoning Cruel Therese had been on purpose, of course. It had taken her a very long time to manage it, countless bottles of wine spilled onto dry and moist soil, floors made of stone and wood, once even over the side of a cliff. Countless lilies ripped into shreds, sometimes with calm, even calculation and other times with the haste of fury. It was on one of her undignified, furious attempts that Cruel Therese finally arrived.

"Iris Witherbone," she said, in a voice as calm and rushing as a night alone on a river-boat, "it seems you do not understand silence as a refusal."

Iris, breathing hard, felt her panting lips stretch into a grin. "Cruel Therese, of all people, I do not. And clearly should not, since you have come. I knew eventually you would come."

"You are not motivated by any urgent need," Cruel Therese said disdainfully. "The first time you tried to summon me, you only wanted to know about the missing pages of an old book so you could carry on with a ritual. My purpose of continued existence is not to attend to the inquiries of lazy academics."

"I realized that, of course. Cruel Therese, I've thought it over. I've thought it over very carefully," Iris said, eyes gleaming almost with tears. "I have a much better question now—questions, plural, if you'll permit, but a singular question if that is all you're willing to answer for me. I've heard most people only ask a single question, and I'm willing to bow to tradition. Me, willing to bow to tradition. You must know it's a great deal to ask for me to bow to anything or anyone but, Cruel Therese, I'm willing to bow to you."

"Your inquiries have changed over time, it is true," Cruel Therese said. (Iris wondered if she knew every question that Iris had ever intended to ask, but oh, of course she would know. She was Cruel Therese. She knew everything, didn't she? Everything.) "However," she added, "the nature of your intent has not changed. I come to those who call on me out of need, wanting to know what to do with their lives, what path they should take, whether they have been betrayed, how they can save themselves. You come to me with nothing more than idle curiosity. I don't see why I should indulge you."

"But you came," Iris said. "You can't refuse me now. You came, didn't you?"

"A spirit or a cursed being can come when called and still refuse a request, unless the nature of their being compels them otherwise or other compulsion is applied," Cruel Therese said. "So it is with me, and there are various other examples of beings with whom it would be the same. Poor Jane is a close analogue, though her existence has taken the form of many people over the ages and so has a different nature from my continuous existence. Or perhaps Kind Alexander, though I would call most lucky if he did refuse their requests, since it is his habit to only fulfill people's desires in the most twisted and sadistic manner possible. Or perhaps Tall Georgiana, though her abilities are fairly limited. Now, in comparison, if you were to manage to summon a faerie, it would only be by finding a way to compel them in the first place, by their name or enough details pinpointing their identity that they could not refuse you, and so you would be able to proceed to request anything else that you wanted from them."

"Who's Poor Jane?" Iris asked.

Cruel Therese tilted her head. "Is that your question, the one you really want answered? I suppose I could answer. I answered a very similar question for Poor Jane herself recently. Maybe you'd like to know about that."

Iris did want to know about that, and the impetuous part of her was willing to let Cruel Therese tell her, but for once in her life she forced herself to practice some restraint. If this was her chance, she couldn't waste it on passing fancies and trivialities. She could get any knowledge in the world right now—if, that was, "You're going to answer me after all?"

Cruel Therese said, "You're right that I did come. Your curiosity and hunger for knowledge has only grown over the years. Such a hunger approximates desperation. I can respect that in a way. Besides, you've already wasted so much wine, and I grow tired of your calling me."

"Does it affect you? My calling, your resisting my call? What has the power to tire a ghost? What kind of existence do you have, anyway?"

"Is that your question then?" Cruel Therese said. "Please pick it carefully. If I hear you calling me again after this, I will be cross, and I am not called cruel for nothing."

Iris knew perfectly well the origin of Therese's moniker and didn't find it all that intimidating. It wasn't as if she were a murderer or some kind of torturing psychopath; she simply was a giver of knowledge that some rejected, and Iris had never rejected knowledge. Still, it had been difficult enough summoning Cruel Therese the first time, and she was well aware she might never manage it again. Closing her eyes and taking a deep breath, she considered all the questions she'd thought of as she summoned Cruel Therese over the years. Queries both academic and personal, though more academic than personal. If she asked Cruel Therese to transcribe all the writings from the Library of Alexandria, would that lie within her abilities? Maybe, maybe not. But fundamentally Iris was a selfish person. She found, thinking it over, that she was no different from those desperates who summoned Cruel Therese to ask about cheating husbands or fatal illnesses or who their true love was or whether they would ever have any children. She had her whole life to search for the academic knowledge she desired—the chase was half the fun of it, wasn't it?—and oh, wasn't that an interesting question...

"Tell me, Cruel Therese," she asked, "What will my life hold?"

Cruel Therese raised her eyebrows. "Is that your question at last? What your life will hold?"

"Yes. I've decided."

"A simple question," Cruel Therese, "but containing multitudes. You are as hungry as I thought—more ask me about the past or the present than the future. But the future is not outside my purview, and indeed there have been those who have asked me about the future before now. I will not send you away unsatisfied. As for what your future holds, well, let me see..." She frowned. "Easier to show you, I suppose."

She put her hand over Iris's eyes, and Iris closed her eyes expectantly, and the visions began.

She saw herself leaving this meeting with a new obsession over ghosts fueled by meeting Cruel Therese. Saw herself going through years and years of research. Reading newer books and seeking out older books, going to abandoned buildings and dark alleys and stinking bogs, trailing tales of hauntings. Sometimes succeeding in summoning ghosts, sometimes not. She saw herself have a long conversation with a particular bog ghost about the types of monsters that lived in bogs. Pivoting her research to focus on those for a while, thinking she would get back to ghosts eventually. Until one evening she would stupidly fall prey to a will-o-the-wisp pretending to be that same friendly ghost, and walk into a bog hole, and drown.

Cruel Therese's hand lifted. "An unfortunate future. Your obsession with ghosts and knowledge will lead to a tragic end."

"The search is worth the risks," Iris said, "but on the other hand, I could be more cautious. There has to be a way to ward off will-o-the-wisps, or defeat them. I will have to research those before looking into ghosts."

Cruel Therese squinted. She lifted a hand. "Wait."

"Ah? Wait?"

Cruel Therese's head was shaking. "The knowledge I have given you is now false. Now that you have been forewarned, you will not die that way. Instead..." She put her hand back over Iris's eyes, and the visions began again.

Now that Iris had already seen what there was to see of ghosts, she would no longer be so interested in looking into them. Some cursory research to verify the memories she'd gotten from her visions—and to clarify them, since the visions were vivid in the moment but later faded—would do the trick. Will-o'-the-wisps, however, were more interesting to her, as were swamps in general. She would get lost for years in books on topography and its relation to legendary beings. Feeling the call of fate, she would hunt down that will-o'-the-wisp and she would extinguish it. She would spend three more years in that swamp, and then leave it, returning to the city. In the city, she would aggressively seek out ghosts and spirits that hovered in urban places, trying to once again illuminate the connection between location and the magic and the creatures that it attracted and created. Growing bold, she would decide the only way to really learn about these things, especially ghosts, was through experimentation. She would decide that the best way to experiment would be to create her own ghosts.

It was illegal, of course. But Iris had stopped caring about law and morality a long time ago.

She would find a location she considered to be quite bright and cheery—the town hall, in fact—and, wondering if it was inherently so due to its location or if it could be altered, and having a strong hypothesis the case was the latter, she would lock and bar all the doors of the building and set it on fire, leading to twelve deaths and ten terrible injuries.

What she wanted to know was whether there would be ghosts lingering afterward. There was in the end one ghost, the ghost of an old clerk who had spent almost her entire life in the building's archives. The woman barely even knew she was dead, and came out eagerly enough when Iris called on her. She did not recognize that Iris was her killer, but said she was lonely. "So few people come to visit the archives these days. These old town records... people don't care about them anymore. Nobody cares about history. But those who don't know history are doomed to repeat it. I've read through so many of these files and there's so much people could learn from them. But no one really cares." Abruptly her face changed, distressed. "My files... my files... oh no, my files, where have they gone? They're burning, burning to ashes, going all away... The memory of this town will be dead and gone forever. They can't burn, no, no, we can't let them burn. Save them. Help me save them!"

Iris spoke to her in a soothing voice, telling her the files hadn't really burned, they were all safe but had simply been moved somewhere else. Eventually the ghost had calmed and then slowly dissipated.

It hadn't been a very enlightening experience, but it did lead Iris to believe that a ghost was more likely to stay where it had been anchored in life than where it had died, though both put together was surely a powerful anchor. This was interesting. It also left her with a little regret. She hadn't considered there were archives in the building before burning it, only thinking of the town hall as being in some senses the grand heart of the city. If she'd remembered the files, she really would have gone through them beforehand—maybe broken in, maybe asked to be admitted—and stolen the ones that were actually important for her own perusal. And now they were all gone. Unfortunate, truly unfortunate.

And then one night very shortly after, her home was attacked. Someone made it past her wards and protections and came upon her in bed. Pulled her out and tied her to a chair and set the house on fire.

"This is for Thomas Falkes," they said, in the calm voice of a professional assassin, and they walked out through the smoke and flames, apparently unbothered.

The mayor who had died in the town hall fire, Iris thought distantly. Aw, shit.

And then she died.

In reality, Iris blinked awake. Her brow furrowed. "Thomas Falkes," she muttered. "That bastard..."

And Cruel Therese sighed, because once again the future had changed, leaving the vision she had shown inaccurate. She put her hand back over Iris's eyes, and once again they were submerged.

In the next life they saw, Iris systematically destroyed Falkes and his entire family, aiming to leave no one alive to avenge them. But this was more difficult than she expected. The mayor's family was well connected everywhere, connected to various noble families and even to the king himself. Eventually she was caught and publicly executed.

Of course, she could learn from this mistake too. And in the next life she saw, she did not pursue the Falkes family at all. She did murder the executioner who would have chopped off her head in another life, though, which put her in a mood of curiosity about the figure dressed in black who would have assassinated her in the world of the town hall fire. Her research led her to quite a few intriguing rumors about a man called Poor John. Why was that familiar? She didn't realize until she also heard about a woman called Poor Jane. These two types of rumors often mixed together. Poor Jane, after all, lived more than one life.

Something, Iris thought distantly, that she and Poor Jane had in common.

She found she didn't want to kill her. Only seek her out. And so she did. In that life, and in the next, and in the next, she always made an opportunity to seek Poor Jane out. And when she didn't, she found they often ran into each other anyway, as if they were bound together by fate. While her subjects of research shifted drastically, while she murdered in some realities and was almost a philanthropist in others (well, perhaps not—but at least she sometimes did no harm), Poor Jane would always still show up, and Iris...

Iris always would welcome her.

After fifty-three realities had passed Iris and Cruel Therese by, Cruel Therese abruptly lowered her hand and tucked it firmly behind her back.

"That's enough."

"Eh? The future hasn't shifted?" Iris found this ridiculous. In the last life she'd viewed, she'd died of forgetting to test the stability of a rope bridge before walking across it. That was a mistake she was quite unlikely to make again.

"It has," Cruel Therese, "but we are through here."

"But you promised to show me what my life would hold!"

"You have seen many possibilities. As for the rest, it is up to you. You can go through life without perfect knowledge, just like anyone else. Perhaps perfect knowledge is impossible." A strange expression passed over Cruel Therese's face. "After all, we all only know what we know, and live life accordingly. No one can know everything. I, too, could not have known what my husband would do to me. I could only do my best with what I did know. That was not my fault." The image of her seemed to shiver. "I could not have known, after all. Only do my best, as I did. So it is with all the living. And after death... one moves on."

Slowly, the image of her began to fade.

"Wait," Iris said, "Wait!"

"Thank you, Iris Witherbone," Cruel Therese said. "You sought knowledge today, but I am the one who has learned. I think from now on... I will rest."

***

Iris had been very annoyed for a while. Cruel Therese was supposed to be the one being who would understand the all-encompassing hunger for knowledge that Iris felt, not some coward who would run away after viewing a mere fifty-three lifetimes. However, she decided eventually that perhaps her expectations had been too high, and after all she was grateful for having been shown what she had seen. Now she knew some people to avoid, knew the products of fifty-three lifetimes of research, and knew certain people she wanted to seek out in her life as well.

Especially Poor Jane.

Poor Jane, who was probably tied to Iris by fate, even if she would never admit it. (Iris knew. She'd tried to tell her in other possible lifetimes, and Poor Jane had always shook her head, sometimes laughed. Oh well.) Poor Jane, who was still sitting on the couch when Iris was finished with her wyrm-scale jelly and came over and snuggled up next to her.

"You smell clean tonight," she observed. "No blood or anything."

"And you stink," Poor Jane said bluntly. "These wyrms…"

"So you can smell it too?"

"I think anyone could smell it."

"But one as magically marked as you can sense it more strongly," Iris mused. "Interesting. Always so interesting, Poor Jane."

Poor Jane elbowed her. "Take a bath."

"If you help me," Iris said. "I'm tired."

Poor Jane sighed deeply. "If you insist."

10

Chapter Ten

James was at a loss as to how to make his excuses properly to his parents, which made Natty roll her eyes. The man had no talent for subterfuge, far less than she would have expected from someone who'd been holding a supposedly clandestine affair for years and should have been versed in this sort of thing. In the end, he relied on Miss Hunt's ingenuity instead. Genevieve told the Earl and Countess of Ilbird that there was a party back in the city that she'd forgotten about, that she'd absolutely promised to attend, and she would need to go back to the city for it—but she would be far too embarrassed to show her face if she returned without her fiancé. After she had gone to visit him in the countryside, if she returned so quickly without him, wouldn't it look as if they had argued? And there were so many stupid rumors about her and James's relationship already, it would be a real shame to let another one get started over nothing.

James's parents hemmed and hawed. The assassin who had kidnapped him was still at large, they said (Natty stared at the wall unassumingly), and he'd come to the countryside for his own safety. In the end, though, the devil they knew frightened them more than the one they didn't. Assassins and kidnappings they barely credited, but gossip they had plenty of experience with. Surely if James stayed in their town house most of the time and only left it for the party and stuck very close to Genevieve at the party, nothing would really go wrong. They would order the footmen left behind at the town house to keep a very close eye on him just in case—for James had also convinced them not to come with him back to the city, arguing that there were also too many rumors that he stuck to his parents' knees lately like a little boy.

It was quite an involved conversation. Natty listened to it with only half attention. She was formulating her own excuses, or rather, coming up with a good explanation to give Angela for why she had associated with—almost befriended—a target and his fiancée, and why letting him go to see Iris personally would be a good idea. For all Angela's dismissive attitude towards Iris, she could be protective of her too, against outsiders and enemies. Of course James was not a threat (Natty couldn't imagine him threatening anyone, let alone a witch of legendary skill), but it might take some doing to convince Angela of that.

In the end, however, it turned out Angela found it all very funny.

She listened to Natty's telling of events quietly, gravely at first and then with a small smile on her face that grew as Natty continued. When Natty had finished, she sighed, shook her head, and grinned. "Ah, Natty. You know, times like these always remind me of... where's that book?"

"Which book?" Natty asked.

Angela got out of the armchair she'd been sitting in and fished around one of their bookcases—mostly crammed with reference materials, some in code—eventually pulling out a novel with its cover half ripped off, paper degrading. Natty recognized it; Angela had given it to her something like five years ago after she had finished it, asking for her opinion on its level of realism and "whether you like this sort of thing." She hadn't liked it much but had still read it compulsively to the end. It had been a tale of a prince whose throne had been usurped, and how with the help of one loyal knight he managed to eventually reclaim it. The prince was a witty, charming type, and horribly in love with the daughter of the man who had stolen his throne. Fortunately, this daughter ended up loving him back, and betrayed her father for his sake, spying on him and scheming against him. There was a happy ending, and the prince and his true love were married, the evil father banished. Natty hadn't thought much of its realism, but she'd rather liked the romance, in a way. She'd been sure the book would end with one of the lovers dead and been a bit surprised when it didn't. "That's probably a sign you don't read much," Angela told Natty when she mentioned this. "It's a sort of a fairy tale. They all end this way." Natty hadn't read many books since then, either, and didn't know if it was true, but sometimes afterward she had thought back on this book, and even reread it once, and she decided she liked that they lived. Unrealistic, maybe, but nice.

"That prince in this book," Angela said, "the princess, too. Such clever, scheming people. They barely meet their match in that evil king, and the author mentions several times that the prince has 'the brains of the Ghensen line'. Isn't it blood that's supposed to be noble, not brains? This author wrote several books, too. More than several. You know I've read about six of them and they're all the same. Such clever, clever princes and princesses and knights and kings and queens. They have such an easy time tricking everyone but each other. Stablemen and butlers and guards and innkeepers always seem to be completely bamboozled by them—the best a soldier without noble blood can be is loyal and strong, but never an ounce of brains in him. You know I think this author writes some pretty compelling stuff, but it's all dumb as crap."

She tossed the book decisively back on the shelf, letting it sit on top of a row of books instead of tucking it back in. "Real life nobles aren't smart, not very. Half of them are stupid, and stupider than the average commoner. They've never had to work for a living or to receive the respect of those around them. But they naturally feel they're better than everyone else, and so they have a certain confidence in their own abilities, their intelligence, and their... shall we say their vulnerabilities; that is to say, they think they don't have any. The only reason I've ever had trouble killing a noble is that they have large households and talented guards—their hired hands give me more trouble than they do. Whereas I was once hired to kill a pickpocket that sometimes frequented the local church, and it took me two months just to find him, and longer to kill him. Did I tell you about that one, Natty?"

"Yes, once or twice," Natty said. "But go on."

"Never mind, not tonight. What I mean is, this James Guarin is the real average noble. He thinks he can find his heart for himself— he's desperate—and he'll be as stupid about it as possible, even co-operating with a woman who tried to kill him, who wants to find his heart for herself. He thinks for some reason he can handle you if things go wrong, when it's twice already *you've* handled *him*." Angela snorted. "Well, Natty, you've got a nice stew cooking, and we'll see how it comes out. As for meeting Iris, I agree that letting him do the spell for locating the heart would certainly expedite things, but we can't let him into Iris's lair. If he does happen to have a brain, he might leak its location to the cops or the church. We'll meet in a neutral location. I'll let you choose the spot."

***

Natty chose a small flat on the other end of her and Angela's street, a flat that had been empty since the couple living there five years ago had been murdered (not by her and Angela. This neighborhood had plenty of its own problems). It was small and decrepit, now covered in dust, dirt and cobwebs, but had enough furniture remaining in it from those times—still a table and a couch that no one had looted from it, as well as a now-mostly-empty bookcase—that she thought it wouldn't be too terribly obvious that not only was this not her or Angela or Iris's home, but it was not even a location they generally used for anything. She spent a couple hours doing a cursory cleaning, and relayed the location through Angela to Iris, as Angela had forbidden her from ever going to visit Iris alone. Iris agreed on it (she was lukewarm on performing this whole spell, as to her it was child's play and not particularly interesting, but would do it for Angela's sake), and so the show was put in motion.

A day after Natty's return to the city, she rented a coach, and with Angela playing the driver, they went over to the Guarin townhouse to pick James up.

He and Genevieve were waiting outside already, Genevieve holding James's arm, less affectionately and more in the manner of a mother concerned that her small child might run away from her in a crowd or be snatched by some stranger. Natty, who would absolutely have snatched James away from Genevieve's supervision given a chance (the fewer people going to see Iris the better, in her opinion, besides which Genevieve was just clever enough to worry her), suppressed a scowl and politely let her and James into the coach.

"You'll have to wear blindfolds," she told them. "You can't know where we're going." Always better to be doubly safe.

James shrugged and agreed, but Genevieve's grip on his arm tightened. "How are we supposed to know you aren't taking us into a trap?"

"There's no way for you to know, I suppose. But it isn't as if I'm tying you hand and foot. Just don't take the blindfolds off so you won't know the location of our hideout. That's all I ask."

Genevieve glanced at James and reluctantly agreed. Natty tied a length of cloth around each of their heads. It was cloth she and Angela usually used for bandages, not uncomfortable against the skin.

When they came to the house, Natty guided each of the young nobles out of the coach, taking their hands and helping them to the ground as they fumbled without vision. James's hand was warm and a bit sweaty, and bigger than she had remembered. Genevieve's hand was cold, and it clenched around hers for a moment, spasmodically, before releasing and fumbling around to again grab hold of James's arm.

Angela stayed out on the coach's seat. Genevieve and James had never met her, and it had been decided that it was safest if they never did. The less they knew, the better. This, of course, made Iris a bit pouty when Natty guided the guests in, but by the time they had taken their blindfolds off, she had summoned up a cheery and welcoming smile. (And Natty had taken the opportunity to lock and bolt the door. It was simple enough to unlock and unbolt it from the inside, but it would still delay someone for a minute if necessary. And if Angela was needed... there was no lock or bolt in the world that could stop Poor Jane if her prey was inside as James was now.)

"Natty has explained to you how all this is going to work?" Iris said offhandedly.

"Natty?" James frowned in confusion.

"Sorry," Iris said, "Rachel. Rachel explained it to you?"

"Not really," Genevieve said. "We know there's a spell James can use to locate his heart but we haven't really been told how it works."

"Not Rachel's area of specialty," Iris said. "My area, of course, and I'll explain it in any level of detail you like. By the way, Mr. Guarin, if you don't mind me doing a little bit of an examination on you when we're finished, I've seen people with missing parts, before, but it still might be interesting to have a look and see what makes your case unique as all cases are unique. Most witches working in this country, most great witches at least, have identifiable patterns in their work. I'm sure I could pinpoint who performed this particular spell. Must be someone in it for the money—I can't imagine what use they'd have for some young earl's heart otherwise. There's nothing that makes your bloodline all that special, my dear, except the name and money attached to it, nothing at all from a magical point of view. If they needed a live human's heart without regard for what human, there are easier ways to go about it. I don't underrate the value of a live heart in certain rituals and recipes but I simply don't think stealing yours is particularly practical. No, they must have been paid or somehow persuaded. Quite pathetic how many people get into this trade for the money, don't you agree?"

"Uh."

"Let's get started," Natty said. "James and Genevieve have to go to a party this evening. It's part of their cover for being here."

Iris smirked.

"What?" Natty demanded.

"Oh, forget it. Let's get started then, right. Mr. Guarin, we'll have to start by drawing a little of your blood. If you don't mind?"

Iris had taken out a long silver pin, the end of which was decorated by a sculpture of a skull with garnets in its eye holes. She gestured James over to the table, where she had set up a porcelain bowl full of clean, clear water. "Your arm," she said, "unless you'd prefer your palm. Some people do, but I don't recommend it except when required. Which in this case it isn't, to be clear."

"My arm is fine," James said, and he extracted it from Genevieve's still-clinging grip.

Iris fiddled around for a minute before locating a vein. This she pricked, and when James, lacking circulation, failed to bleed, she squeezed his arm like a tube of paint until a couple drops of thick blood sluggishly slid out of his skin and dropped into the water below.

"It's necessary for your essence to be in the water," Iris said, "before we scry. In this case."

"Will that be enough? I don't seem to be bleeding easily..."

"Mm, better more than less. Blood is one thing, and closely related to the heart. But for better results, we should throw in a little bone as well."

James paled. Genevieve stepped closer to him. "Bone?"

"A piece of a rib bone of his would suffice," Iris said. "Just a small fragment. I'm not asking you to cut off a finger or anything."

Natty's hand retreated slightly into her sleeve, where at a moment's notice she could withdraw a knife. She and James were cooperating, yes, but if he refused to help with the hunt for the sake of mutual interests, well, there were other methods of persuasion at her disposal. If a knife wouldn't really hurt James, there was Genevieve here too, and Genevieve was perfectly mortal, and if she insisted on coming along, she might as well be of some use.

But after a long pause, James said, "Rachel, you cut me open before."

Natty nodded. It had been more Angela than her, but small difference.

"There was no great damage. I... healed." James fidgeted. "Could you do that, minimizing the damage, again?"

"I understand the human body well enough," Natty said.

James took a deep breath. "Fine. I'll trust you with it."

What a stupid thing to say.

Natty wished that Iris had explained what would be necessary ahead of time; this place didn't have the best set-up. She had James lie down on the floor and take off his shirt. Genevieve flushed but did not turn away. She did not trust Natty's skill at impromptu surgery to not veer straight into murder, apparently, despite knowing the futility of such an attempt. She was right, of course, but Natty still felt the urge to roll her eyes.

"It's going to hurt," she told James. "We could knock you out, and wake you up later."

"No time for that," James said. "It's fine. I trust you." He was on a roll with saying that apparently.

"You could at least have a drink, or..."

Iris was moving forward. "Here," she said. "To numb him." She offered an ointment, and Natty rubbed it over his chest. His chest was warm, and rougher than it had been last time, now with the added bumps of recent stitches. She wondered who had stitched him up. The thread didn't look medical, and the stitches were not entirely even—had it not been a doctor? Who saw the earl-to-be in such a state—who other than Natty, who had already seen him like this against his will and probably didn't count—Natty wondered, and then forced the wondering from her brain. She had to focus.

His flesh was warm and soft, and she wished she hadn't rubbed ointment over it before having to cut it. James reported he did feel numb, so it was for the best. Maybe it would stop him from squirming. But it had peeled away some of her professional detachment, touching him that way, without any violence. Now she had to bring that detachment back, and having discarded it for a moment, it felt unnatural, like a mask or a pair of surgical gloves. It was necessary anyhow. She steadied her jaw and her hand, and cut down through the skin, down and down and down until the knife was stopped by bone.

Even then, it was not so easy. She had to peel back the skin and flesh to get a clear look at the bone. And actually chiseling a fragment away took time and precision. Bone was not something she dealt with—Angela had much more experience. Poor Jane actually ate bones, while apprentices very much did not. Still, after a few minutes she had managed it. She handed the tiny bone shard over to Iris and hurriedly folded the flesh back into place. Iris had a very nice thread and needle ready to stitch James back up. She had been prepared, even if she hadn't told Natty what to expect. The thread even had certain healing qualities, she informed Natty and James, and James thanked her for the consideration.

He put his shirt back on slowly, clumsily. The ointment had numbed more than the area it was spread on, affecting his shoulders and back as well. Potent stuff.

"The scrying bowl is ready now," Iris said. "But you... could be more so. I have a little something that could help put you in the right state for looking for things. Right state for any magic, really. It's a recent concoction of mine, and should be especially helpful for people with no strong magical affinity like you. I've been wanting to give it a whirl." As she spoke, she took a jar out and from the jar, a spoonful of what appeared to be jelly. "Take a taste. Just a little bite should be enough, you'd barely need to swallow. Though please do swallow. And then, we'll be able to find anything you like! Well, practically speaking, the heart will be the easiest thing to find for it's all we've prepared for, but if there's anything else you want to try while you're here, just let me know. I'm in a generous mood today."

James accepted the spoon and ate the jelly. His hands were shaking a little, but he showed no hesitation, though he winced at the taste before quickly swallowing.

Iris grabbed the spoon back and then gripped his wrists. "Feel anything?" she asked, peering at him. "How is it? Lightheaded? On top of the world?"

Had Angela been there, she would have demanded Iris explain what she'd just given James, but Natty was less inclined to question the most powerful witch in their acquaintance. Still, she watched James closely as well. He exhaled sharply and said, "Everything's more... glowy. I don't know."

"Auras," Iris said wisely. "You're seeing auras."

She asked about eight more questions that James only answered vaguely and hazily before glancing at Natty and getting down to business. She pulled James over to the bowl and guided him to put a finger in the water and swirl it around, murmuring words in his ear that he repeated more loudly. They weren't words from a language Natty knew.

James stared at the water. Iris said, "Can you see your heart?"

"No, I can't see it."

"Your blood and your flesh," Iris said. "Ask the water to show you your flesh and blood, to reveal it to you."

"My flesh and blood is here," James said distantly. "Here in this room, one hundred eighty pounds of it. The fragment we removed wants to be returned, it doesn't like being separated..."

"Outside this room," Iris coaxed. "Where is that flesh and blood that is akin to yours but no longer here with you?"

"I see..." James frowned. "My mother and father, they hold my flesh and blood, they are part of me and I am part of them."

Iris sighed. She looked at Natty, and Natty raised her eyebrows.

From a folder she had brought with her, she drew out a map and submerged it in the water. "Your heart. Even if you can't see it, you will know where it is. Here. Point to it."

James stared at the map for a moment, squinting, and then decisively pointed. "Here. It's here."

He was pointing to Ilbird Manor.

"Your heart," Iris said. "Not your flesh and blood any longer. Your heart, that piece which was removed from you."

"Here," James said. "I can sense it."

Iris nodded slowly. "Very good." To Natty she said, "That must be the answer, then. We'll get nothing more definite. The state he's in right now, we're lucky to get a coherent answer."

"From the substance you gave him," Natty said, not quite accusatory.

Iris laughed. "Well, that substance was what allowed him to see at all."

"You wanted to test something stronger than your usual."

"Well, it worked, didn't it? Ilbird Manor. Go there and look, my dear little apprentice Jane, and if it's not there, come back and yell at me all you want. I'm sure even your mentor will want to yell at me. But it's there. James is certain—don't you trust him?" She winked at James, who stared hazily back.

Natty pulled him away from the water. "That's enough. Let's get your blindfold back on and get you home."

***

James and Genevieve stated firmly—well, Genevieve stated firmly, the still-intoxicated James rather hazily—that they would be doing all their heart-hunting alone from this point.

Natty didn't argue with them. It wouldn't be so bad to allow James and Genevieve to take the lead for a bit, watching them quietly from a distance. If they found the heart, she didn't think it would be very difficult for her to swoop in and snatch it away from them before it ended up back in James's chest, and even if it did end up back in James's chest before she could do anything, nothing would prevent her and Angela from then bringing James to Charlotte and seeing how the contract could be fulfilled from there. Angela agreed with her on this point, though she did tell Natty to keep a sharp eye out.

Natty could use this admonition to justify what she did that night.

Though she was on shaky ground.

Restless, she snuck out of the apartment she and Angela shared. She headed to the Guarin town house, crept in James's window, and sat quietly at his bedside. He did not stir at her presence. He was sleeping off whatever weird concoction ("wyrm jelly," Angela had said wisely, on hearing the account) Iris had given him earlier, and probably wouldn't have stirred even if she had yelled or banged a pan in his face. Wary of the house's servants, she remained silent anyhow, sitting motionless at the chair near the foot of his bed, watching him. "Keeping a close eye on him"—yes. She could tell herself that she was worried something would happen to her prey before she and Angela got a chance to pounce, or that he would slip off somewhere other than Ilbird Manor that night and lose her the way that pickpocket had lost Angela for frustrating months on end. She could tell herself that she wanted to observe him, see if the ritual had had any odd effects, see if doing it would somehow set strange events in motion. All this was nonsense, of course. He was sound asleep, Genevieve was off at that party of hers, and there was nothing to threaten him except for Natty herself. But Natty was restless, and though her body could sit still here, her mind could not.

She was watching the play of light and shadow on James's face. His curtains were translucent, so one could not see in or out but moonlight could still enter. The moon was almost full tonight, and the curtains moving a little in the breeze, and so there were shadows moving too, on his face and on the coverlet. His face was still, mostly, but his brow was furrowed. She wondered if the ointment on his chest had worn off, if the wound she had made had begun to hurt. The wound she'd made tonight, or some days ago at that party, when they first met. It had been interesting, seeing how that first wound had begun to heal. She'd never given anyone scars before— her targets died before their wounds had a chance to heal, and those few witnesses she'd only inflicted with injuries, she'd never had a chance to observe at a later date. Then again, James would die soon too, if they really could find his heart. His wounds would never heal fully either.

She closed her eyes for a moment, letting darkness and stillness fill her so completely for a moment that she could believe she was at home in bed. That was a game she used to play when she first started living with Angela. She used to pretend that she was home in her room—her old room, her parents just in the next room over —on the verge of falling asleep, having just had a long, half-lucid dream. It was never a game she could play for long. She was not much of an escapist. But she played it now and then, when she was so overwhelmed with hopelessness that there was nothing else she could do.

It didn't happen often.

Natty mourned her parents in the back of her mind constantly, when she was young, like a never-ending migraine. But she had other things to worry about. At first she spent all her time thinking about how to escape. When Angela read her books, or gave her simpler books to read, about methods of fighting and killing and breaking into houses, she would think about how to apply those methods. When Angela would train her, she worked hardest on strengthening her legs, thinking of how soon she would need to run as fast as she could. And she tried her best to memorize maps of the city and nearby countryside, tried to think up spots she could hide where Angela would not think to look. And she watched Angela, learning her patterns of behavior, when she ate and when she bathed and when she slept, and what she would do with Natty during these times, watch her or lock her up or leave her to her own devices. She thought about each of her escape attempts very carefully. She tried at least once a month, and every time, Angela caught her.

She was rarely punished. Angela seemed to take these attempts as a matter of course. She would not mind either, she told Natty, if Natty tried to kill her. This was also expected. But Natty even back then saw this allowance as what it was, Angela's desire to see Natty become a killer, or at least an attempted killer. She never tried. She made a point of never trying.

Angela deserved to die for what she'd done to Natty's parents, but Natty thought about how Angela had promised Natty she would never grow up to be a "nice lady", and her stomach would clench, and she would promise herself never to do anything her mother wouldn't, no matter how Angela tried to teach her. In her heart she knew her mother would not have cared if she had to kill a murderer in order to escape with her life—would have pitied her, but not judged her. But she didn't want to be another Angela. She wanted to be like her mother, like the self that Angela was slowly peeling away.

She said this to Angela, once, in a fit of temper, after holding it inside herself for years. Angela nodded and asked her, "Do you think that is possible for you?"

"Of course. Just because you think I can't break free of you—"

"I'm not asking about my training," Angela said. "I'm asking if you think you were ever meant to be like your mother to begin with." She leaned back. "Do you know why I picked you, Natty?"

"Because I had nowhere else to go," Natty said resentfully.

"Because you had no one left? Of course not. Do you think none of my other victims have had children? I kill them or spare them depending on the case. And if I just needed an orphan, you know, there are plenty on the streets who would love to be where you are."

"Why, then?"

"I watched your family for a while before acting. Your father was a hearty man, your mother a soft and loving woman. An ideal couple, I'm sure. You were not like either of them. You had a nursery full of dolls and balls and all sorts of toys, but mostly you didn't play with them. You collected pebbles from outside in the yard and put them in rows from smallest to largest. You picked weeds from the garden with seeds on them and plucked the seeds off one by one. You sat around staring at worms that had washed out of the ground in the rain. I liked your attention to detail, your focus. Those are very important things in an assassin," Angela said. "Not violence—not sadism, at least—but focus. And you weren't afraid to fight either. I thought you had the qualities a killer would need, on a basic level. The rest I could teach you. And you've gotten stronger, fitter, better at fighting and running and climbing, in the past few years. You remember most of the maps and books I throw at you too. I wasn't wrong. You'll be a great Poor Jane someday, Natty. I really did pick you because I thought you would be good, not just for my own convenience. And I won't go back on my choice. You don't have to accept that yet, but someday you will. I can wait."

She was patient, Angela. She had her flaws but she was patient. And she didn't lie, at least not to Natty.

And eventually, she was right.

There came a time when Natty learned to see herself the way Angela saw her, learned to relish Angela's vision of her, live for her praise. She was strong. She was clever. She was focused. She was practical. And one day she would be Poor Jane, and she would be good at it.

But sitting here at the end of James's bed, watching his furrowed brow and the shadows licking at his neck and cheeks, Natty wasn't practical, and she wasn't focused, and she wasn't clever, and she wasn't strong.

She was tired. It had been a long time since she allowed herself to see a target as human. It wasn't James that made it hard for her to do otherwise—it was the situation—but perhaps it was partly James too. He wasn't very strong or smart or practical either, even without a heart. He was an idiot, and far too vulnerable to attack. It would be easy to kill him, if his heart wasn't missing, if his heart could be found. Natty didn't want to.

"I don't want to kill him," she whispered, breaking the silence. She wasn't talking to James, who was sleeping. She wasn't talking to the silence, either, to the world, to a god she wasn't sure she believed in. She was talking to Angela, really. Angela, who would shake her head and tell Natty she had to be better. But maybe she could take care of it this time, if Natty really couldn't. She pushed Natty, but never too hard. If Natty asked, she would take over. It would all be done within the week, no doubt. Angela would take care of it.

Natty didn't want that either.

So she sat in the dark and the silence and pretended she wasn't here, until outside the darkness turned into gray, and she forced herself to slink away before the sun rose.

11

Chapter Eleven

Charlotte hadn't really expected to see James Guarin again after their little excursion to watch the boat race.

Well, that wasn't quite true. She had expected that he would show up at the tailor shop again for more clothes. But she had expected that would be it. She would see him sometimes at the shop when he came to get clothes, and maybe she would try to talk to him and he would make evasive answers, and they would both be embarrassed.

But as to anything more, well. Every year a new wave of young nobles came to the capital. Every year the new young men would play games with the local girls, get a little experience before they had to buckle down to courting some young lady in earnest. Some played longer than others. James was timid. Charlotte thought a kiss would be enough to scare him away—and that night, they had done more than kiss, enough that if her brothers ever heard about it, James would be in for a whipping. James was timid, and he'd only even started to open up to her when he was half-drunk, and she had only kissed him for much the same reason. Oh, she'd thought him attractive from the beginning. That was why she'd taken him out. But without the whiskey, she'd never have had the courage to actually do anything about it.

Anyway, he'd said he was in love with someone and they left him. That made her a rebound. She was fine with that, but drunken rebounds didn't outlive the night.

But two days later, she left work to find him standing outside. He already looked embarrassed, so that part of what she had imagined was accurate. But he was grinning, looking at her and then at the ground and then at her again. He was carrying a little bag.

"Hey, little earl," she said. "The shop's closed."

"I know. I was waiting for you."

She'd known that too, but she'd needed him to say it. To admit it.

She didn't make him say why he was waiting for her, though. Instead she asked, "What have you got there?" Wondered if it was another bottle of whiskey. If he thought he could get her drunk and she would just kiss him again, just like that—well. Maybe he was right. She would have to try out the whiskey and think about it.

"Ah, it's a surprise. Maybe we could go get some dinner and I could show it to you?" James said.

Charlotte hummed and tilted her head, considering.

"Or—well, you're probably busy. You can just open it now." And he thrust the bag at her so quickly that she barely caught hold of it before he let go.

Which turned out to be a good thing, that she grabbed it. Or the jar might have broken if it had fallen. For inside, she discovered, was a small glass jar of raspberry preserves.

"You said you liked preserves, but never had time to make them now," James said sheepishly. "I don't know. Apple preserves are kind of pointless when it's apple season, and I wasn't sure what kind you like, but I like raspberries so I hoped maybe you'd like them too."

"My favorite is strawberry," Charlotte said.

"Oh, is it? Sorry. They had strawberry preserves there, at the market, but I wasn't sure what you'd like."

"Well," Charlotte said, "Now you know for next time."

"Next time. Yes. Next time I'll definitely get strawberry." And he beamed.

She ate the raspberry preserves, and the strawberry ones that followed. He bought her strawberry preserves and jam all through the winter, and varying other flavors in addition. He got her peach preserves once, and she didn't much like peaches, but she didn't tell him that. She thought of giving them to her brothers, but she usually ate all his gifts herself, and greedily she didn't want to share her bounty. So she put the jar in a corner of the cellar where it wouldn't likely be found, behind a large sack of potatoes. It was still there even now, though it was probably no good to eat anymore. Even well-made and well-kept preserves didn't last forever.

* * *

Today when Charlotte got out of work, she once again found someone waiting for her outside the shop.

This time, it was Genevieve Hunt.

Charlotte found herself smiling over at her. She couldn't help it. There was a tight, angry, lost look on Genevieve's face. It echoed how Charlotte felt. Of course, Charlotte's smile wasn't out of sympathy, but pleasure. Wasn't that how Genevieve should feel, the pain of abandonment? James didn't love her, had never loved her. He'd only had his heart stolen. Once it was his again, he would return to Charlotte.

She walked over. "Were you waiting for me?" she asked.

Genevieve looked at her.

"Was there something," Charlotte asked, "you wanted to say?"

Genevieve lifted her chin. "I thought I might. But I've changed my mind. You don't deserve anything I could say to you. A person as worthless as you isn't worth speaking to."

"Run along, then," Charlotte said. "I've already said everything I had to say to you too."

"I will love James," Genevieve said. "He deserves to have someone actually love him. And I will protect him." She gave Charlotte a final glare. "You'd better watch yourself, Miss Taylor. I wouldn't need to hire an assassin to take care of you."

Charlotte was ready to retort when Genevieve neatly opened her purse and tilted it to show Charlotte the contents. Tucked between the usual feminine necessities sat a miniature pistol. Genevieve let Charlotte look at it for a long moment before snapping the purse closed, tossing her head, and striding briskly away.

Charlotte laughed. What else could she do but laugh? "Madwoman." She wasn't afraid of her. A high society lady might own a gun but likely wouldn't even know how to use it. What pissed her off more was Genevieve Hunt talking about love. What would she know about? She'd probably never loved anyone in her life.

12

Chapter Twelve

When James arrived back home at Ilbird Manor, his parents wanted to know how his health had been during the three days he'd been gone and how the party he'd attended with Genevieve went.

Avoiding these questions, he steered the two of them into the parlor and sat them down and said, "There's something serious I have to discuss with you."

They exchanged a glance. "If this is about Genevieve, dear," his mother began.

"Oh, no, it's not about Miss Hunt. She's great. She's still as kind and polite and perfect as ever. It's, um. It's about my health, like you were asking. And the assassin—sort of."

"The assassin! Surely they didn't turn up while you were away," his father said, leaning forward. "Were you attacked?"

"No, I didn't see them," James lied. "But thanks to my injury, I was doing some investigation of my own, and I discovered I'm under some sort of curse. My heart is missing. Physically missing. Someone, at some point, took it out."

Another exchanged glance. "Not this again, dear," his mother said. "The other day, when you were very sick after the attack, I know you were having delusions, but you must know that's impossible. Let me check your temperature."

James sighed. He allowed her to touch his forehead, but said even as she did so, "It's not a delusion this time. I don't think it was then either. I've had some people look at me, even cut me open, and they verified it. No, it shouldn't be possible. It's a magical attack. Please, mother. Just give me a chance to prove it to you."

His mother's lips pressed together. "James..."

Gently, he pulled her head down to his chest. "Listen," he said. "You can't hear a heartbeat, can you?"

"You're being silly."

"Mother," James said, "Please. Can you hear a heartbeat or not?"

A long pause. She pulled her head away and looked up at him. And he thought for a moment she would say she could, and wondered what he could say to that.

"No," she said. "I couldn't hear it, but James, that's not uncommon. Sometimes a person's heartbeat is faint, and you know my hearing isn't what it was."

James looked at his father. "Do you believe me?"

His father huffed. "It's not that we don't believe you, it's that what you're saying is unbelievable."

"My chest was cut open," James said. "Through my ribs I could see the open space. It's not there. I can prove it to you more easily than that," he added. "When I cut myself, I don't bleed—the blood won't just come out naturally because the heart isn't pumping it. You have to massage the skin to even get a drop. I can show you. Just give me a knife. Don't worry. I won't cut very deep."

He turned, prepared to head for the kitchen and beg a knife off the cook, but his father snagged his wrist, stopping him in his tracks. He took James's pulse. To James's mother, he said, "I don't feel a pulse either."

"It's gone," James said. "My heart's been stolen. I went to a... magic practitioner to ask them about it, and they confirmed."

The two both eyed him suspiciously at that. "Magic practitioner" was just a nice-sounding way of saying "witch". And no matter how you put it, practicing magic was illegal, as was consulting with someone who did so.

James flushed. "Well, it's done now anyway, even if it wasn't the best idea. They did a ritual for me to discover where the heart was hidden. So we do have a clue. I might be able to get it back."

"You found it?" His father asked. "Where is it hidden, then?"

"Somewhere in the manor," James said. "That's why I'm involving you. I'm sorry, I didn't want to worry you about any of this. But I figured you'd notice if I was turning the house upside down."

"Well, we certainly won't make you search alone," his father said quickly. "Dearest, I'll speak with Mr. Johnson about interrogating all our servants. If it's hidden here, it must have been stolen by one of our own. Perhaps you can get one of the maids—someone you trust—to help you with a search in the meantime. James, you go and get some rest. This all must be very harrowing for you."

"I'm fine. I can help."

"To bed, James," his father said. "In fact, you'd better stay in your room today. I'll send someone to keep an eye on you. If the culprit is in the household, when they realize we're onto them, they might be bold enough to launch another attack."

"There's no point, father. If they really wanted to hurt me, they could just stab my heart and that would kill me easily enough."

Saying this did not reassure his father, whose eyes flashed. "To bed."

James reluctantly agreed to retreat for the time being, but told his parents one final piece of advice—"The, uh, magic practitioner told me that my heart has likely been transformed. It won't look like a heart, exactly. More likely it looks like a precious stone or something similar around the same size as a heart. But no... blood or flesh or... heart."

"Thank you, James. Now, to bed."

"Fine," James muttered, and, escorted by a maid, he went up to his room.

***

He lay quietly on his bed. Unable to sleep. He'd spent most of the trip home thinking about how he would convince his parents to help him with the search. Now he was forced to think about what the implications would be if the search failed... or even if it succeeded.

Finding the heart wouldn't be the end of his problems. How would they even get the heart back into his body? They would have to find another witch, probably, or some "magic practitioner" of another sort. Iris had been very competent, but she'd made James nervous, and besides, he had no idea how to contact her without Rachel's help, and he wasn't going to entrust an assassin with the business of reinstalling his heart. No matter how helpful Rachel had been the past couple days, she had still tried to kill him, and he had no way of knowing if she would do so again.

But if he couldn't put his heart back, or if they couldn't find it, he would be like this forever.

Like "this".

How could he describe how he felt right now? It wasn't quite right to say that since he'd broken up with Charlotte, he'd been feeling more anxious than before, or that he'd become sadder. But he remembered a time when he smiled more easily, more sincerely. Laughed more easily too. He remembered the world feeling more colorful, or as if he could better appreciate its color. He could re-member feeling more of an attachment to people, even to Genevieve.

Lately, he felt so alone, only able to connect with his parents, feeling a stranger to the world whenever he left the house.

Then again, was it really so bad to feel that way? At least since losing his heart he had become more logical. He no longer obsessed over Charlie, no longer wasted hours upon hours not only in her company but daydreaming about her, trying to come up with things to say to her or do for her that would please her, trying even harder to figure out some way that they could be together and be... stable. Good. Something that would last. God, he'd wasted so much time and energy on that, and all of it futile. She'd even tried to kill him when they broke up—how had he ever been in love with a woman like that?

If he regained his heart, would he want to cling to a woman like that again?

If he never got his heart back, he could remain objective and logical, even if it set him apart. He would be better able to protect himself. But no, that wouldn't be permanent. Sooner or later whoever had stolen his heart would use it against him. There was no safety in the way things currently were. And so he had to get the thing back.

He closed his eyes, and stayed restlessly awake.

Until, a little before dinnertime, a maid came to fetch him, saying that they'd found what had gone missing and the master and mistress were waiting for him. It had only been four hours. He got up, stunned, and went downstairs.

**

His mother and father were sitting on the couch next to each other in the parlor, close side by side, waiting gravely. It occurred to James how seldom he saw them sit next to each other. Even at dinner, his father generally sat at the head of the table and his mother at a corner, more diagonal to him than by his side. They were an odd pair, his father much larger than his mother, his face large too and mostly smooth, while his mother was slim and wrinkled and dressed all in quiet pastels.

He came around and stood in front of them, feeling oddly judged. As if they had found his heart only to discover something unspeakably wrong about it. Something wrong not because of the curse, but simply because of who he was and had been to begin with.

"We found the miscreant," his father said abruptly. "It was one of the new boys. Mr. Johnson didn't screen them effectively enough, it seems."

"One of the servants?"

"Who else could it have been?" His father snorted in contempt. "It seems he was lying low and waiting an opportunity to use the heart to his advantage. Probably he intended to sell it to someone wishing to ensnare a young earl sometime in the future... unless he meant to use it on his own account." This last he added with a significant, withering look at James, to remind him that his past indiscretions had not been forgotten.

James shuddered. The possibilities were less than pretty. "Did you ask him? Did you question him yet, I mean?"

"No chance," his father said.

"Ah, well if you haven't yet, maybe I'll..."

"I mean we won't have a chance in the future either," his father said. "He killed himself."

James stared. "Killed himself?"

"We found him hanging in the servants' quarters," his mother said. "He didn't leave a note, but when we searched his belongings, the heart was easily located. You were right that it doesn't look like a heart." She held up what at first glance looked to be a compact mirror, the cover being painted with the image of a rose and the sides made of some golden metal. "It seemed out of place among his things, and we confirmed it has an aura of magic. We may not be magic practitioners, dear, but we know the basics."

There were some basic ways even a layman could identify a magical object. James, if called upon, would probably have spit on it and said a couple words he wasn't supposed to know, and seen if the spit sizzled, one common method.

And the case did seem to be the right size.

"He must have been afraid of discovery," his mother continued. "Bad enough attacking someone so above his station, but to do so with black magic—he must have known he would hang one way or another, and thought it better to do the deed himself."

"Yes," James said faintly. "I imagine it would be very frightening. Mother, who—who was it?"

"The new boy," his mother said. "Leonard. You know, I did think he had a suspicious look to him to begin with. Covetous. I let Mr. Johnson reassure me because of his references, but you see, a woman's instincts are never wrong about this kind of thing."

"Are we quite sure he was the one who stole it?" He could not remember having any recent change of feelings towards Leonard.

"Do you doubt your mother's judgment?" his mother asked, raising her eyebrows.

He cringed.

His father put a calming hand on his mother's shoulder. "You may have a point," he said to James. "We will still look into this further, in case someone left the compact among Leonard's things in order to frame him and escape the blame for their own crime. And you had better still be careful. But for the time being, what's most important is that the heart is recovered. Can't believe you managed to lose the damn thing."

James flushed. "I didn't…"

"Don't be so hard on him, dear," his mother said, and they exchanged another look.

"The question now," his father said, "apart from further

investigation, which I agree is necessary, is what we do with this heart of yours now."

"Ah," James said, "the magic practitioner I saw before, I'm not really sure how to contact them. Perhaps we could ask around and see if anyone we know knows of anyone?"

His mother sighed. "Ask around? It's bad enough you've gotten tangled up with magic to begin with. Keeping it quiet is the only way we can avoid scandal at this point."

"Just some trusted friends…"

"Trusted friends," his mother said, "still blabber."

"Forget all that," his father said. "It's not that we couldn't find someone discreet to help us get your heart back in, James. But are we sure that's the best option for you right now?"

"Are we sure that's…?"

"Of course we had to find your heart immediately," his mother said. "But I'm not sure, dear—well, in a way, isn't this an opportunity for you?"

"Are we sure," his father said, "that your heart is safest in your own hands? Or chest, as the case may be."

James blinked. "Well, where else would it be safer? I mean, people's hearts are meant to be theirs."

"Precisely untrue," his mother said. "Dearest, how many times have we told you? A man should give his heart, as fully as he can, to his wife—or his fiancée, before then."

"Genevieve? But…"

"Miss Hunt is a reliable woman, and I'm sure she could keep your heart very safe," his mother said. "And it would certainly put an end to you constantly running off with other people, wouldn't it? You used to say you couldn't help yourself. Well, this would help you to help yourself, wouldn't it?"

"Maybe," James said helplessly. "But I don't know that Genevieve would like it."

"She'd be amazed. Thrilled," his mother said. "What woman wouldn't be?"

"And it would save us having to find some trustworthy witch," his father added. "I don't believe such a thing exists. If she didn't double cross us now, you could count on blackmail years later. No, better off avoided. You'll thank us later."

"Just ask Genevieve if she'll take it," his mother said. "It will help your marital harmony. Marital harmony is very important to your life, dear. Or do you still not want to marry her?"

Her eyes on James were pleading, almost sad. While his father's eyes were stern.

James swallowed.

**

Genevieve hadn't come back to Ilbird Manor with James, as he had told her it was better if he conducted the search on his own. However, she was staying not very far off, at the very inn that Rachel had been staying at before. James took a horse to go see her. His health was improved enough to ride, and the wind on his face was refreshing, and he was in a hurry. He wanted to get to her before he could change his mind.

His mother was wrong about him. He cared about marital harmony, of course he cared. How often had he wondered if he could ever find a marriage as stable and successful as his parents'? Not just because they had told him, many times, how much they wished for his happiness to be as great as their own. No, there was some greater part of him that longed to be like them, to live that kind of peaceful life. It was only that sometimes he doubted he was capable of it.

If this would grant him the capability, why wouldn't he want it?

And of course he wanted to marry Genevieve. Hadn't he promised he would? Wasn't his word his honor? And not only his honor, but the honor of his whole family. And she was the one who could grant him that happiness. With her, he could finally become a man who would make his parents proud.

Which was what he wanted, of course. It was only his nerves that said otherwise, singing high in his head and chest. Seizing at him, as ever.

When Genevieve held his heart, he was sure she would grant him the serenity she always carried with her. And it would get easier. Everything would get easier.

When his heart was no longer his own burden—when he no longer had a chance to make an idiot of himself—he would be free.

And everything would be perfect.

The wind blew so hard against his face, he was almost scorched with cold by the time he arrived at the inn. He left his horse with the inn's stableboy and went inside, and asked if someone might inform the guest in room twelve of his presence, as he wished to speak with her privately.

Then he leaned against the wall and waited. The compact mirror was in his pocket. Maybe this would be the last time he would have ownership of his own heart. How many people had such an opportunity, to choose who they gave it to? Certainly he'd never had much of a choice about it before. He closed his eyes and tried to feel anticipation.

"James."

Genevieve herself had come down to fetch him. She raised her eyebrows, and he smiled at her reassuringly. The smile she returned seemed almost startled out of her. She led him back to her room.

"Well?" she asked. "Your parents agreed to help you look?"

"Not only that," James said, "they found it. I suppose I should have asked for help from the beginning."

"Really, you found it already? I mean, that's a huge relief to hear. I didn't expect it would be so easy."

"Easy," James said. A man was dead. "True, I barely had to do anything."

He looked at Genevieve and swallowed. She really was very pretty. Her hair neatly woven into a complicated braid, her blue eyes slightly narrowed by her smile, her dimples (many men he knew were very taken by dimples). If he had to love someone for the rest of his life, loving someone like her would surely be an honor.

"Genevieve," he said. "I've talked to—I've thought it over, and I think..."

He got down on one knee. Genevieve took a surprised step back and stared at him as he took the compact mirror out of his pocket. "I want to give you my heart," he said. "This is it. I know it doesn't look like much," he added as Genevieve continued to stare, "and maybe it isn't much, but it's all I can offer you. Please take it, and make me yours."

"James, you can't be serious," Genevieve said. "Your heart is yours. Of course I hope we'll learn to love each other over the course of our marriage, but this is too much. I can't ask you to do something so extreme. You'll end up regretting it later, I'm sure."

"Never," James said. "Genevieve, you're all I want in a wife. You always have been. I want to be right for you and love you like you deserve. Don't you understand that?"

"I don't need more than you give willingly. You should understand that."

"I'm willingly giving you this," James said. "My heart is mine right now. Maybe more than it ever has been. And I'm thinking about this logically, and I'm making my own choice—the right choice—and I want you, and I want to always want you. I'm offering myself to you, Miss Hunt. Don't you want me?"

"Of course I do," Genevieve said, "but..."

James shuffled closer on his knees. He took her hand and pressed the compact mirror into it, then pressed her other hand over it. He kissed her knuckles, and drew away.

"James," Genevieve said, "is this wise?"

She looked very pretty there, with her long, perfectly braided hair, and her blue eyes, and her dimples, and his heart in her hand. Pretty and perfect, and he still wasn't worthy of her, and he still didn't know how he felt about her, but maybe he could be. Maybe he would be soon. Maybe this could fix him.

"I love you," he told her.

He was sure it was true. After all, didn't it have to be?

13

Chapter Thirteen

Infiltrating Ilbird Manor outright for the sake of surveillance would have been too big a challenge for Natty at this point. Instead, she found a nook to hide in on Ilbird Manor's extensive lawn—behind an ornamental rosebush—and watched the search for James's heart unfold with a pair of binoculars. Hm. There was certainly a lot of bustle. She didn't see James or his parents taking part in the action, though, nor had anyone come out to search the garden, which would have been inconvenient for her but certainly what one would expect. Maybe they were putting off searching the grounds until later?

She was keeping an eye on both the front and side doors of the manor as much as possible. If James left she wanted to see it happen; she would have to follow him then, because she would have little way of knowing if he had found his heart or not. And if he recovered his heart, her mission became urgent, endgame imminent.

For a long time, she didn't catch sight of James. At one point a servant left out the front door and hurried off down the road, returning an hour later. But other than that, no one came or left. Inside, chaos reigned; outside, all was quiet.

Until, just as dusk began to fall, she saw James exit after all. He headed for the other side of the building, and then emerged onto the road on a horse, riding off into the forest. Damn it. She hadn't considered speed as a priority for today's mission and had no means of transportation for herself. All she could do was tail him at a run. Well, at least it was no challenge to stay far enough behind him that he didn't realize she was following.

She was fast. Angela had trained her in running with the intent of both catching prey and fleeing a scene, and either scenario required both speed and endurance. She followed the horse until she came to the same inn she had stayed in the last time she was visiting Ilbird Manor—she had a room reserved there now, too, right next to Genevieve's, for the sake of keeping an eye on Genevieve as well as James. She could guess easily enough where James had gone, and quietly made her way up to her room, where she put a cup to the wall and listened for conversation.

James had arrived well before Natty, so Natty was only catching the tail end of what apparently had been a conversation twisty and exhausting, judging by the tired timbre of Genevieve's voice. "I can keep it for now," Genevieve was saying, "since you insist, but in the long run, we'll need to come up with a better option. If you don't want to put it back in your chest, we at least have to find a safe somewhere—or maybe bury it? Just keeping it in my purse isn't safe at all."

"As long as it remains yours," James's voice said, "I'll leave the rest to your discretion."

A sigh.

"Genevieve, I don't mean to burden you."

"It's not that it's a burden. I'm just not sure this is a good choice."

"It is. Trust me. It's the best thing I can do for you—for us."

"James... it's been a long day. Let's talk about it more tomorrow, all right?"

"All right," James said. "Whatever you say. Come to the manor tomorrow, and we can talk as much as you want. My parents will be glad to see you."

"I'll be glad to see them too. I'm relieved they were able to find it so quickly, but I still have some questions for them. And you said this is their advice, too, this..."

"I agreed with them. Giving it to you is the best idea."

"Hm. Well. We'll discuss it. I'll see you all tomorrow."

Footsteps, and a door swinging open and then clicking closed.

Natty listened for a moment longer before leaning away from the wall. Well, things had certainly turned around fast. She hadn't expected James's heart to turn up so quickly, but more than that, why would he think it a better idea to give it to Genevieve than to keep a hold of it himself? They were getting married, sure, but she hadn't gotten the impression at any point that this was a love match, and James was more the independent type, except for how he seemed to rely on—and hate deceiving—his parents...

There was something that itched her about that. She rubbed her head, frowning. Now that she thought about it, it had been itching her for a while, the way James was such an obedient son ever since losing his heart. Was it because he had no drive on his own to be anything but obedient? Still, something about it seemed off.

Not that that mattered right now. What mattered was that Genevieve had the heart, which was strange but all for the best. Her room here at the inn had fewer security measures than Ilbird Manor. And, Natty thought with a hint of spite, it wasn't as if she had any right to the heart anyway, so there was no reason to feel guilty about relieving her of it.

She waited until she was fairly certain Genevieve was asleep.

No sound in an hour, no light under the door in the hallway. No snoring, either, but oh well, Natty couldn't ask for everything.

She walked quietly out into the hall. No one else was out, a piece of luck. Genevieve's door was locked, but that was no real issue. If Natty couldn't pick the lock on the average inn door, Angela would have been embarrassed by her. She had it open in five seconds, and closed it softly behind herself.

Genevieve was in bed, as expected. Natty took a quick look at the things out on the table. It was all stuff that she'd seen the first time she'd searched Genevieve's room, back at Ilbird Manor, standard traveling necessities. Nothing of interest.

Her bag, now. Natty dug through it, placing each object silently on the floor as she took it out. Again, it was all the same, except for a compact mirror.

There was something wrong about the mirror. Or, not wrong, perhaps just unusual. Natty sniffed it, ran a finger over its engraved cover. Opened it up and looked at herself. Unexpectedly she was able to see her reflection quite clearly. The surface of the mirror was glowing in the dark.

She closed the compact, considering. And then a hand grabbed her wrist. She reacted on instinct, grabbing the hand back and twisting the arm it was attached to, putting her attacker on their knees, before realizing it was Genevieve Hunt, who had apparently awoken.

Natty was usually stealthier than this. Maybe Miss Hunt was just a light sleeper.

"Let go of it," Genevieve said from between gritted teeth. (Natty had twisted her arm pretty far back.) "That's not yours to touch."

"Calm down. You know you can't take me."

"You don't deserve to touch him, you murderer. Let go of it."

Natty frowned. "Touch him... you mean this? This is his heart? James's heart?"

"Let go of it!" Genevieve said for the third time, this time almost screaming. Natty let go of her wrist and slid her into a chokehold instead, automatically, knowing that too much noise would attract attention. Fingers scrabbled at her arm, but she was wearing good, thick leather.

She paid more attention to the mirror. Magic, sure. It was glowing, after all, and had that off feeling that magical items often did. But it didn't pulse. It didn't beat. Iris had said that whatever shape the heart was transformed into, it would still beat.

"Don't try to trick me," Natty said. "Where's his real heart? Where did you put it?"

"Let go," Genevieve said, gasping, barely audible. Natty thought at first she wanted to be released, but no—"Let go of it. He's not yours."

She really thought it was the heart. Huh.

Natty released the chokehold, but gave Genevieve no chance to recover before grabbing her wrists and tying them with some cord she was carrying in her pocket. Cord, a knife, a lockpick—Natty kept the basics on her at all times. She tied Genevieve's legs too, but didn't gag her yet. Instead she took out her knife and held it to Genevieve's throat. "James told you this was his heart?"

"Go to hell," Genevieve said.

"It's not his heart," Natty said evenly. "I'm trying to get my facts straight here. He told you it was his heart, and his parents found it for him? They were even the ones who told him to give it to you, weren't they?"

"Why should I say anything to a thief and a monster?"

Natty sighed. She stuffed one of Genevieve's clean handkerchiefs in her mouth to gag her, placed her on the bed, and headed out of the room, back to her own room to fetch a few more supplies before leaving the inn.

***

Thinking about it objectively, with the extra clue in hand, it was all very simple.

Who benefited from stealing James Guarin's heart?

Well, anyone could have benefited, but who had benefited in practice?

The one most hurt (aside from James himself) had been Charlotte Taylor, cruelly cast aside. The one who seemed to benefit the most was Genevieve Hunt, taking Charlotte Taylor's place. But James didn't love Genevieve. Who did he love, then?

Well, he still loved his parents, didn't he? Without a heart, he surely should have become more cold and callous towards them, not suddenly the perfectly dutiful son. Yet he paid close attention to their feelings, their safety, the family honor, even in ways he hadn't before. And they benefited, didn't they, from him leaving Charlotte Taylor—benefited from the engagement with Genevieve, which would bring in the money and business connections they needed to advance their family's financial and social position.

That in itself should have been something Natty and Angela had considered earlier. They had been too caught up in Charlotte's depiction of the situation as a love triangle to fully explore the possibilities, and then Natty had listened too much to James, who would never consider his parents an option. With his heart in their hands he was incapable of suspecting them. But now Natty could see the facts clearly. And there was the additional fact that James's parents had presented him with a "heart" with great certainty, claiming to have tested it, and not only was it not the real heart, but they hadn't even wanted him to put it back in his chest, probably because it would ruin their bluff. They wanted him to believe he had his heart back while secretly still keeping his heart for themselves so that they could continue controlling him even after he'd married and believed his heart belonged to his wife. Probably for the rest of his life.

It was quite a scheme. But now Natty had gotten a glimpse of it, she could rip it all to shreds.

That was what Poor Jane did, after all, to the best laid plans. And even if she wasn't Poor Jane, she was something very close.

Ilbird Manor. It wasn't as quiet as the inn had been. Especially the day after so much bustle, there were some servants still about. A lone guard patrolling the grounds, who Natty knocked unconscious and left tied up behind some bushes. A couple of maids snickering in the kitchen, whom she snuck past without their noticing. Otherwise, though, it was dark and still, and the stillness had a waiting feeling for it. It was waiting for her to do something to break it.

She had earlier gotten a sense of the layout of the place. The Earl and Countess Guarin had separate bedrooms, but they slept in the same one, a chamber not far down the hall from James's room. That, she thought, had a good chance of being where the heart was hidden, if it wasn't buried out in the garden or hidden under a floor panel or some other random location.

This time she had better luck than with Genevieve. Not only was the door left unlocked, but the Earl and Countess were clearly deep asleep. This would give her more freedom to work.

On the other hand, while Genevieve's room at the inn had been sparsely decorated, and contained only a bag's worth of personal items, this room was far more ornate and also far more cluttered. Rummaging through everything systematically would take all night. Natty didn't have time for that. If she couldn't conclude her search tonight—not only of this room but of the entire manor—then the next day someone was bound to notice Genevieve was missing, find her, and learn Natty had taken off with her compact mirror after saying that it wasn't really James's heart. Her prime suspects would be decisively on guard by that point. No, she had to search fast and efficiently. She would risk the chance of disturbing the Earl and Countess's rest and do a little magic that Angela had taught her, a basic spell to locate magical objects within a room. The risk was that she had to murmur the words of the spell aloud, and at the moment it went into action, there was a spark of light on her hand —which she also had to prick, blood or spit being necessary for any spell so hasty.

From there, the magical objects in her vicinity appeared to emit light, but only to her eyes. The spell did not affect the objects themselves, or the room, but only Natty's perception. This was another reason Angela advised her to use it sparingly. Using magic that affected one's own nature was fine for one day, but could build up and have cumulative effects over time. Poor Jane already had enough magic in her being without more being added.

A little, however, was harmless. And could be very useful.

There was a sharp pang in her eyes for an instant as she completed the spell, and she squeezed them shut until it subsided. When she reopened them, she could see two new sources of light in the room, though both faint and hazy. She was not such a powerful magician as to see all the nuances of magical sources the way Iris no doubt could under this sort of influence. She could only get a glimpse.

The first glowing object was slightly hanging out of the closet. It was a shawl—looked to be an old one—made of white and gray lace. With her magic sight, she could tell there was a little something else woven into it, a secret charm, a magical intention. She could not quite glean what, but it did not appear malevolent. Nor relevant. It was hardly the right shape or size to be a heart, its magic signature was faint, and when she touched it, there was no more pulsing than she had noted coming from Genevieve's compact mirror.

The other light was glowing slightly through the crack of one of the armoir drawers. Very slowly and gently she eased the heavy drawer open. The glowing came from beneath a neatly folded shirt, which she lifted aside to discover a watch.

The magic coming from the watch was more intense than from

the shawl by far, even to her unpracticed eyes. But did it pulse? She picked it up and opened it and—yes, of course it pulsed, of course it beat.

It was a watch. It ticked.

It ticked, a bit faster than a watch should have. Some people's hearts, perhaps, would have beat an exact sixty beats per minute, but this one was faster, maybe closer to eighty. As Natty lifted it, the beating hitched for a moment, speeding up, and then slowed back down.

Maybe it sensed it was in danger. "Clever little thing," Natty murmured. She tucked it away in her deepest pocket, and drew out of that pocket her knife.

Her master had accepted a second commission from Charlotte Taylor, after all. Poor Jane's job was never simply retrieval. She had been tasked not just to find the heart, but to kill whoever had stolen it.

Had Natty retrieved the heart from Genevieve, she would not have killed her. The "heart" she had, James had given to her freely. She did not fit the profile of the person Angela had been hired to kill. Angela and Natty would have been forced to investigate further. But it was clear enough that the Earl and Countess had stolen this heart. If they had not performed the ritual to remove it from James's chest themselves, that did not mean they were not the guilty parties. They had found means to have it removed, and kept it hidden away for themselves, even going so far as to produce a fake to throw James and Genevieve off the scent. It was sufficient evidence for action to be justified.

She dealt with the Earl first. She had no particular distaste for killing women, but men often fought back with more strength. She wanted to kill him while he was still asleep. And she almost succeeded. She had slit his throat before he fully woke, but the pain woke him for just a brief second, and he gurgled, limbs twitching, hand moving sluggishly to clutch his neck.

Awakening his wife.

The countess bolted upright and screamed. If she had been a wise woman, her next move then would have been to run. Instead, she lunged. The force took Natty by surprise, knocking her down on the bed. But she quickly regained her senses. She grabbed the blankets of the bed, which were lying between her body and the countess's, and fought to flip the countess over and wrap the blankets around her, pinning her arms and legs to immobilize her. Her knife had skittered off to the side for a moment—now she recovered it, and was about to stab when the door burst open, the countess's scream having summoned a flock of servants. Three men and an old woman in livery. And James.

"Help," the countess was crying. "She killed him, she killed him..."

Natty positioned her knife over the countess's neck. "Stay back, all of you," she called out. "James. Come over here."

He eyed the two of them for a moment, then walked forward, slowly, almost reassuringly. "Rachel," he said, "what are you doing here? You're supposed to be back in the capital with your master."

His gaze was fixed on her. It was as if he hadn't seen his father's bloody corpse, or his crying mother.

Natty swallowed.

His heart was in her pocket.

"Do you love me?" she asked him.

"Huh?"

Too blunt. "Do you want to protect me?" she asked. "Do you trust me?"

"James," the countess was saying, "James, get away from her, get away..."

"Yes," James said. "I do."

"Sit down," she said, and he sat on the edge of the bed. Then, "Close your eyes."

He closed his eyes, and she sliced his mother's throat.

Before the servants could surge forward, she grabbed James and pulled him closer, arm hooked around his chest, bloody knife at the ready. "Don't come any closer, any of you," she warned. "I'll kill your young master too if you do."

"Rachel, what's going on?" James asked. His eyes were still closed, and he leaned into her touch.

"Stand up," she said. "You're leaving with me as my hostage. Then, we have business to settle."

He nodded blindly. They stood, and began to walk, making the servants back away as they passed. She didn't let him open his eyes until they were down the hall and had come to a set of stairs.

***

She took him back to the inn, but by a roundabout route, knowing the servants had watched them leave the estate, even though she'd warned them to stay in the manor if they didn't want James's throat cut open like his parents'. He sat on the edge of her bed as she gathered up her belongings. She'd brought nothing that would identify her, nothing overly precious, but still a few things she didn't want to leave behind.

"Rachel," James said. "There's blood on your face."

She had a bowl of water on the table, brought by a solicitous maid earlier. She dipped her handkerchief in it and removed the compact mirror from her pocket. A heart it was not, but she could at least look in it as she wiped her face off. This inn room was dirt cheap and didn't have a mirror.

"There's some on your sleeves, too," James said. "Not much, but some."

She glanced at it. It had already dried, and her fabric was dark. "Would you be able to tell it was blood if you didn't know?"

James shrugged. "It wouldn't be my first assumption, but you never know."

She changed jackets, folding the one she had on into her knapsack.

"Rachel, you came back to help me after all, didn't you? Even after we told you we didn't need your help, you still came."

"You could put it that way."

A shy smile tweaked James's lips. "Thank you. After we sent you away, I didn't deserve it. But you know, we already found the heart. Ah, actually..." The smile faded. "I gave it to Genevieve. I don't know if I was right to do that. I should get it back."

"No, that was stupid," Natty said. "But it doesn't matter. She doesn't really have it."

James's eyes widened. "You took it from her, didn't you? That's why when I look at you, I feel so..." He waved a hand. "Warm. I don't know. It's like I can see you differently now. Really see you."

"You're not wrong," Natty said, "but not exactly. That mirror you gave Genevieve wasn't your heart in the first place. Your parents tricked you. They were the ones who stole your heart to begin with. I don't know what story they cooked up about finding it, but they had really kept the heart to themselves." She took the watch out of her pocket. "Here it is."

He studied it, hands folded behind his back. "This watch... My father said my mother had bought it for him for his birthday. He has it on him all the time."

"Your heart," Natty said. She almost told him to hold it and see if he could feel what it was. But that would have been incredibly stupid. She couldn't lose control of James. She shouldn't have taken the heart out in front of him to begin with—it would be far too easy for him to snatch it away and run away with it.

Maybe she wanted him to.

But he only nodded slowly. Then he seemed to shudder. "My

parents told me that the servant who stole my heart killed himself. They must have killed him to cover up."

"Did you see the body?"

"No."

"Maybe they lied and there is no dead servant," Natty said. She didn't believe that; a lie that big would have come out eventually, as the other servants in the household would of course have gossiped about it. But it would be all right to let him believe this lie for now. It was like covering his eyes again.

What a silly urge. Scowling, she said, "Anyway, we'll be going to the capital now. We should get this business done with."

"Returning my heart to me?" James asked. "I don't know. Maybe you could keep it. I... I feel like it belongs with you, if anyone. Though I suppose you might not really want it."

"You're an idiot," Natty said. "Did you forget the first time we met I tried to kill you?"

"Yes," James said. "It wasn't a good first meeting. But I'm still glad we met. I think it must have been fate, no matter how it came about."

"Fate is the delusion of fools."

"Sure. I'm deluded," James said. "I've lived with different delusions all my life." He leaned closer. "Keep my heart, Rachel. Even if you would never love me back, I don't want it returned. Keep it."

"You've misunderstood," Natty said. "I never intended to give you the heart back. Did I ever claim I would help you with that? Charlotte Taylor hired me and my master to bring this heart to her."

"Ah." James's face fell. "So you'll give it to her."

"No," Natty said. "She may think we will. But before she hired us to retrieve the heart, she hired us to kill you by stabbing you through the heart. And once we've accepted a commission, we never turn back. Do you understand? I'm taking you back to the capital to kill you."

James looked at her.

Natty held out the heart in front of her, loosely. He could easily snatch it and run away. Then she would have to chase him, but maybe she wouldn't be fast enough. Then she would have to find him if he got away, but if he hid well it might take hours—days— weeks—maybe even forever. Maybe she would never find him.

"Will you kill me yourself?" James asked. "With your own hands?"

"Me or my master."

"You should do it. Stab my heart through like you did at that party. It's right, I think. I was meant to die then, at your hands. We should close this circle. I won't blame you," James said earnestly. "It's how it's meant to be."

Natty let out her breath in a slow hiss. "Even under the curse," she said, "shouldn't you want to live?"

"I don't know. What do people want to live for? All my life, I've lived for other people. If I can't live for you, I don't know if there's much of a point. Dying for you is just as good, then."

"There are plenty of things to live for!" Natty said furiously. "And you only started loving me less than an hour ago! You can't say that's the reason why! There must be other things."

"I don't know," James repeated. "I just feel empty." He smiled at her, then, and he was right. It was a hollow smile. "Maybe," he said, "I've been empty forever."

"Why don't you even try to take it?" Natty said. "Even if you love me, or you trust me, there should be some part of you that would try. You're fucking human, aren't you? Well?"

"I'm tired," James said. "What would I do even if I could escape you? Where would I go, and what would the point be? Rachel, you said we should go to the capital and be done with this. I think you're right."

Natty's hands spasmed around the watch. She wanted to shove it in his hands. She wanted to hurl it out the window.

She took a deep breath. In the capital, Angela was waiting. When she returned, when the mission was over with, when James was dead, Angela would still be there, and everything would return to normal. Natty couldn't fail her just because getting to know her target a little better was making her emotional.

"We should leave now, then," she said. "They'll be hunting for us here soon. We can't stay the night." She put a couple last things in her pack, and hauled James to his feet. "Let's go."

14

Chapter Fourteen

When Angela dropped by to report to Charlotte Taylor this time, she noticed a change in the woman. Previously, her attitude on seeing Angela had been completely grim, whether in resolute anger (as the first time) or conflicted fury and desire and regret (as the second). Now, she still looked resolute and grim, but there was a hint of anticipation in her eyes too as she let Angela in the window.

"Did you get it?" she asked. "I mean, did you find the heart?"

Angela nodded. "It had been enchanted to look like a watch. I have it back at my headquarters."

Charlotte sighed. "Excellent! Thank god. But why don't you have it with you?"

"Your commission to me," Angela said. "You want it completed at the earliest possible date?"

"Yes, of course."

"It seems to me you may wish James Guarin to be present himself at the decisive moment," Angela said, "considering the details of your request. Do you wish to be present as well?"

Charlotte's brow wrinkled. "I would have to be, wouldn't I? I told you to recover the heart and bring it specifically to me."

"That was not all you asked for," Angela reminded her. "I am a killer, not a hound that chases down your little sticks."

"Right," Charlotte said. "I asked you to kill whoever had stolen the heart. Have you done so yet?"

"They are dead."

"Was it Genevieve Hunt? She came visiting me the other day, you know. Such arrogance."

"No."

"Who on earth was it then?"

"Mr. Guarin's parents."

"His parents!" Charlotte exclaimed. "Really? Them." She considered. "I should have known. They've always been controlling, and they've always had it out for me and James. Still, magically removing his heart is too far."

"They're dead now," Angela said, "so you might consider their crime paid for."

"Serves them right."

"Perhaps."

"Was it quick, the way you killed them?"

Angela hadn't been the one to kill them, but according to Natty's report, "Yes."

"Hm," Charlotte said. "It's what James would want, I guess. He always did love them."

Angela wondered if that was why he had never noticed the change in his affections as regarded his parents when his heart was stolen, or if the spell had simply been strong enough to override any usual observations. Well, it hardly mattered at this point. Nothing about the former Earl and Countess mattered anymore.

More to the point, "When will it be convenient to meet you and bring this matter to a close? I will be bringing James Guarin with me as well as the heart and an associate of mine."

"An associate?"

"As she was involved in the heart's recovery, I feel it only fair she be allowed to see the mission completed."

"Hm. Fine, but it's a bit of a crowd." Charlotte pursed her lips. "There's a spot underneath the bridge where few people go except during festivals. I used to meet James there in private. Let's meet there tomorrow night—"

"I know the spot you mean, but I don't think it will serve."

"Why not?"

"Not so private as you say. Boats pass by unpredictably."

"I don't mind boats passing. There's distance. They won't recognize us; all they'll see is a quiet meeting. People conduct private business there all the time. Anyway, it can't be here. There's only a certain number of people I can sneak in without my brothers noticing."

Angela nodded. "You're the client. What you say goes. Tomorrow at eleven o'clock, I will meet you there."

"Not midnight?" Charlotte asked. Almost teasing.

"Why delay? We should only wait until the road and river are quiet. The stray bystander, we'll have to risk, but you say you don't care about that. We will simply have to do this as discreetly as possible. You know, even if you don't kill anyone yourself, hiring an assassin can still get you in a lot of trouble, Miss Taylor."

"I know. We'll be careful."

Angela nodded.

Charlotte probably still didn't understand what the nature of their meeting tomorrow night would be. Still didn't understand that when you commissioned Poor Jane, there was no taking it back. But it was not Angela's responsibility to remind her of every detail of the contract. She'd asked the girl if she was sure at the time, and reminded her of their pact more recently as well. Was she meant to spell it out? And if she did, Charlotte was bound to get upset and make a huge fuss before the mission could be completed.

The mission was primary, the client secondary. She would complete her task tomorrow and deal with Charlotte's wrath afterward. If she made too much trouble, well, she wouldn't be the first client Angela had been forced to eliminate when their arrangement was over.

Angela was more worried about Natty.

Natty had arrived at the hideout that day in the early morning hours, James Guarin in tow, a heart turned into a watch tucked into a deep pocket. She summarized the events of the past day to Angela with great frankness, uncaring of James sitting only a couple feet away. "He no longer cares if he lives or dies, and he'll die soon," she said when Angela brought it up. "Let him listen if he wants to. He won't do anything to stop us."

James smiled when Angela glanced over skeptically. "I really won't," he said. "I wish Rachel only the best."

"Her name's Natty, actually," Angela told him, and when Natty flinched, she said, "If it doesn't matter what he knows, why would him knowing your name matter either?"

"Fine," Natty said.

The job was nearly complete, and Natty had done an excellent job. But despite Angela praising her, she was not pleased with herself. She was tense, and irritable, and sat close by James and kept on staring at him even though she claimed to have him well in hand. (She hadn't even bothered tying him up.) And for the night, she said he would sleep in her room with her. "I can keep an eye on him."

"You'll be sleeping. I'll watch him."

"I can handle him," Natty said. "He won't try anything on me. You've trusted me this far with this job. Let me finish it."

Angela hummed, but allowed Natty to keep James for the night after all.

It was true Natty had done very well so far. But with the tension she was holding in, something was bound to snap.

***

Angela, Natty, and James went to the meeting spot a half hour ahead of time—or rather, they went to hide in a corner from which one could see the meeting spot, a little ways away from the bridge. It wouldn't have been the first time Angela went to meet with a client only to discover she'd been set up for an ambush or an encounter with the police; these attempts were generally clumsy, in her experience, but she still preferred to avoid them. They would wait and watch Charlotte arrive, and then emerge to meet her.

Natty was still tense, and as they all crouched together, she had a hand on James's knee. Not particularly suggestive, but proprietary, almost reassuring. Maybe it did reassure James, but it didn't reassure Angela.

James himself was jittery. The prospect of death, he had accepted, but meeting Charlotte worried him. He hadn't seen her since their breakup, and he'd mentioned to Natty a couple times that he wondered how she would react to seeing him again, how he might feel, even though he was only capable now of truly loving Natty and not susceptible to Charlotte's charms. (As far as reassurance went, this last comment seemed calculated to reassure Natty, which was ridiculous.) Natty told him after he'd brought it up a couple times to shut up. They were hiding and even if he was nervous, talking wouldn't help and might bring them to someone's attention. Then she squeezed James's knee.

Charlotte arrived a few minutes before the hour, and actually sat down under the bridge. Angela marveled at her composure—most of her clients would have stood or even paced while waiting. But then, Charlotte had always been something of a cool customer.

She motioned to Natty and stood, while Natty pulled James up behind her. They made their way down to the spot under the bridge. Charlotte on seeing them stood, but she did not walk forward to greet them, waiting instead. Angela approved.

She reached out towards James when they converged, as if to hug him or clasp his hand, but then she drew her hand away when he only looked at her awkwardly. "James, I'm sorry," she said. "I should have known something was wrong, the way you left things. I did know it wasn't like you, but some things are just a bit fantastical for me to dream up. I would never have imagined your parents in particular would do such a thing to you."

James shrugged. "Well, I do wish you hadn't set out to kill me. But it's too late to change that now." He glanced at Natty, and she nodded—what that meant, Angela wasn't sure, but apparently he could guess. "I never hated you for any of this. Please remember that, now that it's over. Though I couldn't love you anymore, I never hated you."

"James..." Charlotte turned to Angela. "Your commission's complete, I'm satisfied. Now give me the heart so we can bring an end to all this madness."

Natty had James's heart in her pocket. She took it out now, but when Charlotte stepped forward to take it, Angela blocked her. "Not so fast."

"Not payment," Angela said. "But the commission is not, as you said, complete. There is still one step further to go. Have you really forgotten, Miss Taylor?"

Charlotte frowned. "Forgotten what?" She kept looking over Angela's shoulder at James and Natty rather than at Angela. Still not taking the situation seriously.

"The details of your commission," Angela said. "Retrieving the heart and killing the thief who stole it were aspects you added later to the original task. But the first thing you asked me to do, Miss

Taylor, was kill James Guarin. You asked us to stab him through the heart—well, I'm afraid one cannot really stab a knife through a watch, but there are still plenty of ways to demolish it. Perhaps you have an opinion on which we should use."

Charlotte gaped. "I—I told you to kill his parents, though. Not him. I took that back."

"Poor Jane does not accept reversals of decision," Angela said patiently. "Additions to the commission, yes. Cancellation? My dear, I made an oath to fulfill the mission. It cannot be stopped by something as puerile as you changing your mind."

"I…"

"Let me make it simple for you," Angela said, when Charlotte continued to simply gape. "No takebacks. There is no question whether I will kill Earl Ilbird here. The only question is how."

"What if—I won't tell you how," Charlotte said resolutely. "You can't kill him unless—what if I say he has to die of old age, what then? You can't kill him then."

Angela sighed. "The details of a request are often complicated and impossible to fulfill exactly. Poor Jane's vocation is one of reason; if I can't handle the details, at least I'll still complete the mission as well as I can. I can't stab him through the heart as you originally requested, but I can still say the words you requested—Charlotte Taylor," she said to James, "sends her love. And," she added to Charlotte, "Perhaps if you can't stab through a watch, you can still smash it with a knife if it's sturdy enough. It shouldn't be that hard."

She had drawn her knife already when Charlotte lunged at her with a wordless cry. It was easy for her to flip the knife and punch it straight through Charlotte's bodice, through skin and flesh and deep into her stomach.

Charlotte sank to the ground, gasping and choking and grasping at her stomach, at the knife. "You… How can you attack me? I'm the one who summoned you!"

"You're a client, not my master," Angela said. "Anyone who interferes with the mission must be removed. You clearly won't be reasonable, and as you said, you already paid me. If you put pressure on that, you may live through the night, if you get medical help. I would try not to move too much. You can leave as soon as I've completed the task and you've confirmed its completion."

"Don't fight, Charlie," James put in anxiously, "Just let her end this. It's better that way."

"You idiot," Charlotte said. "I wish..."

She trailed off as Angela turned around to face Natty, who was still holding the watch.

Natty earlier had held the watch out so that Charlotte could see it, but now she held it close to herself, pressed against her chest, one hand folded over another. Angela put her own hand out and raised her eyebrows. "Natty."

Natty's lips were pressed tight together. She took a step backward, instinctively, right onto James's feet. As he shuffled back and braced her, muttering awkwardly, she said, "Angela."

"Give me the watch."

Natty was silent for a moment. Her hands were clenched and trembling. "I can't," she said at last. "Not this time. I can't."

"Natty, you know our rules."

"You killed the ones who stole the heart and brought the heart back. I already stabbed him, too, at the party. You could say we fulfilled the mission's requirements already."

"Poor Jane isn't done until the target is dead. You know that very well."

"Master, please."

"If you don't want me to kill him," Angela said, "then you will have to stop me." She raised her knife, and looked at Natty questioningly.

Natty's face screwed up, brow furrowing and mouth flattening, and then she was shoving the watch back at James, who dropped it, and lunging at Angela. Getting close quick, stepping inside her reach, one arm reaching up to strike Angela's knife arm, the other punching at Angela's sternum. Angela let the watch fall, unworried, let the knife fall from her jarred hand—Charlotte Taylor was far enough away that she'd have a hard time grabbing either while putting pressure on her stomach—and turned so that Natty's gut punch only brushed at her side, and hit Natty's face with the heel of her palm. Caught a foot when Natty stumbled back but used the distance to ready a kick. Knocked Natty over, and kicked her in the head for good measure. Not very hard, just hard enough to make her ears ring, and stun her for long enough for Angela to do what she had to do.

James was frozen, staring at the watch and at Natty and Angela and Charlotte. Lost. Angela picked her knife back up and took a step towards him, towards the watch lying between them.

There was a loud crack.

Angela was confused for a moment. She recognized the noise, but she hadn't brought a gun with her. Natty hadn't either, she was sure, and Charlotte probably wouldn't know a pistol from a petunia. But it had been a gunshot. She knew that.

It took her a moment longer to recognize the pain in her chest as a bullet wound.

She stumbled back, clutching at her chest, hands growing red. The bullet had hit her heart, or damn close.

How ironic.

"Master!" Natty was beside her, grabbing her shoulders, and she realized she'd fallen to her knees. How pathetic. How weak.

But then, all Poor Janes ended this way. All humans.

Poor Jane had a particular talent, too, for the judging of injuries, for telling when they were serious, when they were trivial, when they were fatal. She could tell, by the feel of the wound, by its placement, by the amount of blood pumping out of her—she wasn't going to make it. She didn't have long.

"I'm sorry, Natty. Quick. If you cut my throat now, you can still be the one who killed me. My successor. I promised."

But Natty was shaking her head, helplessly. At a better time, Angela was sure she would have followed the order as she was trained to, but today she was already acting on emotions, letting herself be weak. She would regret it later. But Angela wouldn't push her now, not in her last moments. Natty could hunt down the killer and take back her inheritance in her own time.

"I'm sorry," she said again. "You were good, you know. You're so good. Thank you for being my apprentice."

She closed her eyes, and let herself slip away in Natty's arms.

15

Chapter Fifteen

Rachel had tied Jenny tightly. She spent hours working her way free of the knots and the gag, cursing Rachel and cursing herself for having been so stupid as to not safeguard the room against intruders. For being unable to protect James's heart for even a single night, after he had asked her if she would keep it for him for an entire lifetime.

She heard Rachel's return some hours later. At that point she had managed to untie her legs but not her hands—it was easier for her to reach the knots on her ankles than to work her fingers around the tighter knots securing her wrists. She was full of regrets about that now, overhearing Rachel speak to James—James, here and so close! —in the next room over, knowing she might be able to walk over to the door and even make her way out, but with her wrists tied, she'd never be able to fight Rachel and get James's heart back. Maybe she wouldn't have been able to beat her hand to hand, but she had a gun beneath her mattress. She'd been groggy earlier and hadn't even thought to get it out before alerting Rachel to her presence, but now she might have been able to take Rachel by surprise—and finally take her out.

She fought with the knots on her wrists and eavesdropped at the same time, ear pressed against the wall. Rachel had found a new "heart", which meshed with her tale about the compact mirror not being James's real heart at all. But that paled in significance compared to Rachel's plans. She was going to take James away with her and kill him, and James, eerily infatuated, wasn't going to do anything to resist her.

She fought with the knots and failed to escape them before she heard Rachel and James quietly slip out of their room and down the hallway. Still, she did not give up. She knew one thing at least: Rachel had said she would take James to see Charlotte before killing him, Charlotte and her mysterious master. If Jenny could intercept them, she could still rescue James then.

***

By the time she had wrestled herself free, James and Rachel were too long gone for her to shadow. She packed her gun and the necessities she'd brought with her efficiently, but forced herself not to rush. Setting up a meeting with Charlotte would take Rachel time, as would meeting with her master. Jenny therefore had some time to act, and it was important for her to keep her head. Rushing wouldn't help with that.

On the other hand, she couldn't waste time either. She asked the one inn worker awake at this odd hour whether it would be possible to get a coach at this time of night, and on hearing the answer was negative, asked the price to hire a horse. She was not the fastest horse rider, but she went riding at the park regularly when in the city, and raced with friends when she was home. She would do.

She made it to the city in less than three hours, and realized she did not know where Charlotte Taylor lived. She nearly cried. Calm, she told herself. For this mission calm was needed. If she did not know where Charlotte Taylor lived, she still knew where to look for her. She went to the tailor shop where Miss Taylor worked, and stood around the corner, waiting, until the night turned to dawn and, soon after, the shop opened its doors to customers.

She had intended, as soon as it opened, to go in and inquire about Charlotte Taylor's whereabouts, though despite wracking her brains she could find no good excuse for her to need the information. This turned out, however, to be unnecessary, for before the shop had even opened, among the slow trail of employees dragging their feet in the morning light, Charlotte Taylor arrived with a spring in her step and a smile for the coworker she ran into at the door.

Was this the look of a woman who had just watched her former lover die? Jenny didn't think so. Certainly Charlotte harbored hatred toward James, but even so—could she go to work so cheerfully knowing he had died only the night before?

Jenny doubted it.

She kept a close eye on both doors of the shop, front and back, watching from a café that was across the corner and had a large, open window. The waiter got a little snappish at her when she'd been sitting there for a few hours, but she gave him a large tip, and purchased an expensive lunch, and he shut up about it, saying she could stay as long as she wanted and he hoped she would enjoy herself. This last doubtfully, as the intent way Jenny constantly stared out the window could hardly escape his notice. Enjoying herself was the last thing she was doing today.

She had barely slept for ten minutes last night, and as the day passed, she grew at first exhausted and then, overcoming her exhaustion, tense and headachey. Her focus waxed and waned. She worried that Charlotte would come out and she wouldn't notice it. She worried maybe Charlotte had snuck out already. But in fact Charlotte emerged from the shop a short time after it closed in the early evening hours, and Jenny hurried out of the café to follow her.

Charlotte went home. Or at least, that was all Jenny could figure. She went to a small house in a not-so-nice area of the city. Jenny hesitated, unsure whether to enter. Was this where Rachel would bring James? If so, Jenny could not wait uselessly outside while he was murdered. If not, though, going in would alert Charlotte to the fact that she was being followed prematurely. And if Rachel was already in there—her and her master—the odds of a fight would not be in Jenny's favor.

She was about to burst inside, and had her hand in her pocketbook where it could hold her concealed gun, when Charlotte, having been inside for only a few short minutes, emerged back onto the street. She had changed clothes, out of her work outfit and into a nice dress made of dark brown material, and a coat and bonnet of similar colors. She began to walk towards the center of town, and Jenny followed.

When Charlotte wandered into a bar, she almost groaned. She couldn't enter here subtly, not in the fine clothes she was wearing, not without calling far too much attention to herself. She could watch through the window, and she didn't think this was a place Rachel would choose to arrange a murder, but perhaps Charlotte would vanish off to some private upper room, and how would Jenny keep up with her if that was the case? Though at least she could wager Rachel wouldn't slaughter James as soon as he and Charlotte laid eyes on each other. "Settling business" would surely involve a few more formalities than that. Still. Jenny fidgeted, and rubbed burning eyes. The night was late, and the fumes of this part of the city were noxious.

The sun had long since set and the night grown cold, yet the bar was only growing livelier, when Charlotte again left the bar. Earlier she had walked at a meandering pace, almost wandering. Now she walked with purpose, and Jenny's heart quickened as she followed.

They came to a spot near the river, or more specifically near a bridge that crossed the river. Charlotte went to stand underneath the bridge, and Jenny found a spot some distance away and waited. Was this the rendezvous point at last?

Sure enough, after a couple minutes Jenny saw a group of three approach Charlotte. James she could recognize easily from a distance. Rachel looked a bit different—the clothes she was wearing, perhaps, or simply the darkness of the night. Then there was a third figure, tall, wearing a long, black coat and a short, black hat. That had to be Rachel's master.

Jenny took her gun out of her purse. She aimed at Rachel, who was standing the closest to James at the moment and was the most likely to stop him if he tried to run. Not that he was going to run, from what Jenny had overheard in the inn. At the moment, the effects of Rachel possessing his heart had quelled any attempt at rebellion.

Three enemies. Rachel, Rachel's master, and Charlotte. Jenny's gun held four bullets, but she still hesitated to shoot. She didn't know which held the heart and where they held it—if she were to shoot the heart itself, hiding in an inner pocket, by accident, it would be all too ironic. And she didn't know, once she revealed her presence, how the rest of the group would react.

She hesitated when Rachel took some indistinct object out of her pocket—the heart, most likely, but Jenny couldn't really see it from here—but raised her gun when Rachel's master raised her knife. Only then Charlotte tackled her and ruined the shot. A moment later, Rachel and Rachel's master were grappling as well. Jenny wouldn't have minded killing either of them, but with the movement and the overlap of their bodies, she would have a hard time lining up her shot.

Finally, Rachel's master had cast both Charlotte and Rachel aside and raised her knife again. As she raised the knife, Jenny adjusted her gun, braced herself, and pulled the trigger.

It was a hit.

The woman fell.

Jenny's heart was racing, but her mind was clear. Rachel next, that would be best. But Rachel had crouched down over her fallen master, and Jenny couldn't get a clear shot. And it was hard to even tell from this distance what James and Charlotte were doing. And the heart had to have fallen on the ground somewhere by now. She ran down towards the meeting place where the three figures were milling about. She was about halfway there when her chest began to seize with a burning pain. Had someone shot her too? She hadn't heard any sound. But these were dangerous people. What kinds of weaponry they had on them, she didn't, couldn't know.

She made it to them regardless, and leveled her gun at Rachel's head. "Hand me the heart," she said, for she could see it on the ground between Rachel and her now still and silent master. A watch, the glass cracked from a fall. "Or I'll shoot you in the head."

"You're the one who killed her," Rachel said.

"I did," Jenny said, fighting to keep her voice even when the pain in her chest was such that she could barely breathe. "And I'll kill you too. I don't want to, but I will."

Rachel touched the heart. "I'll give this to James. It belongs to him. Not to you or me or... her." She glanced at Charlotte, who was wounded as well, and who was watching them with a glazed fascination.

"Fine. James?"

James walked over. His face was stunned. Rachel handed him the heart, and he took it and slowly backed away.

"Now," Jenny said, "We go..." Her breath shorted again. "To the..."

Her vision blacked out, and she heard a surprised exclamation as she collapsed. The voice, she could not distinguish.

***

Her chest burned, her head ached. When she opened her eyes,

the world around her would appear blurred and yet too bright, and then suddenly too sharp. It was easier to close them. Her limbs shuddered with a surge of adrenalin and twinged with aches dull and sharp in turn. It was easier to lie still than try to move them. Yet she knew she couldn't lie still, couldn't keep her eyes closed; knew she was in danger.

She felt, for a long, disjointed moment, a point of metal rest against her throat. This didn't frighten her more than everything else; if anything, it calmed her. Danger gained a focus, and her wild anxiety cooled—she didn't move to grab the knife at her throat, nor to scramble away, but felt ready to do so at any moment. When the point of metal left again, her focus again collapsed, and reality again became a blur.

When she came to her senses at last, she was in a quiet room. The walls were covered in old wallpaper which looked like it had once been purple and brown but might conceivably have included some gold as well, long dulled into an ugly beige.

The place was unfamiliar, and yet she could tell something about how she was seeing it was still different. The ragged texture of the wallpaper was too sharp. Her head hurt.

She was lying in an unfamiliar bed. She sat up, pushing aside a navy comforter. Saw a figure sitting at the end of the bed, blinked, and recognized it as Rachel. Except she could see Rachel now more sharply and precisely than before, despite the light in the room being poor, and could spot some differences from how Rachel was usually: she was wearing a long, thick coat despite the room being warm, and her hair was a little wet, though it was pulled back in a braid, and her eyes were red with the peculiar redness that followed crying.

They were intently focused on Jenny now, even more intently than when they had first met, when Rachel had searched her and practically seduced her, albeit unintentionally. Jenny swallowed.

"What did you do with James?"

"He had his heart," Rachel said. "I let him go. What else should I have done? He took that Miss Taylor with him. One can hope he'll watch his back, but it's not my affair. It was more necessary to take care of you." She stood, and formally bowed, bowing as a man would rather than curtseying. "You killed my master. I should salute you. You are the new Poor Jane."

"...what?"

"My master carried a curse," Rachel said, "that has been passed down for many generations. The carrier of Poor Jane's sigil must take up the task of killing for patrons who offer them bone, blood, and coin. You will be cursed with a thirst for blood, but also blessed. You'll have greater physical and emotional strength and endurance than the average mortal, and a longer lifespan. You'll become a perfect killer."

"You—me? I'm not..."

"Poor Jane's sigil is passed down to the person who killed the last Poor Jane," Rachel said. "My master always meant for me to kill her eventually. That's why I was her apprentice. But you killed her, so now it's you instead. You're Poor Jane."

Jenny brought her knees up defensively. She looked around the room to see if she could locate her gun, but it was missing, taken from her while she was unconscious. Damn it. "So, what—now you're going to kill me?"

"No," Rachel said. "I should, maybe. But then again. I don't really deserve to."

"Deserve? What does an assassin know of who deserves to live or die?"

Rachel's reddened eyes gleamed. "It's not that you deserve to live. But if I deserved to become Poor Jane, I should have killed my master. It's what she would have wanted. Instead, I tried to oppose her with no conviction because I was too soft to kill my target. The opposite of what Poor Jane should be. You were able to kill your target without flinching—all I could do was flinch."

"Ah," Jenny said. "I see."

She'd gotten herself through and out of many an awkward and precarious conversation in the past. However, these had been within her own social circles, where all danger lay in implications of impropriety, veiled insults, offensive implications, undesirable connections. And while she had once felt a connection to Rachel when they met, being honest, she did not understand how the woman's mind worked. Was she meant to comfort Rachel now? Say that she was in fact a very good assassin most of the time, or tell her that it was better not to kill people anyhow by most standards of human morality? Or was she meant to boast about her own prowess, or to underplay it and apologize, call it a moment of desperation? Unable to figure out the most appropriate or desired response, the response that would not change Rachel's mind on killing her, she said, "What do you want from me, then?"

As it turned out, frankness was not a bad tack to take. Rachel calmed, and said, "I will be your apprentice and your servant. You have the guts to be Poor Jane but don't know what it means; I have the skill and the knowledge but not the resolve. I can teach you how to be a good Poor Jane, and serve you in any way you wish. I think if I couldn't kill my master, it's what she would have wanted."

Jenny folded her hands.

Her mind, still only half awake, was churning at a million miles a minute.

She'd received many compliments, back-handed compliments, and straightforward insults since debuting in society. Never had anyone looked in her in the eyes and told her she had the potential to be a good assassin, and not because of any particular skill, but because of her guts—that was to say, some innate brutality. She felt that Rachel had peeled away her skin and looked at her naked, saw her as part of her had always guiltily felt she was. Vicious. She hadn't hesitated to shoot Rachel's master out of any qualms of conscience, only waited for the proper moment to arrive. A slew of other moments went through her head: The day her father had first taught her to shoot, the satisfaction of it, the first time she'd shot a deer when they went hunting together, the day he'd given her the little pistol and told her it was no good for hunting but could be used in self-defense, the satisfaction at feeling it in her palm. More than that, maybe, the way she'd felt grabbing Tiffany Botts by the hair and making her grovel and apologize. There'd been satisfaction in that, too, in seeing her hurt and afraid. For a moment.

No one had ever seen that darker side of her before. Not so clearly.

For a moment she liked it. For a moment, she reveled in the feeling of Rachel's reddened eyes fixed on her, in the idea of becoming like Rachel, working together with her. *"I will serve you in any way you wish."* The words had an attractive ring to them. Wasn't a part of her sick of all the petty niceties that composed her life? It was certainly something to have someone look at that guilty part of her and say it was good. *"Anything you wish."* The thought was heady.

But then there were other words that came to mind too. Words she had held in her heart her entire life.

"The queen of the world has to be patient and kind."

The woman who had yanked Tiffany's hair and made her cry wasn't the woman she wanted to be.

"I can't do that," she said. "I can't become this—I can't become some kind of an assassin. There must be some way to get this sigil you're talking about off. To break the curse. All curses can be broken, right?"

Rachel said, "The sigil of Poor Jane has endured for more than centuries. For thousands of years, millennia, it has been passed down from carrier to carrier with no disruption. The legacy you hold, people would and have died for. They've craved the kind of power you hold."

"That's abominable," Genevieve said. She was sure her face didn't reveal the thrill that Rachel's words gave her. Sure, because her face and body were as still as stone. "Certainly I can't allow such an abomination to continue. I will not be a part of perpetuating such horrors. If you wish to continue this line, then kill me! Otherwise, I'll end this curse even if I have to kill myself to do it."

Rachel glared, jaw clenched.

There was a strange pleasure in this too. In Rachel's eyes on her.

In the thought of Rachel killing her, not because she was in Rachel's way, but because it was personal. Because she had what Rachel wanted and was what Rachel aspired to be.

Killing herself, on the other hand, repulsed her. It was something wretched, ruined women did, not respectable girls like her. And the things people would say... But they would be wrong, anyhow, because if it was to save lives that she killed herself, it wouldn't really be suicide, would it? It would be martyrdom. There was something noble in that too.

She looked Rachel calmly in the eye, and watched Rachel's face crumple and grimace and distort, flush and pale. Until at last she stood and turned away and told Jenny, "There may be a way to draw the curse off of you."

"So there is a way."

"Maybe. I don't know. Iris Witherbone once said she could do it. If you are truly certain that—"

"One does not have to think carefully about something like this," Jenny said sternly. "What's right is right. Take me to Iris Witherbone and we'll do whatever must be done to... cut our ties."

Rachel nodded. "I—In the morning, then. You collapsed earlier. You're drained. You should get some rest."

Crazier than many other things that had happened this week,

an assassin telling her to rest. But again, Jenny felt the urge to obey her. Of course, she had no way of finding Iris Witherbone on her own anyway.

***

The place Rachel took her to in the morning was not where they had met with Iris Witherbone previously. While Jenny had been blindfolded at the time, and might not have recognized a difference between streets or buildings, there were more stairs climbing up to the front door, and when Iris let them in, she could tell even at a glimpse that the interior was much better decorated as well.

Iris did not say much before ushering them in, but when she had shut the door, she said, "So Poor Jane has been reborn, now, and the cycle has left the previous Poor Jane behind."

"You can tell," Rachel said.

"There's not much I can't sense about a powerful curse," Iris said, but her arrogance lacked conviction. There was a dull pain in her eyes as she looked at Jenny. "And this was all inevitable, sooner or later. The real surprise is that you're with her, Natty. And why bring her to me?"

"Miss Hunt doesn't wish to carry the sigil of Poor Jane," Rachel said. "You said once you could remove it."

"I could," Iris said. "I'm surprised you'd offer. And that you haven't killed her yet, to inherit it yourself."

Rachel said nothing.

Iris tilted her head. "If you had inherited the sigil, I would never have taken it from you, you know. That would be the least I could do to honor your master. She would have been furious at me depriving you of your rights, even if you requested it, even if you begged me. But since it's someone else... frankly, if you'd come here for another reason, I would have found a chance to take the curse off her anyway. Maybe not while you were around, dear. But it's too good a magical bounty to turn away."

"I thought it might interest you," Rachel said. "If it's not enough in itself, we can pay for the service."

Iris dismissed the offer with a snort. "I'm not like you or your master, you know. I'm not driven by money, even if it's useful. A favor to a friend, a chance to increase my power—those things are far more convincing. And if you don't intend to follow your master's footsteps, you should save your money. With your pride and your background, you won't find it as easy to make your own way in the world as you think."

As she spoke, she walked further into the house. Rachel followed close behind, and Jenny trailed a few steps back. The way the sigil affected her seeing had distracted her on the way here, but in this house it was much more intense. Practically everything she looked at, from a decorative plant to the sofa that Rachel and Iris had settled on in the living room by the time she arrived, had some strange brightness or shadow to it that instinctively she knew to be a sign of magic. It was dizzying. She sank into a free armchair, forcing herself to sit up straight. Rachel had already seen her weak, but Iris had no need to know how off balance she was at the moment.

Iris murmured something in Rachel's ear, Rachel only replying by shaking her head. They looked each other in the eyes for a moment, and then Iris stood, lightly touching Rachel's shoulder as if for support. "Poor Jane, there are some preparations I have to make before I can remove that sigil from you. I hope you and Natty can entertain yourselves. Please don't touch anything; you won't like the consequences."

Rachel and Jenny spent the next few hours entertaining themselves by staring at the walls, the floor, and the ceiling, and occasionally glancing at each other before looking away again. Jenny occasionally bit back a question, reminding herself she couldn't expect Rachel to be honest with her anyway.

Iris's instructions, when she returned, were blunt and obscene.

The first thing she ordered was for Jenny to take her clothes off. Iris needed free access to her chest.

Jenny told herself to consider Iris something of a doctor, though Iris made no such excuses herself, made no real effort to make Jenny comfortable. The way her eyes rested on Jenny as she undressed was some combination of hungry and angry, and it made Jenny shiver.

She cleared the center of the room and made Jenny sit on the floor. She sat down in front of her, eyes still fixed on Jenny's chest. On the sigil. Jenny had gotten a look at it before coming here, and didn't like the sight. But to Iris, it seemed intoxicating.

"Poor Jane," she said quietly. "Ah... I've seen fifty-three possible worlds, and never seen you carry this sigil before. But my Poor Jane was in all of them. If you had known her as I knew her... but then, that's impossible. No one else ever could and no one else ever will. And it is done now, as all things must end. But I'll keep one memento for myself, at least."

With that, she abruptly leaned forward and latched her teeth to Jenny's chest, biting hard enough to draw blood. Jenny gasped and grabbed her shoulders. The teeth did not sink down once they had pierced skin, but the position... Iris's mouth did not circle Jenny's breast like a suckling baby, but bit the flesh above. Still far too intimate a place. She bit down on the sigil, blood seeping slightly out of the wound, and sucked.

A pressure built up in Jenny. A tension, at first an itch and then growing to pain, as if the energy in every part of her body had surged into her chest and then into the very pin-sized spot where Iris's teeth had pierced her. It warred against itself there, and Iris sucked harder, and she felt—felt it flow out, slowly, roughly, into Iris's wet and waiting mouth. Poor Jane's essence, excised from Jenny's body little by little until Iris had swallowed it whole.

At last Iris leaned away and even stood, body swaying. Her mouth had a couple drops of blood on it. She swallowed again, compulsively. "Poor Jane," she said. "Mine." She laughed headily. "Mine forever, darling, forever as we were meant to be! And who's to say, Natty—maybe we will meet again. Could Cruel Therese really grow bored after fifty-three lives? How could she? No, this is just another dream, and when it is over and another starts, we will meet again. But in this life and the next and the next, she will be mine forever." She laughed. "Mine, mine..."

Rachel, who had been sitting warily on the sofa all this time, stood.

Iris waved a hand. "See yourselves out. Come back soon, Natty. You're always welcome here. After all, your teacher lives in me."

Rachel tossed Jenny her clothing, and she shakily dressed. They left together. On the street, Rachel said, "It's gone now. I saw... it was like the ink of a tattoo was sucked out of your skin." She closed her eyes. "Poor Jane is really gone forever, now."

"Thank you," Jenny said, "for helping me."

Rachel's eyes opened. "It wasn't for you. You and I—let's never meet again."

***

A few days later, Jenny was visited by James Guarin.

He had come to break off their engagement. Jenny was less surprised than perhaps she should have been. She felt... a bit relieved.

A bit sad. There had been things, with James Guarin, she had been looking forward to.

But a bit relieved, still.

He was still carrying a watch with him, unsure what to do with it. She offered to take him to Iris Witherbone, knowing now where the witch lived. James shook his head at that. He didn't trust her, and Jenny couldn't blame him. He said he'd try his luck elsewhere.

Jenny wished him the best.

The break-up didn't stain her reputation as badly as her distraught parents expected it to. James Guarin was a man in mourning, and some irrationality was to be expected. Moreover, he had an unreliable reputation to begin with. It was believed by many that Jenny had dodged a bullet. Her friends fawned over her, comforting and flattering. Tiffany Botts even had the audacity to say she'd known James was a bad apple all along and that was why she'd "done her best to warn her dear friend off." An outrageous claim, but Jenny allowed it.

She enjoyed the sympathy. She was, after all, somewhat worn, if not heartbroken. She would rest a while before thinking what to do next. Her parents had some ideas about other possible connections. But she was still young. There was no particular rush.

16

Chapter Sixteen

Regaining possession of his heart hurt James in stages.

When he first took it from Natty, he barely felt anything. Stunned, dried out, weary. A little more frightened than he'd been before, a little less willing to die. A little more worried about Charlie, who was lying on the ground with a knife in her gut.

He was frightened for Genevieve, too, who had collapsed after brandishing a gun at Natty. Frightened of how Natty might retaliate. He said, "Please..."

Natty looked at him. She was holding Genevieve in her arms, having caught her as she fell. "What."

"Don't hurt them anymore," he said. "If you're going to kill me, just kill me. There's been too much violence already."

Natty looked over at her master. (Angela, she'd called her earlier.) Dead. "No one else has to die," she said. "Not tonight. Take your lover and go; I'll clean up here."

Lover—did that mean Genevieve or Charlie? He stepped closer. "Listen, I—"

Natty stood, hefting Genevieve in her arms. "Killing Poor Jane leaves you... affected. It's better if I take care of her for now. I won't kill her. You have my word on it."

He didn't love Natty anymore, with that dazed, stupid, cursed infatuation of earlier, but for some reason he still felt like he could trust her. "All right," he said. "Be careful with her. She's a good woman."

"She killed my master," Natty said, and whether that was a rebuttal to the need to be careful with her or the claim she was a good woman, James couldn't tell. At any rate, he had more urgent matters to take care of than Miss Hunt. Genevieve had merely fainted, but Charlie was on the verge of bleeding out.

He carefully picked her up, telling her to put her arms around his neck for support. In the past he'd carried her a few times, flirting, playing around. Usually he'd carry her on his back, which was the easiest way, but right now he couldn't have her stomach pressed against his back for fear it would agitate the wound there. So he carried her in his arms instead, trying to keep his pace steady and not jostle her too much.

"James," she said, voice syrupy and pained, "James, do you love me?"

"Shh," he said. "We need to get you to a doctor."

On the street he flagged down a coach and ordered the man at the wheel to take them to the nearest doctor he knew of. Fortunately, although the area beneath the bridge was secluded and out of the way, the bridge itself was near the center of town, and so they did not have far to go. They were brought to a small, well-to-do house, and the coachman was kind enough to knock for them since James's hands were full of Charlie. The doctor who answered looked as if he'd been about to go to bed, but while he frowned at the late arrivals, he did not seem overly surprised either. He had to get a lot of late-night emergencies.

He had James take Charlie into his workroom, where he and an assistant could perform immediate surgery. His assistant lived with him, and so was also on hand, though considerably more flustered. They both kicked James right out to the parlor to wait for results, promising they would do their very best.

So James waited.

His heart was in his pocket. If he slipped his hand in, then between his fingers, he could feel its ticking. He remembered a couple times he'd seen his father fiddle with it in a similar manner, staring at its face compulsively—his father who had never cared much about time had developed what he'd seen as nervous tics in relation to this particular watch.

Had it frightened him, holding his son's life, heart, soul in his hands?

Had he been more afraid that he might hurt his son, or that he might be found out?

Had the idea of taking James's heart in such a manner been his idea or James's mother's?

They must have agreed on it together; neither one of them was likely to be forced into such a subterfuge unwillingly. James's mother always told him that a marriage was only harmonious when decisions were made in tandem, so when he got married he would have to respect his wife and listen to her wishes. This in relation to Genevieve, to his engagement to Genevieve.

James's father had craved the connection with the Hunts, but his mother had been the one more set on the marriage. Yet most of the time, she hung away from doing anything less than respectable, and dark magic was hardly within the realm of respectability. His father's idea, then, or his mother's? James couldn't decide.

Not that it mattered now. Not that he could ask them, either. They were dead.

Dead.

He leaned forward, resting his head in his hands.

The past few weeks felt like a dream to him. How he'd thought about his parents during that time, how he'd felt about them—when he thought about it now, it had been different. He'd always wanted his parents to be proud of him, but it had been some time since that had been his driving motivation. He'd realized ever since Eric that there were parts of himself they would never accept. Slowly he'd begun to accept that lack of acceptance. His parents had known, of course, that while he loved them he did not always obey them, that while he loved them there were other things and people he loved more. That while he loved them, his world had, over the years, centered around them less and less.

For a few weeks—it was as if he had reverted to childhood, that neediness he'd felt towards them. It made him shudder a little. And yet it had felt natural. And yet to know they loved him too—to know they finally approved of what he was doing, to feel no guilt towards them, no anger—had felt so good, so right.

Now he knew they had never grown to approve of or trust him. They had only come up with a new way to control him. If that was love, it wasn't a kind of love he could recognize.

But they were dead now, and there was no holding them accountable, except in the bloody way Natty had already done.

No holding Natty accountable either—she'd vanished, and she was stronger than he was any day. He could report her to the police, and he would, but he doubted they'd ever find her. If they did, if she hanged for what she'd done, wouldn't she hang for having saved him? Didn't he owe her?

He would still report her; no doubt his servants (his, now!) had talked to the police already. But part of him hoped they would fail.

Natty had saved him, in the end, from his parents. Hadn't killed him, though her master had wanted to. Angela was another person too dead for James to blame anymore. He could still be angry at

Charlie, maybe. She'd tried to kill him, and then tried to save him, and mostly made a mess of things.

Charlie. He closed his eyes. Thought of warm beds and the taste of jam on freshly made bread. Lips on his, the smell of the river.

She'd tried to kill him.

He understood it in a way. She'd loved him so much she hadn't been willing to let go. That was how much he'd wanted someone to love him, after Eric. It was how much he'd thought he loved her.

But with his heart now his own, he found the old love kept there had tangled into snarls. It was unwilling to enter the room where she was under surgery, to wish her well, to long for a life together again.

When the doctor exited, he told James she would survive, would wake up soon. James could wait if he wanted. James asked for a pen and paper. He wrote a letter, sealed it in an envelope, and gave it to the doctor along with all the money he had on him. The money to pay the doctor's fee. The envelope for Charlie, when she awoke.

He didn't think he could bear to see her.

***

The Ilbird manor was a large and empty place, now.

Most of the servant stayed. James was well liked, and although the transition to him being earl would be rough—he had little idea how to administer an estate, and ended up foisting most of the work on his father's secretary—they knew they could count on keeping their positions, and that he would be a reasonable master. The servants stayed, and were very sympathetic towards the poor new Earl of Ilbird, who had lost his parents and been kidnapped and nearly murdered himself, who was so deep in grief he had broken off his engagement and spent hours locked up in his room reading books he had found in his parents' room. What the books were about, they didn't wonder; they figured he simply wanted to understand his deceased parents better, as he had not in life. They weren't far wrong. He had discovered several books relating to magic and was trying to figure out what exactly they had had done to him and how to reverse it without the help of someone like Iris Witherbone.

As yet, he had nothing.

It had been a few weeks since his parents' death when he made his way to that not-quite-familiar-yet tavern. He was wearing less noticeable clothes than last time; not as fine but also not ripped or stained with blood. The couple of men he bumped into on his way to the bar still seemed to notice something amiss about him. Maybe it was his high-society accent, or the melancholy on his face. They turned away from him with an expression that was just shy of openly scornful.

At the bar he asked if Delia or Laurie were in. Delia, he was told, was off tonight. As for Laurie, he had shown up just a little ago, not that he was staff. But he came here many nights after work. He was no heavy drinker or high-stakes gambler, but he liked to have a single beer and play a round or two of cards. Today he was already engaged in a game at a corner table, but if James liked, the bartender was willing to go over and let him know a gentleman at the bar wanted to speak with him—in exchange for a little, hm, recognition of the favor.

James gave him a generous tip. He was an earl now and could afford it. The bartender grinned and made his way over to the corner table immediately.

James sighed.

He hadn't come to the bar to drink anything, and was surprised when Laurie, on joining him, offered to buy him a drink.

"Ah, it's not necessary. I have money on me this time. If anything, I owe you..."

"You paid me well enough last time," Laurie said. "And it's not about payment anyway, not really. You're a guest here, of sorts. Or at least you don't come often, and I assume you came to see me. Doesn't that make me your host?"

"Well, not exactly. And I don't mean to impose."

"Go ahead and impose," Laurie said. "What should I get you?"

"Bourbon, then."

Laurie ordered.

"I heard about your parents," he told James. "Ill fortune seems to be following you lately. First the attack on you, now this."

"The events weren't entirely unrelated."

"No?"

"I'd rather not go into it."

"Well, I won't interrogate you. I'm sure it's hard to talk about."

James hadn't talked about it all yet with anyone. He nodded. The drinks arrived, and he sipped his bourbon. Not bad.

"Well, why did you want to see me? You don't seem to be in the mood for talking, so I assume there was some specific purpose. I hope it's nothing medical this time. You know, I'm really not a doctor."

"Ah, no, not that. Though to be honest, you did at least one thing better than our family doctor. You noticed my lack of a heartbeat."

"That," Laurie said. "Right. That was strange." He gave James a questioning look.

James didn't feel like explaining that whole mess right now either. "I was wondering—you and Delia seem to know a lot of people around the city. Do you know anyone skilled and trustworthy who deals in magic? There's a task I need done, but I can't think of who to go to, and frankly I'm not even sure who to ask."

"Magic? Well, that's a tough one. I won't say I don't know people. I have sort of a reputation for that, actually." Laurie pondered the question. "I know some people who are skilled and some who are trustworthy, but no one who's both springs to mind. Why do you ask?"

"Just a quandary."

"And if I asked you if it had to do with your heart, and the kidnapping, and the attack on your parents, you might say it isn't unrelated either?"

James hummed noncommittally.

"I'd help you if I could," Laurie said. "But frankly, these days, finding an upstanding magician's like finding an upstanding building with a rope bridge as its foundation." He sipped his beer. "You might have better luck outside the country. Somewhere the laws aren't as tight."

"I've been thinking about it," James sad. "It does seem the obvious answer. And I'd like to get away for a while." He sighed. "I'd still be going at it blindly, though. No one to take with me either, except maybe my butler. And I doubt he'd approve. My servants don't know about any of this, and I'm not sure I want them to. Going alone, though..." If nothing else, dealing with even the most respectable magician alone seemed dangerous.

"I'm sure you could find a companion," Laurie said. "If you paid for expenses, who wouldn't want to go traveling for a while? Maybe all your high society friends aren't the adventurous sort, but even in this tavern I can think of a few men here tonight who'd love that kind of an adventure."

"Ah, really?"

"I could recommend someone," Laurie said. His lips quirked. "For that matter, there's someone sitting at this bar who'd be very interested."

"Ah," James said. "Really."

"If you really wanted some company," Laurie said, "and you cared to ask."

In James's pocket, the pace of his watch's ticking quickened. His heart was resting against his thigh, yet he felt it in his throat at the same time, waiting for him to take a chance, open his mouth, and let a little of it out into the world again.

17

Chapter Seventeen

Natty had been forced to take care of the new Poor Jane's situation immediately, before she woke up from her dead faint and caused a world of trouble. For that reason Natty had not immediately been able to take care of her poor master's body. Now she remedied that neglect. She had left Angela's body hidden behind some shrubbery near the river, and returned now with a rowboat to take it down the river to a spot where she and Angela had dumped many bodies over the years.

Angela had never shown any particular regard for this spot, but neither had she ever cared what happened to her body after her death. She had told Natty once to please God not try to hold a funeral or get her interred in some sort of Christian cemetery, as it would be a farce to pretend she had any chance at a Christian sort of heaven after the sort of life she'd lived on Earth. "Besides," she said, "who wants to spend eternity around a bunch of other bodies, watching people drop off flowers? You wouldn't like it either, Natty, admit it. It's simply dull."

Natty had gone to visit her parents' grave a few times over the years. It was very nice. The cemetery was well-tended by the local undertaker, and occasionally received flowers from friends and distant family. She had to admit that sort of thing didn't suit Angela, though. Angela's friends in life had been few and far between, and not particularly sweet or respectful of the dignity of the dead. Natty had no intention of telling any of them that Angela was dead to begin with, except Iris, who hadn't been concerned about the body anyway.

It was more fitting to leave Angela here, among the skeletons and decaying corpses of her victims. Among her trophies, in a sense; among kindred spirits, in another, if one counted her a victim of Poor Jane's curse as well. Among, in short, her work, the thing that had made her life worth living.

"I can't say I'll pray for you," she told Angela as she heaved her body over the side of the boat, "but I'll remember you. In some ways, I will always be what you made me."

She did not row away for a while, observing a moment of silence. When she did so, she knew she would not be returning to this spot to visit. What was gone and done was gone and done.

***

She would forever be what Angela had made her. That was useless to deny. She would never be able to walk among people without counting weapons and places where weapons might be concealed, enter a room without cataloguing exits, touch a person's wrist without calculating the force and angle necessary to snap it. At the same time, she was not and never would be Poor Jane, and to become an assassin for as trivial an object as monetary payment would, she felt, be degrading Angela's teaching. She could not become what Angela had really wanted her to be—why chase a shadow of that glorious dream?

No, she would hold Angela's teachings in her heart... and pursue her own future.

And so, the day after laying Angela to rest found her in a nicer dress than she had worn in years, carrying a light suitcase full of unincriminating belongings. (The incriminating belongings she had left in her and Angela's hideout, for which she would continue to pay rent until she was surer of her situation.) She hired a carriage to take her to a town a few hours away, dropping her off at an address she had had memorized for years but never visited.

She knocked.

The man that answered the door had grayer hair than she remembered. He smiled at her in bewilderment. "Good evening, miss. May I ask how I can help you?"

She had perhaps dressed a little too nice. In her mind, Uncle Emmanuel was always the rich uncle, so well-dressed and so smart and worldly wise. To her grown-up eyes, though, he was just another middle-class merchant, and she had dressed almost as a lady.

"Hello," she said. "You may not recognize me, but we knew each other years ago. My name is Natalie Packer. My mother was your sister Elizabeth. I think I look like she used to. I don't know. It's been so long, and I've been out of touch with anyone who knew her."

The man's eyes widened. "Elizabeth's daughter?"

"Yes, that's me. Natalie. Natty, if you like. I—you used to buy me candy, sometimes. And once you helped me catch a frog, and I was going to keep it as a pet until my mother forced me to let it go. Do you remember that?"

"Natty. Little Natty? Dear God, we thought you were dead." He opened the door wider. "Come in. No—here, come hug your uncle. Natty."

His arms were not as strong as Angela's, and she knew as she held him that she could easily have sunk a knife into his back or snapped his neck. But he was warm, and soft, and safe, and so for a moment, she was warm and soft and safe as well.

Thanks for reading!

Thank you for reading my book! I hope you enjoyed it.

If you did (or if you didn't!), you might consider leaving a review on Amazon, Goodreads, or elsewhere. Reviews help a self published author like me gain visibility and find more readers like you. They mean a lot to me <3

About the Author

Melody Wiklund is a writer of fantasy and occasionally romance. In her free time, she loves knitting and watching Chinese dramas. And she's never summoned a spirit or an assassin... or at least so she claims.

You can find Melody online on Instagram @melodywiklund. She also has a website: melodywiklund.wordpress.com.

More Books by Melody Wiklund

A WOUND LIKE LAPIS LAZULI

Ricardo Montero is a painter of great repute, favored by the king of Salandra and chosen by him to paint the ceiling of a temple dedicated to a sea goddess. When he mysteriously goes missing, his friend Beatriz enters a competition to paint the temple in his stead. But when the sea goddess herself gets involved in Beatriz's painting, and in her life, Beatriz finds herself in over her head. Hopefully the woman she's falling in love with can help her keep afloat.

Meanwhile, Ricardo has been kidnapped by one of the king's enemies, a woman who claims the kidnapping is purely to spite the king but who seems obsessed with Ricardo himself. Under pressure and learning secrets he never wanted to know, Ricardo fights to maintain his loyalty to the king and control over his feelings and his life.

ELEVEN DANCING SISTERS

Erin has a good reason for sneaking into a fae castle: her sisters—princesses of Erdhea—have been secretly visiting it for months, and she just knows they're in trouble. Unfortunately that's not an excuse she can give fae lord Desmond when she gets caught. Because Erin is a princess too, and whatever schemes Desmond has, Erin wants no part of them. Instead, she tells him she's a simple war nurse, and offers no excuse at all.

Desmond can't have humans wandering in and out of his castle, not when the Fae's presence in Erdhea must remain hidden. He needs to know how and why Erin sneaked in. But before long, his concerns about Erin are blooming into interest, then fascination, then something else altogether. Under the eye of a lovelorn fae lord, can Erin keep her secrets? Will she even want to?

9 781088 044735